"OH, NO," GROANED AKIRA TOKAIDO.
"IT'S A

Multiple Unresponsive Airc acronym for the alert.

The phone shrilled at Kurtzma a new alarm went off on his computer. And then another.

"Bear?" Barbara Price was on the phone. "Are you seeing what's happening in China?"

"China?" He scanned the next alert. It reported a large-scale oil pipeline break. His brain tried to play catch-up. Multiple aircraft—and then an oil pipeline?

"What the hell is that?" demanded Tokaido, standing at Kurtzman's shoulder and stabbing a finger at a list of numbers on the screen, "I wrote this routine. Why the hell don't I get what it's showing?" Tokaido liked his world of iron-fisted cybernetics control. There was nothing worse than when one of his own apps went rogue.

"No," Kurtzman said. "It's working."

"Then what is *that?*" There were six items on the screen. Then there were seven.

"Pipeline breaches. Each a different one."

Tokaido glared at the computer. Of course he'd programmed the thing to display multiple catastrophic oil pipeline breaches, should they ever happen simultaneously. He'd just never dreamed that would ever happen.

"Talk to me, Bear," Price snapped. "I'm on my way. Do you see what's happening in China or not?"

Kurtzman paused. "Everywhere but," he replied grimly.

DON PENDLETON'S

STONY

AMERICA'S ULTRA-COVERT INTELLIGENCE AGENCY

MAN®

INCENDIARY
DISPATCH

A GOLD EAGLE BOOK FROM

WORLDWIDE®

TORONTO • NEW YORK • LONDON
AMSTERDAM • PARIS • SYDNEY • HAMBURG
STOCKHOLM • ATHENS • TOKYO • MILAN
MADRID • WARSAW • BUDAPEST • AUCKLAND

Recycling programs
for this product may
not exist in your area.

First edition August 2012

ISBN-13: 978-0-373-80434-4

INCENDIARY DISPATCH

Special thanks and acknowledgment to
Tim Somheil for his contribution to this work.

Printed in U.S.A.

INCENDIARY DISPATCH

CHAPTER ONE

The gunner stood alongside the open archway, ears tuned to the subtle sound of movement on the linoleum floor. The sound stopped. His enemy was hesitating. That hesitation, the gunner thought, would cost him his life. He twisted his body into the opening, already hanging on to the trigger of the Heckler & Koch MP-7. The rounds ate into the wallboard and bounced off the floor. But then the gunner laid his eyes on the source of the noise—an office chair rolling slowly in his direction. His final four rounds slammed into the padded back, and the office chair reversed direction as if kicked.

His enemy had vanished and his gun was empty. Very amateur, he thought. Could you tell it was his first time with a machine gun?

The amateur machine-gunner spun back into the cover behind the wall and grabbed for a spare magazine, but then he saw the shadows move and a heartbeat later his chest collapsed in on itself.

The amateur machine-gunner didn't feel the pain but he felt the damage. Internal organs were mutilated, and blood cascaded from his chest. The sound of the blast seemed meaningless.

Then came his enemy, across the room, his face revealed in the glow of light from an exit sign. Blond hair and blue eyes. Cold eyes. The gunner knew he had been outmatched from the beginning.

He was sinking to his knees. He was as good as dead. Was it an honor or a mark of shame that he had been executed with a single shot?

"One shot," he said, then toppled onto his face, surrounded by blood.

"What was that about?" There was another man in the shadows, and the gunner, now dead, hadn't even known he was there.

"He was admiring my efficient use of ammo," Carl Lyons answered. The large blond figure crouched to pat down the corpse.

"Meanwhile he wastes a bunch of rounds offing this fine piece of ergonomic Broyhill furniture," said Hermann "Gadgets" Schwarz, a slim man in wire-rimmed glasses.

Lyons came up with a cell phone and a thin wallet. He tucked them away for later examination and followed his partner into the next section of the lab.

Schwarz heard someone coming, approaching with quick, light steps. These guys, Schwarz decided, weren't that good. This one was heading for the sound of the gunfire, and felt safe approaching from behind a steel fire door.

Schwarz quickly reviewed the people occupying the building. Himself, Carl Lyons and one more teammate, Rosario Blancanales. One company president sprawled dead in his own executive offices on the top floor. One intruder killed by Lyons.

That left two more intruders unaccounted for.

The approaching footsteps didn't sound like Blancanales. Schwarz waited as the man reached the other side of the fire door, paused, then pulled it open slowly. The door was silent. And it was heavy-duty steel. It should have protected the intruder.

But it didn't. Schwarz gave the door an abrupt shove. He heard the steel clatter against the gun in the intruder's hand. He heard the clonk of a skull hitting the door, then the sound of a body bouncing against the painted cinder-block wall.

Schwarz slammed his foot into the door, crushing the body behind it, then nudged away the submachine gun that clattered from a limp hand. He reached around the door and dragged out the intruder, who had enough life left in him to struggle a little. Schwarz walked the attacker back to join his partner and sent the broken man crashing to the floor with his face in the expanding pool of the dead man's blood.

The attacker sputtered and retched as his wrists and ankles were bound in plastic restraints. Then he was wrenched by one arm and landed hard on his back. He gasped for air, inhaling more of his dead companion's lifeblood. That stopped when a large, compact wad of paper was forced into his mouth, wedging it open, and he wheezed around it.

The slim, unassuming man standing over him put a finger to his lips and pressed the business end of a Beretta 92-A1 into the man's blood-smeared face. The man nodded, now very interested in cooperating.

ONE FLOOR UP, Blancanales paused to listen. The gunfire and the commotion of a quick take-down had come from directly below where he was standing.

"Two down," said the voice of Carl Lyons through a microtransceiver in his ear.

Blancanales didn't respond. Two down meant only one to go, which had to be the nervous-looking figure who had just retreated into a corner at the far end of the hall, where a protruding brick wall gave the man some cover. It also made him more vulnerable to unseen approach.

Blancanales stepped out of the blackness of his own shadowy alcove in the lab hallway and moved forward carefully. Despite a head of gray hair he had the agility and grace of a young man and moved silently.

But he didn't need to. His prey was cowering in the darkness, speaking in hushed whispers to someone on a radio or phone.

The man never heard Rosario Blancanales approach on the other side of the protective wall and eavesdrop on his conversation.

Blancanales was a former Black Beret, highly trained, well-educated in a broad scope of esoteric subjects that, for whatever reason, might be useful in a black ops situation. That included languages. Blancanales was fluent in a few and functional enough in many to order a taxi in most parts of the world. But he didn't recognize the language that the man on the other side of the brick wall was shouting into his cell phone. Something Scandinavian. Whatever the man was saying, he was getting more agitated by the second. Then he was pleading. *"Nie! Nie!"*

Blancanales knew those words without knowing the language they came from. He was saying "No! No!" And he was practically begging with the person on the other end of the line.

Blancanales didn't know what was going on. He didn't know why these men were here or what their purpose was. And he knew they weren't exceptionally skilled intruders. Blancanales didn't feel like he was in an especially dangerous situation—

Until now. Suddenly there was a knot of dread sitting in his gut. Something bad was about to happen.

Whatever it was, maybe he could stop it.

Blancanales slipped around the corner of the brick wall. The intruder's combat shotgun was tucked uselessly under one arm, the cell phone in the other hand. The look on his face was one of sheer terror, but the terror had nothing to do with the unexpected arrival of Rosario Blancanales.

Blancanales disabled the man with a knee-shattering kick. The shotgun clattered away. The man collapsed and grabbed at the useless leg. Blancanales kicked the man's right hand, shattering fingers, further damaging the knee. The man was groaning and sobbing until Blancanales demanded his attention by securing his shattered hand to his good one in a plastic cuff.

The soft-spoken Hispanic could be amazingly commanding when he needed to be. The Beretta handgun helped.

"Talk to me."

The man was hyperventilating. A question came from the fallen cell phone.

The wounded intruder shouted at the phone.

The display showed the call had been disconnected. The intruder's eyes widened and he forced himself onto his stomach and began crawling for the stairwell entrance.

Whatever was about to happen, this man considered it worse than the chance of being shot in the back by Rosario Blancanales.

Blancanales touched his transceiver. "Lyons! Schwarz! Get the fuck—"

He heard what sounded like a hiss, but loud as thunder, and the stairwell at the other end of the hallway filled with impossibly brilliant orange and the air distorted from the heat waves that rushed at Blancanales with immense speed. He ducked for cover behind the brick jut-out and let the tsunami of convection pass him. The atmosphere became so hot that his skin burned.

But the worst of the heat wave was gone. The intruder was a pathetic, broken thing crawling down the stairs and Blancanales let him go. He rushed down the hall, to the stairs that had filled with brilliance and become dark again. The air became hotter with every step he took.

"Carl, copy! Schwarz!"

No response.

"Stony, I can't raise them. We've got trouble. Some sort of explosive."

"Understood," said the calm voice of mission controller Barbara Price. "Carmen's trying to raise them."

"Heading into the blast source," Blancanales reported. "Damned hot." He thundered down the stairs, trying to make sense of the ovenlike heat and the lack of a flame. He'd expected a firestorm.

"Lyons? Gadgets?" Blancanales found a fallen weapon, one of the intruders' combat shotguns. Just beyond it was the scene where the burning seemed to have started. Two intruder corpses were on the ground, cooked black, their clothes incinerated. The cadavers were pocked with deep, smoking craters. The room was in flames—plastic furniture, the wallboard, even the steel cabinets appeared to have already melted and sagged. Blancanales felt as if he was cooking in his own skin. He looked into all the corners, searching for his teammates.

"No sign of them yet, Stony," Blancanales announced.

"No response," replied the cool female voice in his ear.

"Lyons! Gadgets, damn it!" Blancanales shouted. He raced to the far side of the room. It was one of the omnipresent steel fire doors.

And it was burning.

He shouldered through it, into the next section of the labs.

"Lyons!" Blancanales demanded of the roaring fire. Hungry flames were growing fat on shelves of stored paperwork. The heat was almost unbearable. The floor was covered with smoking, foot-wide craters. What were those all about?

Rosario Blancanales was suddenly angry. What the hell was going on here? Who the hell were these amateur intruders and what kind of freakish explosion had just gone off?

And where had Lyons and Schwarz been at the time of the explosion?

His arrived at another steel fire door. Why the hell were the fire doors freaking burning? Blancanales knew what an incendiary grenade did—spit out molten metal bits that burned through anything they touched. This was way more than a few incendiary grenades. There were *streaks* of burning steel.

He kicked the door savagely with the bottom of one foot, opening into a jungle of fire, where some kind of electrical system had spilled out ropes of bundled wire that now burned floor to ceiling along with the furniture, books and lab equipment. Clouds of acrid smoke were collecting at the ceiling. Blancanales tried not to breathe but the wisps that he did inhale felt toxic and the blast of heat almost bowled him over. Something burst nearby, spewing orange, red-hot worms.

"Lyons!" Blancanales bellowed. "Schwarz!"

Then something big came leaping through the vines

of fire and crashed at Blancanales's feet. It was Carl Lyons, tangled in a strand of burning cable. He rolled away, extinguishing the flames that clung to his black BDUs. Blancanales snatched off a tangle of wire but a strand of melting insulation stuck to Lyon's clothing like glue.

Then Hermann Schwarz charged through the flames, rolled once and was back on his feet, making a quick search of his body for anything that was still on fire.

"No way out!" Schwarz shouted over the heightening roar.

"Yeah, this way, come on!" Blancanales led the way back in the direction he had come. The conflagration in each room had grown progressively more intense within seconds. The fire was reaching out as if trying to grab them.

Blancanales heard a crash behind him. Carl Lyons had just dumped his pack to the ground. Lyons, without slowing, unceremoniously snatched the small pack off of Schwarz's shoulder.

"Huh?" Schwarz demanded, shielding his eyes from the horrific heat and stinging fumes, but he could see that his pack was smoldering.

Blancanales slipped off his own smoking pack and left it in the room with the corpses of the two intruders. The room was biggest of the lab workrooms and it was an inferno. Blancanales felt his skin cooking and his lungs were exploding as if he were drowning—but he didn't dare take another breath. One inhalation of the superheated air might just drop him in his tracks. His vision was a mass of orange and black. He saw the stairway entrance framed in fire and staggered into it.

The temperature was cooler and he allowed himself a sip of air. It was still so hot it burned his nostrils and he slowed to watch behind him. Schwarz came through. A heartbeat passed.

Then Lyons.

They called Lyons "Ironman." It had been his nickname since long before any superhero movie and he had earned it by toughing out some of the most horrific battles any soldier had ever endured.

But now it looked as though the Ironman was about to crumple. Blancanales shoved Schwarz ahead and got behind Lyons, shouldering into him to keep him moving. The climb up the stairs seemed interminable, then they were into the upper hall. No sign of flame. But the wall trim along the floor was smoking.

"Go!" Blancanales ordered, shoving Schwarz and Lyons, and it was like trying to keep a pair of drunk wrestlers in motion. The trio staggered down the hall. Blancanales felt his feet burning. The sticky rubber toes of his boots were melting. Something liquid sloshed onto the floor and sizzled and Blancanales smelled griddled blood.

Somebody was bleeding buckets.

Lyons seemed to swerve slightly and Blancanales grabbed him around the waist.

Lyons grumbled something about being okay, and then they were in the exit stairs.

There was a rush of air behind them. The stairwell they had left seconds before went up in a fireball. A roar of flame erupted below them. The walls around them were now on fire. They careened down two flights and reached the landing. They saw two doors. One had a darkened exit sign. Smoke poured from the second door and Blancanales swore he actually saw it bulge.

"Out!" he insisted. The three of them pushed through the exit door.

Blancanales felt like he was in paradise—he gratefully inhaled the sweet, cool air of the Georgia night.

He stumbled over a body. It was the intruder whose knee he had shattered. The man had managed to crawl down the stairs and onto the grounds surrounding the Solon Labs. He was either dead or had passed out from the pain. Blancanales grabbed the man by the collar, intending to drag him farther away from the burning building.

But the body seemed to weigh a ton. Blancanales couldn't budge him, and a quick pulse check told him that man was beyond help.

It also dawned on Blancanales that it wasn't the body getting heavier that was the problem. It was himself, getting weaker.

Then he saw another spill of blood. It was *his* blood, and a lot of it.

No wonder he felt weak.

Blancanales collapsed alongside the dead intruder.

CHAPTER TWO

Lyons, Schwarz and Blancanales were members of Able Team, a supersecret covert-operations team based at Stony Man Farm.

Carl Lyons was fighting to sit upright in his helicopter seat without the seat belt. But he wasn't sure Rosario Blancanales would even be able to stay alive for the next twenty minutes.

"Rosario's in bad shape," Lyons said into the mike on his headset.

"What is the nature of his injury?" Barbara Price asked.

"We haven't figured that out yet. Gadgets is working on it."

Hermann Schwarz had Blancanales strapped into the seat beside him and was ripping the man's blood-drenched shirt off in shreds. "No broken bones. No sign of head trauma. But I can't find the wound!" he said in frustration.

Then he found it. The last strip of the black BDU blouse came off Blancanales's torso and there was a long, deep channel of black meandering across the man's side, just above the hip. With the removal of the shirt, blood poured out of the wound.

"Jesus!" Schwarz stormed, covering the wound with his hand and squeezing the ripped flesh together to halt the bleeding.

Lyons watched the flow of blood from between Schwarz's fingers. He watched the color drain out of Schwarz's face—but it wasn't as gray as Blancanales's.

"We found the wound. We don't need a burn unit," Lyons said into the mike. "We just need a lot of blood."

"Understood," Price said. "Putnam General Hospital in Eaton. You're five minutes away."

Jack Grimaldi, the ace Stony Man pilot, manhandled the controls and pulled the helicopter in a turning decent. "Tell them to be ready in three minutes, Stony," he said.

"There's no helipad," Price added.

"Like I need one."

Stony Man Farm, Virginia

BARBARA PRICE hit the switch and brought up the image on the main plasma screen in the War Room. It showed an office in Washington, D.C., and Justice Department official Hal Brognola looked at her from behind his desk. The Potomac was barely visible in the windows behind him.

The communications line between the big Fed's office and Stony Man Farm was highly secure. Brognola was, after all, Director of the Sensitive Operations Group, the ultracovert intelligence agency so secret that its existence was known, ostensibly, only to the President of the United States. And the President was the only person Brognola answered to.

Stony Man Farm itself, tucked away in Virginia's Blue Ridge Mountains, was the hidden base of the Stony Man antiterrorist, anticrime operation. The property had remained secure enough over many years to still be viable as the group's mission center—but that meant diligently and constantly diverting attention away from the Farm and its activities.

Sometimes it was simply impossible for SOG operations to remain invisible.

"They landed in the parking lot?" Brognola asked, chewing an antacid.

"There was nowhere else for them to land," Barbara Price said.

To be accurate, Jack Grimaldi had put the helicopter down in a section of decorative landscaping between the parking lot and the hospital emergency entrance doors. It was twenty feet closer than landing on asphalt, Grimaldi had explained. Twenty feet less distance they'd have to transport the wounded Blancanales.

"How's Rosario?" the big Fed asked.

"He'll be okay. He made a serious dent in the inventory of the blood banks in Putnam County. And the medical staff has been asking a lot of questions about the nature of his injury."

"I'd like some explanation on that myself."

Price strolled to the large conference table in the empty War Room. She was dressed in a conservative skirt and rather plain white blouse, but still managed to look stunning. She took a thin report from the table and brushed back a strand of honey-blond hair to read it.

"The doctors are calling it an incision caused by burning plastic material. The wound was clean-edged—clean enough that the escharotomy was a comparatively minor process."

"Escharotomy?"

"The surgical removal of the skin killed by the burn. They wanted it off of him as quickly as possible to avoid infection. They also wanted to examine the material imbedded in the eschar. We didn't permit that. We had the tissue samples sent to our medical staff. Rosario is resting. Unless there is infection in the wound, he'll be on his feet in a matter of days."

"Good to hear." Brognola tapped his desktop with a very expensive pen. "Dr. Solon?"

"The video from Able Team confirmed it was his body in his office."

"Huh." Brognola didn't like the sound of that.

The lab in Georgia had been researching weaponized thermite for the U.S. military. At least, that was what it had been contracted to do. But it looked as though the prototypes and research they were presenting to the U.S. military had actually been compiled offshore—probably in China.

Worse, the technology that the U.S. government was sharing with the lab was being funneled somewhere else.

It had been a brilliantly executed subterfuge and might have remained undetected if not for Stony Man Farm's watchful cybernetic systems. One of the routines did nothing but sample telecommunications from around the world, looking for new kinds of security. Whenever it found one, the Farm would try to decrypt it—and one such call came to the personal phone of Dr. Anthony Solon.

The scramble was one of the most sophisticated the cybernetics experts at Stony Man Farm had ever seen. It took the team two days to crack it, and when the next scrambled call came to Dr. Solon, it was descrambled and recorded.

Just in time. Solon was getting out. A "special team" was coming to help remove equipment on loan from the U.S. government and to get Solon to safety. This special team would be on-site within hours.

Brognola and Stony Man Farm had their own team on the ground—Able Team. Schwarz, Lyons and Blancanales had observed the arrival of three hardmen in a rented SUV and plenty of heavy gear in their backpacks.

They weren't Chinese.

And they weren't there to extract Solon along with a piece of classified U.S. equipment. They were there to erase the evidence—starting with Solon. They had shot him in the back and left him dead in his office.

Then they had proceeded to place a number of incendiary devices throughout the building.

Somebody had set them off by remote control, not bothering to wait for the intruders to get to safety first. Schwarz and Lyons had found themselves fleeing from a chain of incendiary blasts that had driven them deep inside the building—and far from an escape route.

Just seconds after the incendiaries ignited, Blancanales had chased after his teammates and led them out. All three had suffered superficial burns to the skin. It was the best they could have hoped for. Seconds later and they would have been cooked.

The special team sent to clean out Solon Labs hadn't been so special. Just a bunch of handymen sent to shoot a corrupt scientist in the back and drop off a bunch of remote-controlled incendiary devices. The thermite incendiaries had done their job. The lab was burned to the ground. The only evidence left was the unidentified corpse on the lawn and a few unexceptional personal items carried out in Lyons's pockets.

"Akira's working on the cell phone as we speak. He's not optimistic," Price noted.

"Then we've got nothing," Brognola complained. "There's some serious high technology being exported by this operation and we don't even know who they were. Only that they're hostile and very determined to cover their own tracks."

"You're right," Price said. "That's all we've got."

CHAPTER THREE

Northeastern Vermont

Abraham Clay liked New England. This wild and wooded spot in northern Vermont was beautiful. Especially in the autumn. He really loved it when the colors changed. But there were other places you could go to watch the change of season. There were only a few safe spots where you could go digging up the Portland-Montreal pipeline.

This spot was ideal. Twenty miles from any sizable towns. Unincorporated land meant little likelihood of state or federal rangers nosing around. Chances of being spotted were slim to none.

He'd come to this spot months ago with his ATV and yanked the warning signs out of the ground. If he'd been arrested then it would have been simple vandalism.

Nobody had noticed or bothered to replace the signs. If somebody caught him digging here now, they couldn't exactly claim he was doing anything dangerous, because there were no markers visible in either direction to tell him that there was a crude oil pipeline not three feet below where he was standing.

So his ass was well covered in case he got caught. And he wasn't going to get caught anyway.

He waited awhile, chomping a protein bar, which helped reinforce the image he was going for: casual hiker. He was in his North Face boots—cost him a cool $170—with a water bottle on his belt and a bright yellow Garmin geocaching GPS unit hung around his neck. Hell, the Garmin GPS had been cheaper than the damned boots.

If anybody caught him, he'd claim he was looking for the "Lewis's Ninth" cache. The geocaching website gave it a Terrain Rating of 2 stars out of 5 and a Difficulty Rating of 5 out of 5. In other words, a reasonably easy hike to the spot, but once you got there you'd have a hell of a time actually finding the cache itself. And the coordinates led right here. And there was evidence of something being buried in this spot. That's why he was digging here, Officer.

Abe Clay had come up with the strategy before he'd even started this project. It sounded reasonable. He'd posted the fake entries to the geocaching websites himself. And after several digs, he had never once had to use the excuse, because he had never once been caught.

After waiting a suitable interval, and hearing and seeing no signs of anyone in the vicinity, he checked his watch and got to work. He unfolded his shovel, scraped off the thin layer of vegetation, and dug into the rich earth. Eighteen inches down, he hit metal.

Another reason this spot was ideal: uncharacteristically aggressive erosion in this vicinity in the past few years had brought the pipeline much closer to the surface than it was supposed to be. Thank you, Hurricane Irene. Clay found it pretty easy to get the erosion reports from the Vermont Department of Environmental Conservation. Overlay those with the publically available reports of the exact routes of the Portland-Montreal pipeline, look for population densities and scout the sites months in advance, including pulling up the warning signs that have been hastily staked after Irene washed away most of the original.

The same process had worked in Maine.

This was his final placement. He cleared the earth around the first pipe, the eighteen-inch pipe, and as he moved the dirt he found the bigger, twenty-four-inch pipe. He took a quick look around, found he was still in the clear and snatched the charges from his backpack. They were in small black plastic bags.

Inside was a device that was no bigger than his fist and looked like some sort of computer accessory. Black plastic, with a curved profile and a USB port inside. Clay flipped the switch on the device.

This was the only time he got nervous. He didn't understand exactly how these things were engineered, but he did understand that the ignition power source was inside the device itself. What if there was a problem inside the device and powering it up caused premature ignition?

But, like all the times before, the device's only response to the powerup was the glow of a yellow LED.

Next Clay turned on the cell phone. It was one of those prepaid cell phones. Not many bells and whistles. You couldn't play Angry Birds on the thing. But one feature it did have was exceptional battery life—the longest standby-mode rating in its class.

Finally he attached the cell phone to the device with a short USB cable. To tell the truth, this part made him nervous, too. The phone was supposed to get the call, and that call would somehow send a signal through the USB cable telling the device to do its thing. What if the act of plugging in the cable somehow gave some sort of signal to the device that it should do its thing now?

But the only thing that happened was that the LED

on the device changed from yellow to green. All systems go. He placed the phone and pushed the device with some force against the metal shell of the twenty-four-inch pipe, and poured on water.

After a few seconds he released his hold on the device. The foamy stuff on the bottom of the device reacted with the water and made it into a strong adhesive. The device wasn't going to come off unless you cut it off.

He repeated the process with a second device. The phone powered up, the LED turned green, the device was adhered to the eighteen-inch pipe. Clay carefully filled in earth all around the plastic devices, not quite burying them completely. He jumped to his feet and looked at his watch.

Three minutes, fifty-eight seconds! His personal best. And now he was done. Devices buried in eight different locations along a hundred-mile stretch of the pipeline in Maine, New Hampshire and Vermont.

He'd seen some really pretty scenery, too. And somehow, knowing he'd be one of the last people to see it in its pristine state for a long, long time, made him appreciate it that much more.

Maybe he would take up hiking for real.

After all, he had invested in these kick-ass hiking boots.

And with all the money he'd just earned for himself, he'd have lots of free time.

London

THOMAS HAMMIL WAS TAKING a risk and he knew it. But if he pulled it off, the payoff would be huge. And he'd be out of this stinking job and out of stinking London and they could all go to hell.

He'd given them a lot of his life and got nothing back.

He'd given to his country: He'd served in the Royal navy, but they'd tossed him out like he was garbage—no money and no rank.

His mates, the boys he'd known since his school days, looked down their noses at him ever since he'd come home from his military stint. They said they believed his version of the story, but they'd been cool toward him. Every once in a while they'd been into their pints and one of them would say something sort of snidelike, and then Hammil would know they really didn't believe his side of the story at all.

Clara? He couldn't even remember why he'd married her. She was a shrew, that one. He'd spent seventeen years living in the same disgusting little row house with that woman and he couldn't take another day of it.

He hated them. The lot of them. He hated bloody England and he hated this bloody company. Been with this bloody company eighteen years and him doing the same job today as when he'd started. Hammil was bossed around by a bunch of little turds ten years younger than him. And just lately somebody had been passing around a printout of one of the little turd's pay stubs. The little turd—his direct supervisor—was making twice what Hammil did.

BirnBari Expediting Services should have been paying Hammil that kind of money. Hammil should have been getting a check from the Royal Navy all these years. Hammil should have had a wife who wasn't a sow and a home that wasn't a pigsty and mates who didn't call him Hammy to his face—and worse things behind his back.

One thing he had gotten for all his years with Birn-Bari Expediting Services was a lock on the head expediter position. Not that he got to tell any of the other expediters what to do. He wasn't a boss. Just highest on the seniority list. What it boiled down to was his pick of the shifts and four thousand pounds per year more than the regular expediters. Not much.

And the company trusted him. He'd done his job right for eighteen years without any major screwups. Nobody watched him anymore. Nobody checked his work.

The whistle told the crew it was lunchtime and the young ones began wandering off of the floor.

"They're buying us lunch today, Hammil," reminded one of the other expediters.

"Not for me," Hammil said, and patted his stomach. For weeks he had been complaining of stomach problems and he'd been skipping meals. His coworkers had been telling him to see a doctor. The playacting had worked. They were used to his skipping meals now. Nobody thought anything strange about it—even on the one day of the month when the company paid the food tab at the pub next door.

Hammil was alone in the large distribution room.

He kept working like normal for several minutes. Just in case somebody forgot something and came back for it. Or whatever. Nobody did. The big warehouse got a kind of feel to it when it was empty of people. The sounds became bigger, in a way.

Hammil darted to the rear, peered out the back and found the lot empty. It took him less than fifteen seconds to retrieve a cardboard box from the trunk of his old Nissan. Then he was back inside. He stopped and listened. No sound. He was still alone. He spent another thirty seconds stuffing items from the box onto the shelves, then he ripped up the box and crammed it into the trash.

He was doing it all the way it was supposed to be done. Exactly the way they had told him to do it.

Next he began making his rounds again. He drove his cart up and down the aisles, grabbing items off the shelves per the manifest in his hand. It was for a cargo flight to Istanbul, leaving at 6:05 in the evening. Hammil knew the flight times by heart, and he knew it was three hours, forty-five minutes to Istanbul.

He had been instructed to follow some very simple rules when choosing the flights. They had to have a scheduled takeoff between six and eight in the evening. They had to be nonstop flights. They had to be three hours or longer.

This one was perfect.

Next came another cargo flight. Departure: 6:45. To Moscow. Again, an ideal fit. One of the packages went into the shipping crate for the Moscow flight.

The packages were in BirnBari Expediting Services boxes. They had official BirnBari bar-coded labels. Inside each box was an identical set of items: a cell phone, nail clippers, an expensive electric toothbrush, two new white button-down shirts, two tasteful silk ties and a bulky tablet computer. It was the kind of package some well-to-do travelers preshipped when they went on a trip to save them time going through security at the airport. If somebody opened this package and glanced at the contents, he'd see nothing alarming.

But the tablet wasn't what it seemed to be. And it was plugged into the cell phone. And both the cell phone and the tablet computer were in sleep mode. If one of the boxes was opened and the contents examined closely, it would definitely raise suspicion.

Hammil had to hope and pray that wouldn't happen. And there was no reason it should. BirnBari Expediting Services had a stellar security reputation. Hammil had never been considered a security risk.

The next flight on the manifest was to Paris. Too short. He loaded the cargo crate without adding one of his special packages. The next one was to Glasgow. No way.

The next was to Delhi. It was a passenger jet. A nine-hour flight departing at 7:30 p.m. Christ, it was an A380. You could cram more than five hundred passengers into one of those monsters. He swallowed hard. For the very first time, Hammil began thinking about the true repercussions of what he was doing.

But he loaded up the shipping crate anyway, adding his own special package, and carted the crate to the loading dock, sealed and ready for the aircraft.

Hammil packed nine more crates by the time the day shift began returning from lunch. Six crates had his special packages. Three of those were for passenger flights.

Which left at least six of his special packages still on the shelves in the big warehouse at BirnBari Expediting Services.

Hammil had been instructed carefully. He had been informed that there would almost certainly be more packages than he could ship out. As long as he shipped out most of them, he shouldn't worry about it.

But now he was worried about it.

"Hammil!" It was one of the young guys on the day crew. Just some brainless bloke with a girlfriend and a bad complexion. "You look like hell! You feel okay?"

Hammil got off the cart and leaned with his hands

on his knees. He was supposed to act sick. But he didn't need to act at all.

"Hey, you want a drink of water or something?"

They were gathering around him now. The blokes on the day crew. Including the young turd who managed the shift.

"Your stomach acting up again, Hammil?" The shift manager, in his tie and jacket, was crouched next to him, looking at him worriedly. "You need a doctor."

"I'm okay." But his arms were shaking. That wasn't a part of his act. "Need to lie down."

"Take the rest of the day, but only promise me you'll set up an appointment with a doctor already."

"Yeah. All right." He stood. He wavered a little. They were all gathered around him. There were thirteen of them. There were still six of his packages left on the shelves in this very room.

"You need to go to the hospital," said one of the faces.

"I'm okay. Really."

"How about I drive him home?"

"Fine," said the shift manager.

"No. I'll drive myself. I'm not that bad off." The thought occurred to him that this lot would be gone in the late afternoon. An entirely different bunch of guys would be working this evening, in the room with the packages. These guys would be at home or at the pub or—somewhere else.

Which did make him feel just a bit better.

The shift manager was still walking with him as he got into his car. "I'll be fine. I'll call for an appointment."

He drove away, and the more distance he put between himself and BirnBari Expediting Services the less awful he felt. Everything had gone smoothly, except for a brief case of nerves. If only he had time to stop for a pint—but that would have to wait until later.

He didn't go home. He would never see his pigsty row house or his miserable Clara again.

He took the M11 out of London and never looked back.

LEWIS CHARD HAD NEVER earned so much money for so little work.

Fourteen devices placed on six cars and eight homes, all belonging to employees of BirnBari Expediting Services.

The homes were no problem. He didn't need to break into them, just get close enough to deliver the device. A few miserable dogs yapped at him when he crept up in the middle of the night. If the miserable dogs woke any of the homeowners, they'd find nothing suspicious. Chard was away in seconds.

Putting the devices on the cars was riskier, but his contacts had told him exactly when the cars would be unattended. Apparently lunch would be paid for by the company today. Chard was told to wait for the shift to go to lunch, and then wait for one last bloke to step outside to get something out of his car. Chard didn't ask questions, although it seemed an odd bit of staging.

So, sure enough, the shift workers went to the pub next door, then one fellow darted out the back door and grabbed something from the back of his car. After that, Chard put a device on all six cars without delay. The devices were magnetized. They were primed. The LEDs were green.

Lewis Chard was driving away from London before the lunch shift was half done.

He considered the fact that one of the cars he had

rigged belonged to the man who had ducked out the back. The car had also been parked at one of the row houses that he had rigged with a device the night before.

Whoever had arranged this whole affair really wanted that one guy dead.

Qingdao, China

ZHANG JEI DUCKED into the park off of Xilingxia Road and sprinted through the darkness. The night was black. There was no reason for security this far away from the city center, the seaports or the airports.

His reef walker shoes were in his pants' pocket. He pulled them on, then removed his slacks and shirt. He was wearing a wetsuit underneath. He stuffed his clothing and city shoes into his backpack and stepped into the cold waters of the bay.

The backpack floated behind as he paddled patiently into the blackness. There was no water traffic in this area. Too many rocks this close to the shore.

The illuminated face of his TomTom waterproof GPS unit led him effortlessly to the Farallon MK-8. The neutrally buoyant DPV—diver propulsion vehicle—was fully charged.

It started with a touch and hummed with power, like a sea snake. It was black aluminum and weighed almost 130 pounds with the battery.

The battery was key. Zhang had a lot of distance to cover before sunrise. The MK-8 had fantastic range—three miles. That was more than enough.

Silently, in darkness, he let the DPV pull him through the waters of Jiaozhou Bay, toward Berth 62.

Zhang Jei considered himself to be an extremely lucky man. He had been at the right place at the right time with the rare combination of attributes needed for this particular task. They'd needed someone skilled in stealth diving and DPV use. Someone who didn't have qualms about a long-distance solo operation. Someone who had demonstrated a certain degree of ruthlessness.

Zhang Jei was all those things. Trained by the People's Liberation Army navy for out-of-area operations, he had been part of the insertion teams on the Somalia shores that had successfully taken out a group of pirates preying on Chinese cargo ships. He'd earned a medal for it.

Then came the operation in North Korea. He'd been part of a three-man nighttime insertion—two divers and an army sniper. To this day Zhang Jei didn't know the identity of the North Korean official they were supposed to have killed, or why—only that the man had somehow become a severe hindrance to effective Chinese/North Korean relations.

But the mission went all to hell. The sniper missed. Twice. The man was just sitting there in a parked military jeep and still the sniper missed.

Before a third shot could be fired the North Korean target had been hustled into hiding and twenty North Korean special forces operatives were in pursuit of the Chinese sniper team.

The sniper surrendered to the North Koreans. Maybe he thought the People's Republic would negotiate his return. The other diver found himself surrounded by special forces operatives and shot himself in the head. It was a wise choice, in Zhang's opinion, knowing that sniper would have endured months of torture and questioning before ending up just as dead.

Zhang had made it back to the shore and into the water and then he'd just swam. He'd come ashore at dawn and collapsed in a stand of vegetation near a noisy little factory village. Throughout the daylight hours he'd been roused from unconsciousness by the occasional screech of bending metal. That night he'd stolen into a shabby building and eaten putrid food, then taken to the ocean again.

It had taken him days to work his way up the coast, moving ever slower as his energy waned. He'd spent his last two nights on a makeshift float and kicked relentlessly across the tide.

The North Koreans patrolled the waters, but one man, in the water at night, could sneak through their guard. When the virtual wall of North Korean ships was behind him, Zhang Jei knew he was back in China.

But as far as China was concerned, he was dead. They had abandoned him. He would abandon them, as well. They had trained him to survive and thrive in darkness and secrecy, and he would make the most of it.

By the time he had wandered into Qingdao he had murdered three men and stolen their identities, as well as enough cash to live a comfortable lifestyle. His fourth victim was the most carefully chosen. A traveling man, recently widowed, no family, with a little inherited money. Nobody would miss him. That man had been the real Zhang Jei, but now the corpse of the real Zhang Jei was disintegrating in the East China Sea.

He had operated in the vicinity, taking on some dirty jobs for local officials and local drug organizations. Just enough to provide a comfortable income without making any unwanted alliances. It was learned that he was skilled at killing.

The job tonight was his biggest paycheck yet. He could live on the profits for a year or more.

If the man who now went by the name Zhang Jei was

afraid of ghosts, he would have been worried about the decomposing corpse of the real Zhang Jei coming up and snatching him by the ankle.

But the man now known as Zhang Jei didn't care about ghosts. Even if they did exist, no animated corpse could move as fast as the DPV.

BERTH 62 WAS FAR OUT into Jiaozhou Bay. It was a mechanical island large enough to dock an oil tanker up to 280,000 deadweight tonnage. It had four off-loading arms and pumped out huge volumes of crude oil. Still, for a ship like the *Northern Aurora,* it could take days to get in, get unloaded and get out of port.

She was a VLCC, a Very Large Crude Carrier. She was unexceptional in her class, one of about five hundred VLCCs plowing the world's oceans. Still, any vessel capable of carrying two million barrels of oil was impressively large when seen from the waterline.

The massive shape loomed over Zhang Jei, but he couldn't afford to admire it. He had a job to do. He floated on his back and removed the first device, placing it against the hull of the *Northern Aurora.* He dipped the device in the ocean to wet the foam backing, then pressed the foam to the hull and applied pressure. The foam cells burst and the encapsulated cyanoacrylate adhesive reacted with the water. In seconds, it was stuck in place. And it was never coming off.

The green LED inside waterproof plastic casing told Zhang Jei that the electronics were operational.

He swam along the hull, towing the DPV, making no sound loud enough to alert the security guard on the deck far above him. None of the bay patrol craft came close enough to spot a black-suited man in the black water alongside a black ship's hull.

He put the second device in place 141 feet from the first one, and then a third. It wasn't difficult, but he was careful. Soon all six devices were in place. Zhang Jei pulled a last phone from the pack—a waterproofed satellite phone. He dialed the number he had never dialed before.

He didn't know who had hired him. He didn't know why they wanted to sink the *Northern Aurora*. All he knew was that they had put a quarter-million dollars in his bank account already, and were obliged to pay him that much again when the job was done.

"Are they in place?" The man spoke English.

"They are," Zhang Jei said.

"Wait," the man said.

Zhang Jei didn't wish to wait.

Then the man said, "We see a problem. One of the units is not responding."

"Which one?"

"Do you want the serial number on the device?" the man demanded. "I can provide that if you think it will somehow help you determine which one of the six is not responding. Did you in fact note the serial numbers on the devices as you were placing them?"

Zhang Jei felt chagrined. He had asked a stupid question.

But he was feeling something else, too.

Maybe the question hadn't been the stupidest thing he had done this day.

Ramvik, Norway

THE YOUNG MAN muted the phone and gave Olan Ramm a wicked grin.

"Zhang, finally?" Ramm demanded. He was a blond, emaciated man with a cadaverous face.

When the young man spoke he sounded like British gentry. "He's only three minutes late. He's all done."

"Then we are all done," Ramm said, feeling almost euphoric.

"All done. All in place. Nothing left to do except make some phone calls," the young British man said.

"Let's make them, then," Ramm said.

The young man unmuted his telephone.

Qingdao, China

"THE PROBLEM SEEMS to have righted itself. Thanks so much for your services, Mr. Zhang."

Zhang saw the connection get cut. The screen went dead. And Zhang knew he had made a very bad mistake. He grabbed the control handle on the MK-8 and started the motor. It pulled him away from the *Northern Aurora* at full speed. Which wasn't going to be fast enough.

Ramvik, Norway

IT WAS 4:03 P.M. in Northeastern Vermont.

It was 9:03 p.m. in London.

It was 5:03 a.m. in Qingdao, China.

It was 10:03 p.m. in Ramvik when Olan Ramm made the most anticipated phone call of his life.

CHAPTER FOUR

Stony Man Farm, Virginia

He was a powerful-looking man, even confined to a wheelchair. Aaron Kurtzman was the top cybernetics expert at Stony Man Farm, and as such he was tapped into a dizzying array of electronic intelligence feeds. His fingers moved deftly over a wireless keyboard.

One of those feeds had just beeped at him. He had hundreds of alerts programmed into the system, but this one he recognized.

So did the Japanese man at a nearby terminal. The alert had played over his earbuds, interrupting the music. "Oh, no," groaned Akira Tokaido. "It's an MUA."

Multiple Unresponsive Aircraft was their internal acronym for the alert.

Their dynamic search routines assessed all the data coming into the Farm, looking for patterns, any sign of trouble. Any unresponsive aircraft could signal trouble, but the truth was that aircraft went unresponsive every day. A bad radio, a storm, a flight crew in an animated discussion about yesterday's game—anything could cause an aircraft to be unresponsive for a little while. Stony Man Farm's MUA alert didn't trigger when just one aircraft went unresponsive somewhere in the world.

But when there were several at once, it demanded

immediate attention. If they'd only been able to track MUAs in 2001....

"Airbus out of Heathrow, en route to New Delhi," Kurtzman said out loud as he sped through the feeds highlighted by the alert. "Cargo flight out of Heathrow to Istanbul."

"Cargo flight, LHR to MOW," Tokaido announced. LHR was Heathrow, MOW was Moscow. "Passenger, LHR to CPT."

CPT was Cape Town. And again out of Heathrow. Somebody had just exploited a huge hole in Heathrow security....

"Passenger!" Tokaido blurted. "CDG to SXM!"

It took an extra second for that to register. Vacationers to St. Maarten—out of Paris. Kurtzman felt sick. Then his own screen showed him a new window. Passenger. MIA-GIG.

"Miami!" he shouted. "That's a GPS tracking beacon response failure."

Kurtzman wished every aircraft on the planet was equipped with a device like that, constantly transmitting its exact location. The truth was, most aircraft had beacons that didn't go off until there was trouble. And sometimes the trouble happened too fast for the technology to activate.

The phone shrilled at Kurtzman's elbow and at the same time a new alarm went off on his screen.

And then another.

"Aaron?" Barbara Price was on the phone. "Are you seeing what's happening in China?"

"China?"

He scanned the next alert. It reported a large-scale oil pipeline break. His brain tried to play catch-up. Multiple aircraft—and then an oil pipeline?

"What the hell is that?" demanded Tokaido, now standing at Kurtzman's shoulder and stabbing a finger at a list of numbers on the screen.

"I wrote this routine. Why the hell don't I get what it's showing?" Tokaido liked his world of iron-fisted cybernetics control. There was nothing worse than when one of his own apps went rogue.

"No," Kurtzman said. "It's working."

"Then what is that?" There were six items on the screen. Then there were seven.

"Pipeline breaches. Each is a different one."

Tokaido glared at the computer. Of course he had programmed the thing to display multiple catastrophic oil pipeline breaches, should they ever happen simultaneously.

He'd just never dreamed it would actually happen.

"Talk to me, Aaron," Price snapped. "I'm on my way. Do you see what's happening in China or not?"

"Everywhere but," Kurtzman said grimly.

Washington, D.C.

THE SUNNY AFTERNOON turned dark.

"Jesus!"

Hal Brognola was in his office when he heard the expletive issued out in the hall. It reached him through two closed doors. Now somebody was running. Now somebody was sobbing.

The big Fed in the big office overlooking the Potomac felt his stomach churn as he snatched up the remote and stabbed the power button.

"—ruptured and exploded. We're trying to get out but it's moving fast."

It looked like a small-time TV newscast. The title at

the bottom of the screen read, Live in Shambert: Protesters Want Mayor Dubin's Resignation.

What was on the screen was nothing as mundane as a protest against a local politician. The cameraman was trying to keep the image steady as the news reporter steered the van through black smoke.

"We heard the snaps and then we saw it coming down the hill. It didn't take but a minute. Every building in the town's on fire. We must've seen twenty people just get drenched in it. They're still burning. No way to get to them. We're trying to get out. Look at that!"

The camera swung to look out of the front windshield and for a moment there was the image of a street. Hundreds of gallons of black oil channeled between burning buildings and flooded through the streets. Running people scattered, but not fast enough. The burning oil tide swept over them. The camera caught the image of a woman twisting and staggering until the belching smoke masked her.

"Not getting out this way!" The reporter slammed the van into Reverse and whipped it around and into a side street.

And the image vanished. "We're getting word from Houston of another oil fire, this one at an oil terminal station…"

The big Fed grabbed at the phone to make a call, but it was ringing when he touched it. It was the Stony Man Farm mission controller, Barbara Price.

"We need to shut down airspace, Hal."

Brognola scowled. "Airspace? This some sort of aerial attack?"

He heard Price use a word that Barbara Price didn't often use. Then there was a rush of words in the background. It was Kurtzman.

"Hal," Price said calmly but firmly. "We have several incidents under way."

"Top priority?" Brognola demanded. He could hear the urgency in her voice; there was no time for a debriefing. He was going to have trust her judgment—and he did.

"We've got many unresponsive aircraft alarms in the last few minutes. Half of them are out of Heathrow. Others are over Brazil, Africa, the Atlantic—"

"I thought the MUA alert system wasn't supposed to work that well?" Brognola demanded, almost defensively. His mind was spinning.

"It's working better than we had hoped, unfortunately," Barbara Price said. "Six ELTs have activated, matching the MUAs. But only we know about it, Hal—because of the MUA alerts. Global air traffic control doesn't yet see how widespread this emergency is. We need a global alert. We need airspace shut down. If we can get one more aircraft out of the sky before it's attacked…"

"I'm on it."

Brognola snatched up a second phone and dialed the President himself.

"Yes, sir. Right now our number-one concern is the aircraft. We believe at least six aircraft around the world have been downed. Yes, sir, some are passenger jets…. We don't know."

There was a pause.

"We don't *know*. We can't wait for the aviation authorities around the world to make these connections themselves. This attack is still going on."

But even as he said it, Brognola wondered if it was true. The muted TV was showing a rotating series of nightmare images. Burning land. Burning people.

Burning ships. Had everything really burst into flames simultaneously? If so, was the attack done?

The President hung up. He would make calls. Personally. He would ensure that warnings were spread around the world within minutes. Commercial aircraft would be lining up to land all over the planet. Air force patrols would take to the air by the thousands, looking for signs of attacking or suspicious aircraft. The response would be worldwide and as instantaneous as any global mobilization could possibly be.

Brognola looked at the clock.

It was 4:26 p.m.

The shadows were growing longer in D.C.

Stony Man Farm, Virginia

AKIRA TOKAIDO'S BASIC skill set was in computer hacking, and right now he was tearing open digital security walls with all the finesse of a belligerent fifteen-year-old. It was somewhat amazing to watch his process. He would stare into one monitor, pull up a new attack report, then pound the keys in front of him, opening government and commercial systems with equal speed and ease, dismantling their firewalls in minutes, digesting the intelligence inside in search of anything that would help. He'd then dismiss it and move on to the next attack report.

So far, he'd come up with nothing. Neither had Carmen Delahunt nor Huntington Wethers, two other members of Kurtzman's cyberteam. They were tearing through report after report in the Computer Room, looking for any electronic signature, any puzzle piece, any clue.

Barbara Price was doing what she could to simply organize what they knew so far.

The sheer number of the attacks was staggering. Pipelines all around the world. Oil tankers on every ocean. Aircraft—at least one on each inhabited continent.

She brought up the live video feed from China. It had been the first attack report that she had seen, and only because she had been watching a live news feed from BBC Asia, almost at random. They had news crews in Qingdao—at a hotel on the bay, in fact. It was the sudden bright light, not the noise, that had roused one of the news crew, who'd promptly set up a camera at the window of his hotel room and begun taping the burning of Jiaozhou Bay.

The *Northern Aurora,* which had been sitting there, waiting for some paperwork to go through so it could off-load a million barrels of crude oil, had burst into flame in the predawn night.

The BBC replayed its first minutes of footage and Price paused the playback herself. The massive oil tanker was a black hulk in the black night, but six gaping holes were open in its side, exuding orange flames that were licking off of spilling oil. The holes had been spaced with a precision that was unsettling.

"Easy," sneered Tokaido, looking at the video on the well-mounted video screen. "You could put them there with a rowboat."

He was glaring at the screen, his eyes glinting. The young Japanese hacker looked—what? Enraged?

Tokaido had been with Stony Man Farm for several years. He had seen much. Why, Price wondered, was he taking this one so personally?

Or was that just her imagination?

Tokaido abruptly thrust his finger at the frozen image of the tanker on the huge plasma screen.

"Fucker!" he snarled.

The way that Tokaido went back to his computer, Price thought he was going to start pounding the keys with his fists.

Wethers, Delahunt and Kurtzman had all stopped what they were doing. Kurtzman met her eyes before he returned to rattling the keys of his own terminal.

Price hit Play and watched the playback from China. The local time code started at 4:06 a.m., the moment the quick-thinking BBC staffer got his camera going. By 4:33 a.m. local time the black hulk of the *Northern Aurora* had vanished behind a lake of flame. The lake spread. Price watched with horrified fascination as the orange brilliance illuminated the shore and the buildings and then seemed to swallow them up. There were explosions. Ship after ship was being consumed in the flame. At least two more oil tankers were engulfed and burned until they blossomed and added their own fuel to the flames. The voice of the reporter standing behind the camera described the oil spill's creep along the shore of the bay. Buildings were being set ablaze. Thousands being evacuated from the shoreline as the fire jumped to the buildings and spread inland.

The vivid image of the bay was of half blackness and half conflagration, but the blackness continued to shrink. The fire seemed to have sensed the voyeurs in the hotel and was coming after them.

"We're leaving the camera," the reporter said. It was odd, hearing the voices of a bunch of Brits in a hotel room. The oil fire itself was silent.

"Let's go!" the reporter said a moment later.

Then viewers around the world heard the door to the

hotel room open and slam shut. There were no more voices. Just the camera's unique view of the fire that seemed now to reach to the horizon.

The attacks had happened less than an hour ago. The damage still had a long way to spread.

Over the next twenty minutes the satellite-fed footage of the flames crawling to the hotel was dramatic and terrifying. Then a new kind of smoke appeared in front of the fire. Close-proximity fumes. The hotel itself was finally burning.

CHAPTER FIVE

The rugged British commando, leader of one of the deadliest paramilitary units on the planet, was drinking on the job.

Drinking heavily. He upended the bottle and sucked out 500 ml of the brown liquid and kept sucking until the plastic bottle collapsed noisily upon itself. Then he released it into a trash can beside one of the computer desks and savagely twisted the plastic cap off of a second bottle.

The big plasma screen had been replaying news feeds from all over the world for three hours. How many times were they going to show this bloody piece of video? It must have been the tenth time he'd seen it.

But he couldn't look away.

It was the video from the reporter and his cameraman out of a small station in Casper, Wyoming. They'd driven pretty far out of their way to get some video of a protest staged against the mayor of a little town called Shambert. Protesters didn't agree with his budgeting priorities.

Then the pipelines blew and a sea of flaming crude oil swamped the town. The reporter and his cameraman had been broadcasting live as they careened wildly through Shambert, trying to find an escape route.

"Get 'em!"

It was already a famous sound bite. It was the cameraman shouting as a group of young men staggered into the streets, faces covered by their shirts from the already acrid smoke. For a second, you thought the cameraman was telling the reporter to just run the young men down to get out of town faster.

But the reporter was stomping on the brakes and the cameraman was shouting again. "We gotta get 'em!"

The cameraman screamed out the window. The young men piled into the news van. They screeched away—but maybe the reporter and cameraman shouldn't have been Good Samaritans. Maybe they shouldn't have taken those precious seconds to pick up those young men. Maybe they could have saved themselves, at least, if they'd had a few extra seconds to spare.

There was one way out of town left to them, and the oil was already advancing. The reporter tried to drive through the wall of flame. He had no other option. And he did manage to make it through. He reached the other side of the fire. But the van became drenched in burning oil. The men inside were shouting. It was mayhem.

Thank God the news network stopped the tape before the shouting turned to screaming. Once those men started screaming, the camera had continued to operate for eleven seconds. It sent eleven seconds of live video and audio around the world to millions of viewers. A lot of people had listened to those five men die.

The big Brit with the bottle had seen some seriously bad things in his life, but he never again wanted to hear the screaming of the men in that news van as they burned.

There was a different tape now and some female reporter was running down the latest list of attack sites. It just went on and on.

"What is that?"

Carl Lyons was there, staring at the Brit's freshly opened bottle. It was red and sported a bright white logo in Arabic.

David McCarter waved the bottle dismissively. "Egyptian Coca-Cola. Carl, do we have *anything* to go on?"

"Not yet. They're tearing it up back there." Lyons nodded back into the depths of the Farm. McCarter understood what he meant—the cybernetics team ripping through the systems of the world in search of clues.

"What about arrests?"

"I just got here three minutes ago. I don't know a thing."

McCarter shook his head miserably. "How's Pol?"

"Been better," Rosario "Politician" Blancanales answered, trying not to limp when he came into the War Room.

"You been cleared by the doc?" Lyons demanded. "I thought you were on bed rest for another forty-eight hours."

Blancanales's attention was engaged for a moment by the bottle in McCarter's hand, then he said. "I'm good to go. We got a target?"

"No," Lyons replied. He wasn't fooled for a second by Blancanales's evasive response.

Blancanales's circulatory system had been severely compromised. At the little hospital in Georgia, they had pumped every pint of compatible blood in the medical center into Blancanales before his skin began to resume something like its normal color—Lyons never would have thought Blancanales's Hispanic complexion could have gone as pale as it had been when they'd first run him into that little E.R. They'd performed a quick, temporary stitch-up job to close the wound. Hours later, Blancanales had been transported to a larger hospital in Atlanta, where a surgeon sliced out a thin millimeter of dead flesh on either side of the wound, along with the blackened particles of burned material that had cut into him.

Blancanales hadn't even noticed it—the moment when he was cut open by an orange-hot fragment of flying debris in the bowels of Solon Labs.

Lyons and Schwarz had fled the explosions deep into the lab and found themselves surrounded in flames. Blancanales rendezvoused with them there, in the biggest lab, where all kinds of equipment and materials were igniting, burning, melting and bursting. Something had exploded and Blancanales got in the way of a piece of shrapnel that burned through his armor, his clothing and his skin.

Blancanales was herding Lyons and Schwarz out of the building as the building burned around them. Blancanales hadn't even realized he was losing critical quantities of blood out of the sizzling gash in his side.

"Barb—" McCarter said as the mission controller entered the War Room.

"We should have everybody on-site in twenty minutes," she announced. "We'll debrief then." She looked at Blancanales. "Didn't know you'd received medical clearance, Rosario."

"All this is looking a lot like what we saw at the lab," Blancanales said, waving at the big plasma screen and images of burning. Pipelines. Harbors. Ships. People.

"It does, on the surface," she agreed.

"What about below the surface?"

Price shook her head slightly. "We just don't know."

THE TIME CODE on the screen read 7:35 p.m.

The War Room hosted a full house. David McCarter's Phoenix Force teammates were present. The three members of Able Team were there.

Aaron Kurtzman was there with the Stony Many Farm cyberteam. Carmen Delahunt, a vivacious redhead, was a talented analyst. Huntington Wethers, a dignified black man, every inch the UCLA cybernetics professor that he had once been. And there was Akira Tokaido, the Japanese hacker. The man was snapping at the touchscreen on a tablet computer, looking as grim as anyone had ever seen him.

Hal Brognola was on the screen from his office in Washington, D.C. Barbara Price, as mission controller, was the one that everybody started unloading on.

"First things first," Price said. "We're going to go through a list of incidents." She looked around at the gathering of faces. "It's a long one."

And indeed it was.

"Thirty major pipelines are out of commission," Price said. "In nearly all cases, the sabotage occurred in semiremote areas where the explosive devices could be, we assume, placed in advance. It's also clear that some locations were chosen for their geography—the places where the oil flow and fire could do the most damage."

"Like in Wyoming," said Hal Brognola.

"Yes," Price said. "Like in Wyoming. We're still receiving information from around the world, but there appears to be a standard approach to the sabotage. A series of small explosive devices were placed along the pipelines in advance, where they waited for a signal to detonate."

"Does anyone have one of those devices?" Brognola said.

"As far as we know, most of the oil fires continue to

burn and no investigation teams have been able to get to the scene of any of the actual explosions."

"What about Alaska?" Brognola demanded.

"No." Price looked at the screen. Video pickups shifted automatically even when Brognola's image moved from one screen to another. "The pipeline attacks followed certain patterns, from what we can tell. The explosives detonated simultaneously—maybe as many as twenty to thirty small explosions at once. More in some cases.

"The pipeline in Wyoming was opened up at approximately thirty-four locations over a distance of two miles. The oil spilled out under the pipeline pressure. There are block valve stations on the line that responded to the pressure drop automatically and immediately shut down oil flow. However, at least fifteen of the explosions took place uphill of the station that is supposed to protect the town in case of a pipeline breach. The next station shut down the pipe, but the volume of oil remaining in the pipelines was considerable and was gravity-fed into the town. Gravity-fed oil flow from punctures on the east and the west of the town fed the fires on the town limits and trapped the population inside."

Price was now looking at the surface of the War Room conference table, not at any of them. She opened her hand, a hopeless gesture. "The town was surrounded, blocking all escape routes."

The room full of people was silent for a moment.

"Anybody get out of that town?" Carl Lyons asked.

"It's still burning."

"Oh."

"It's important to note that most of these attacks were not intended to result in significant loss of life," Aaron Kurtzman said. "Most of the pipeline attacks were not in populated areas. The intention was clearly to put these pipes out of commission. The same intention was behind the sabotage of oil tankers. We have a number of oil tankers burning or sunk, including several tankers that were nonmobile—used only for storage, not oil transport. In some ports, the damage is so widespread that it has not even been determined yet whether there was one ship sabotaged or more than one."

"Obviously," Price said, "whoever did this wanted to cripple the movement of oil and get the attention of the world. They wanted there to be no doubt in anybody's mind that they had the means to do it."

"So if they wanted to stop the movement of oil," asked Rafael Encizo, one of the Phoenix Force commandos, "why'd they hit all the aircraft? A passenger jet to India, a passenger jet to Brazil—plus a cargo flight into Moscow? What am I missing here? What's the purpose?"

"Terror is the purpose, we must assume," Barbara Price said. "Whoever did this wanted the world to know they could hit anywhere. Anyplace and anybody."

"Which brings up the big question of who?" Brognola said. "Unfortunately, we've got precious little to go on."

"How can that be?" Carl Lyons demanded. "You don't set off five hundred bombs at once, all around the world, and not leave some evidence."

"Of course there's evidence," said Gary Manning, Phoenix Force's demolitions expert. He was a veteran of the Royal Canadian Mounted Police, where he had once served as an antiterrorist operative. He was a hulking, burly, square-jawed figure, often subdued compared to some of the other figures in his team, but never hesitant to say what was on his mind. "Half those hot spots are still burning. You think there's been time to go in and sift through the wreckage?"

"FBI forensic demolitions analysis teams are on-site at five pipeline explosions, including at a Trans-Alaska Pipeline site thirty miles north of the Yukon River," Brognola said.

"The blasts were all planned for maximum destruction. In Alaska, it seems the planning went awry," Price said. "The pipeline wasn't ripped apart as thoroughly as some of the others. It appears that only about a third of the explosives in the series actually detonated."

Kurtzman typed a command into the interface board built into his wheelchair. The onscreen image of Hal shifted to a secondary screen and a map of Alaska showing a red, thick line that indicated the route of the Trans-Alaska Pipeline System appeared on the main screen. He zoomed in on Fairbanks, then followed the trail of the pipeline north until it crossed the Yukon River and headed north another thirty miles.

"It looks as if most of the pipeline explosives included twenty to thirty shaped charges designed to go off simultaneously," Price explained. "In Alaska, an estimated ten charges detonated simultaneously. The pipeline was damaged seriously, but not on the scale we've seen elsewhere around the world. We have video. Bear?"

She nodded to Kurtzman, who brought up shaky aerial footage of empty landscape. "A station in Fairbanks rushed a chopper to the scene as soon as they heard about it," Price said. "They started taping when they saw the smoke." The video shifted to show a flaming, billowing canal of black oil covering the ground and surrounding what was apparently an undamaged section of the pipeline. The destroyed section of the pipe appeared small, but it was difficult to grasp the scale from the shaky camera.

Then the pipe split open and more oil flooded out.

Manning was leaning forward on the table, watching the video intently. "So the charges didn't go off when they were supposed to, but as soon as the fire catches up to them they ignite."

"That's what we think happened."

"You said ignite," stated the black Phoenix Force commando, Calvin James, who had once been a Navy SEAL.

"That's what I said—ignite," Manning agreed. There was a moment of silence as they stared at the screen, and the pipeline broke open farther downstream. More oil spilled out and the flames intensified.

"That's a pretty damned efficient release of energy," Manning pointed out, "even going off at the wrong time. It didn't send oil spraying in all directions. It just opened up the metal."

"Low explosives engineered to just break the shell?" James suggested.

"Maybe. But nah," Manning said, frowning at the screen. "Got any more of those on tape?"

"You're in luck," Kurtzman said, nodding at the screen. There was a cut and the shot changed. Now the camera was zooming in close to the pipe. The men in the news chopper were interested in the damage being done to the pipeline, just as Manning was. The image was shaky and smoke-blurred. They couldn't make out anything actually attached to the pipe. The pipe was cooking in the flames from the spreading oil underneath it, then a bright white streak appeared on the surface of the metal and it grew into a narrow opening in the pipe. Oil, no longer under pressure, oozed out, and the conflagration quickly wormed its way inside and ripped the pipeline wide open.

"What the hell was that?" growled Rafael Encizo. Stocky and powerful, he'd been born in Cuba and spent plenty of time rotting in Castro's prisons. Castro couldn't kill Encizo, but only made him stronger. Encizo was a naval tech specialist, as much at home in the water as on land.

"Virtually no visible fragmentation," Manning pointed out.

"These bastards were trying to be neat about it?" McCarter demanded.

"They were trying to be efficient," Manning said with a grim smile. "You go setting off five hundred devices at a time, you need to control costs. You figure out just exactly how much explosive or incendiary you need, you figure out how to make it do exactly what you want it to do, then you use just enough each time to do your dirty work."

A man in a cowboy hat had been stretched out in the chair alongside James. As the others kept their eyes glued to the progressive damage playing out along the Alaskan pipeline, the man in the hat now walked around to stand behind Akira Tokaido.

Thomas Jackson Hawkins knew quite a bit about electronic communications—military, civilian and industrial. He watched intently as Tokaido played with some communications schematics out of Alaska, using computer models of communications infrastructure to replicate the simultaneous detonation of hundreds of bombs around the world—a type of communication whose failure could lead to the partial misfires that had occurred in Alaska.

"What about the lab in Georgia where Rafe got burned?" Hermann Schwarz was asking. "Gary, they were specializing in incendiary research."

"I've looked at the reports. I don't know what the hell that was all about. It was damned suspicious, for sure. But what were they trying to accomplish by bringing in foreign-made military research and prototype? I couldn't figure it out."

"What about the prototype devices they supplied the military?" Schwarz asked. "Any good?"

"No. They were shoddy," Manning said.

"But could their prototypes do that?" Schwarz persisted, nodding at the screen where the Alaskan pipeline continued to open again every few minutes.

Manning shrugged. "I doubt it."

"Would you like to see one of the devices from the Solon lab in Georgia?" Kurtzman asked.

Gary Manning blinked. "You have one?"

Kurtzman grimaced. "Don't worry. It's not live."

Carmen Delahunt was already slipping out of the room and was back in a moment with a plastic crate. She opened it and removed several items packed in gray foam: a wallet and a cell phone, both removed by Carl Lyons from the intruder at the lab. There was also a small, engineered device composed of three plastic discs held together by three plastic screws. Delahunt handed it to Manning, along with a printout of the functional characteristics of the device.

"One of the prototype samples from the lab."

Of the dozen people in the War Room, not one took notice when the time code on the various computer screens changed to 8:00 p.m.

Manning sneered at the prototype. "This?"

"Looks like a Big Mac without the all-beef patties," Schwarz muttered.

"It is *not* more sophisticated than it looks," Price said.

Manning spun the screw, examined the interior. "Nonmetallic. Cavity for ignitables. So what? How much taxpayer cash did this cost us?"

"Could it have been used for the attacks we just saw?"

"No," Manning said. "It's too small and it won't create a directed ignition. You'd need specially shaped charges of thermite or something to make those holes."

"You sound pretty sure," Brognola interjected.

"I know it would make things simpler if we could target your lab in Georgia right now, but it's not adding up," Manning said. "Maybe this was a diversionary tactic. They wanted to create the prototype to show just how inept they were when it came to engineering weaponized incendiaries. That would explain why they would trying to submit something like this as an advanced prototype." Manning was arguing with the schematics sheet in front of him. "Yeah. They must have known this was crap when they sent it into the DOD. They did it on purpose."

"Everything about that situation was damned odd," Lyons growled. "I bet it was those hamburger incendiaries that they had rigged to go off on us. They were throwing shit in all directions."

Manning shrugged. "You load it up with thermite, it would be a great arson tool," he said, sliding the clattering plastic piece across the conference table. "For getting through the A53 carbon steel they use for structural steel pipes—no way. Not the precision punctures we just saw happen in Alaska."

"We're getting bloody nowhere," David McCarter grumbled. He got up, paced behind the table and sucked on his Egyptian Coca-Cola until the plastic bottle collapsed with a fingernails-on-chalkboard crackling noise, then stopped when he was the center of attention of every person in the War Room.

Except for Akira Tokaido and T. J. Hawkins, who were jabbering quietly together and poking at the tablet screen. There was a dull but tangible frustration in the room.

Despite the vast inventory of attacks that had just occurred, no action plan presented itself. This was not a group of people accustomed to doing nothing.

Still, not one of them noticed when the time code on the computer screens turned from 8:02 p.m. to 8:03 p.m.

The phone that Carl Lyons had lifted from the attacker in the lab in Georgia began to ring.

Everybody in the room looked at it.

T. J. Hawkins said something under his breath.

Akira Tokaido's hand froze over the tablet.

There was a beep from a computer. Then the peal of an electronics alarm. And then another. The phone rang again.

"More attacks?" Kurtzman exclaimed.

"Shit!" Akira Tokaido said. "Coming through the fucking phones!" He sprawled over the conference table, grabbed the phone from Solon Labs and leaped behind one of the nearby terminals. The phone rang again. He snatched at a USB cable and jabbed it into the phone.

Kurtzman wheeled into position behind a computer of his own. Brognola, having vanished offscreen, saw none of the action.

"You getting this?" the big Fed's voice demanded. "We've got railroad and bridge alerts! Are you getting this?"

"Incoming calls setting off the devices," T. J. Hawkins explained as the cybernetics crew seated themselves at any terminal that happened to be available. "Akira and I were discussing that possibility just before the phone went off."

"Tracking the incoming call," Tokaido said, his voice on edge.

"What good will that do?" Manning asked Schwarz. "The calls won't all be coming from the same number."

"They're originating *somewhere,*" Schwarz said.

The phone was still ringing.

"Tell me you got something, Barb!" Brognola barked from far away in D.C.

"Got it!" Tokaido said. "Tracking back!"

"How far can you get, Akira?" Price asked with an unreal calm.

"I don't know!"

"Bear?" Price urged.

"We're moving!" Kurtzman said. "We're getting through!"

"Through to what?" Brognola asked.

Barbara Price shook her head at him. She wasn't going to ask for an explanation right now.

"Got the bastard!" Tokaido said.

"Seeing it," responded the low, calm rumble of Huntington Wethers. "Identifying that picocell as a nanoGSM. Sending you the serial number."

"I'm accessing the OMC-R," Tokaido said.

Hawkins, standing at Tokaido's shoulder, made a face at Schwarz. "He can access the Operations and Management Center-Radio?" he whispered.

"I'm in," Tokaido crowed. His fingers stabbed at the keys. He spoke angrily at the LCD screen. "You are *not* getting past me *again*."

His fingers stopped. He sat there staring at the screen. Kurtzman pushed back from his monitor.

"Okay, it's off," Kurtzman said. "He turned it off. Akira, you did it. It's off."

"Yeah. I know."

"Holy shit. That was fast-ass hackwork, my friend," Hawkins said, clapping Tokaido on the shoulder.

"Yeah." Tokaido didn't seem to share Hawkins's enthusiasm. He began typing again furiously. "Gonna cover my tracks."

"We know where the picocell is, right?" Schwarz demanded.

"I can give you a street address," Wethers confirmed. "In Barcelona."

"Let's go get that damned box!" Hawkins said.

"Will it do us any good?" Price asked.

"It just might," Kurtzman said. "The picocell, the base station controller—the radio operations and maintenance hardware give us a way into the system."

"Sounds like a weak link. As soon as they know it's compromised they'll stop using it. Or incinerate it," Price suggested.

"Maybe not," Tokaido announced. "There's a power outage in that end of the city. They'll have battery backup but I told the Operations and Management Center for the nanoGSM to take steps against a surge. Maybe they'll believe that was the reason their signals stopped going out."

"A power outage caused by?"

Tokaido grimaced and held up ten wiggling fingers, then kept typing.

"They'll never believe the timing was coincidental," Price replied.

"I'm creating a record in the OMC of several hours of power fluctuations on the grid," Tokaido said. "If I'm this terrorist, then I'm gonna dedicate my picocell to my own job. I'm not sharing it with anybody. Which means the picocell's had low-volume traffic all day until the high volume of signals at 8:04 Eastern time. I'm making it look like the thing was cycling on and off. When the high volume of calls started, it was too at-risk and the system shut itself down again."

"A good IT guy will see through it."

"They might see through it anyway," Price snapped. "But we'll be there if they're not. Phoenix?"

"We're gone," McCarter snapped, and the room cleared of the five members in seconds.

"Carmen?" Price said.

"Transport to Barcelona is standing by for Phoenix Force," Delahunt replied. Aircraft, like almost all dedicated Stony Man resources, had been standing by since the first attack. "Ground transport will be waiting for them in Barcelona."

"Can I get an update here?" Brognola said.

Price walked to the screen and quickly summarized the rapid-fire chain of events. "We tracked down a specific picocell as the source of the calls going out. A picocell is a phone cell system. An office building might have one for dedicated mobile phone traffic. The hardware's not large."

"How large?" Brognola asked. "Would it need a dedicated IT room? Extra air-conditioning? That kind of thing?"

"No, Hal," Kurtzman broke in, wheeling away from his desk. "The picocell itself, the operations and maintenance hardware, the base station, none of it's bigger than a PC tower. The biggest piece would be a battery backup. That's a 150-pound box, maybe."

"Think they'll buy the story about the power fluctuations?"

"If they have enough IT skill to look into the source of the problem, and not so much they analyze operational logs—maybe," Kurtzman said.

"Or maybe they'll play it safe and just burn it down. They'll have backup phone systems," Brognola said. He was staring at his own offscreen monitors. Barbara Price didn't know what he was looking at. She would have time, soon enough, to assess the latest series of attacks.

"We're working on tracing the destinations of the phone calls," Kurtzman announced.

"I'm into the Mobile interface," Tokaido announced. "I'm looking at the call traces."

Kurtzman nodded. "Hunt?"

"We recorded some of the outgoing calls. This one to Chicago. It's not voice. Sending commands to some sort of smartphone app. Pretty specific set of commands."

"This is a call that went though?" Kurtzman asked.

"Yes." Huntington Wethers turned to the big screen and brought up a computer map of Chicago, then zoomed in tight. "Right here," he said.

"Railroad," Kurtzman observed.

"Commuter rails have been hit heavily in the last ten minutes," Brognola said. "Two commuter trains derailed in Chicago."

"Mile southwest of the Metro Wrightwood station," Wethers clarified.

"That's one of them," Brognola confirmed.

"We did intercept calls that did not go through,"

Kurtzman stated, but there was a slight question in his voice.

"Yes," Tokaido said. "Should I trace them?"

"How?" Schwarz said, suddenly alarmed.

"I gotta place a call."

Silence.

"Several of the numbers are 703s," Tokaido added.

"It appears—*appears*—that an app is used to ignite the devices. We'll know more after we analyze this phone." Kurtzman nodded at the phone on Tokaido's desk—the one from the lab in Georgia.

"But it could be just the incoming call itself that does it?" Brognola asked loudly.

"Possible."

"Allow any incoming call to start the ignition? That would be a foolish risk for the attackers to take," Schwarz said.

"But not out of the question," Price said.

"I'm calling this," Brognola said. "I do know the risks. I know we could be setting off one of these devices. We must follow this lead."

"You're gambling," Price said.

"I know," Brognola shot back. "Make the call."

Tokaido hit a key. The call went through. The ring came through the speakers on his monitor. It rang. And rang.

"Does that mean it didn't detonate?" Brognola said.

"Maybe," Kurtzman responded. All eyes were on Tokaido as he tracked the signal, hit an impasse, typed out commands and continued to track.

"Got it!"

"Here it comes," Wethers said as he pulled up the map on the big screen. "It's the rail line, short distance from Franconia/Springfield Station, in Springfield, Virginia."

"Checking the emergency bands," Carmen Delahunt said. "Police and fire are relatively quiet in that vicinity."

"We're your gophers," Carl Lyons growled.

Price glanced at the time display. "Move fast."

CHAPTER SIX

Stony Man pilot Jack Grimaldi zipped them on a straight-line northwest flight over Virginia. Grimaldi was another veteran staffer of Stony Man Farm, one of many recruited back when Mack Bolan, aka the Executioner, targeted the Mafia. Grimaldi had been a Mafia pilot, but Bolan had convinced him to switch sides.

When Bolan's efforts shifted from mobsters to terrorists, and when the covert agency now based at Stony Man Farm was assembled to coordinate the activities of Bolan and the teams of black-operations commandos he had recruited, Grimaldi was on board.

His toy for today was an MD-600N, a sweet piece of helicopter engineering from McDonnell Douglas. It was fast. It was quiet. It didn't look military. In fact, Stony Man had nameplates at the ready to make it look like a news chopper or a local SWAT mover. Today, there was no logo. Nobody was supposed to be in the air—nobody. Around Washington, D.C., the no-fly zone was being enthusiastically enforced, and it took some quick behind-the-scenes work by the Farm before the Army UH-60 Black Hawk that was trying to force them to land got a cease-and-desist order.

Able Team exited the helicopter before the skids fully settled on the parking lot of an abandoned warehouse. Blancanales got behind the wheel of a black Explorer, a vehicle with run-flat tires, power-boosting accessories under the hood, and body panels that were designed to withstand bullets and shrapnel.

They drove less than a mile and Schwarz and Lyons exited the vehicle near the station. The big Alexandria, Virginia, parking lot was eerily quiet. The trains were not running today, and wouldn't be running anytime soon. Schwarz and Lyons avoided the security personnel posted at the station and slipped through the darkness and into the weeds before stepping onto the tracks.

"We're on-site, Stony," the Able Team leader said into his headset.

"We're tracking you, Carl. You're a hundred feet away and closing."

Lyons's MV-321G Gen 3 night-vision goggles were equipped with infrared illumination. The plan was for him to use night vision while Schwarz conducted a naked-eyes search. So far the track was so well lit by overhead lighting that Lyons didn't need the NVGs.

They watched the tracks, looking for signs of devices that didn't belong. Tokaido's little track-back trick had triangulated the location of just one of the cell phones. The reports of the latest wave of attacks—including derailments on several commuter and cargo railroads in the United States and around the world—suggested there would be half a dozen devices planted along the tracks. Whoever was doing this, obviously wanted to do the job completely.

They were still ten yards from the location of the specific tracked device when Schwarz froze.

"I think I've got one."

"Show us, Able," Price said through the headset.

Schwarz pulled out a video camera, offering far higher resolution than the video feed from the lipstick-size video pickups on his headset. He pointed it at the device nestled against the steel rail of the Fredericksburg Line.

"Manning is seeing it. Cowboy's here, too," Price announced. John "Cowboy" Kissinger was the Stony Man Farm armorer.

"Looks like a rock," Gary Manning announced from his seat on a jet over the Atlantic Ocean.

"I'm no ballistics expert like Gary," Kissinger said, "but I'd have to agree that it looks like a rock."

"You're a big help," Schwarz said. "Can't thank you guys enough. See the plastic foam on the bottom? It's adhered to the metal. Bonding agent of some kind. They have it glued to the track itself so they can be sure the rail is damaged by the blast."

"Gadgets," Manning said, "you can't touch that thing. What if it's got a motion-sensing trigger?"

Schwarz snorted. "It's super-glued to the rail of a commuter train line. It's been getting rattled for days."

"Gadgets—" Lyons said.

"Hey, you don't have to tell me to be careful," Schwarz said. "We don't have to touch it. We'll move it from a distance."

Schwarz pulled out a small, dense wedge of steel on a metallic spike. He pulled a safety strip to activate it, then impaled the thing in the ground, within a half inch of the device on the rail track.

They moved away from the device, along the curve of the track.

"Able Three here," Blancanales said on the line from his lookout in the Explorer. "Get to cover. Company coming. Two white males."

Schwarz and Lyons blended into the bushes.

"They're walking the rails," Blancanales added from

his vantage point. "They might be Virginia Railway Express track inspectors."

"That's to be expected."

"Looks like one of them is armed."

That was hardly out of the question either, Lyons thought, given the state of high anxiety in the nation and the fact that railroads had just become demonstrated targets.

"Any other equipment, Pol?" he asked quietly.

"No."

"Doesn't make sense," Lyons commented. "Patrols should be obviously armed. Inspectors should have equipment."

"Let's ask them," Schwarz suggested, extracting his Beretta 93-R, a handgun based on the well-known Beretta 92. One serious difference in the design: a selector switch that enabled the handgun to fire three-round bursts.

Rosario Blancanales left the Explorer and followed the path taken earlier by Lyons and Schwarz. He moved quickly. There was a dull ache from the sutures in his gut. A dull ache was nothing compared to the pain he'd woken up with after the firestorm in Georgia.

He didn't like what was happening. More than that, Blancanales knew that Stony Man was in a bad, bad place. What intelligence they had so far served them little in tracking down whoever was causing this mayhem. They needed information. They needed a source.

"Able Three here," he said quietly. "I'm in position alongside the tracks."

"Don't engage," Lyons said.

"Don't plan to," Blancanales replied. "I'm concealed. I'm the fly on the wall."

The two men approached. The one in front had a firearm held close to his leg, on the far side of his body where Blancanales only glimpsed it. The other followed a few steps behind. The body language of the follower said "nervous."

They were moving quickly now, half jogging. There was no cover here, unless they decided to crawl through the bushes where Encizo was camped.

Blancanales kept his mike wide open. Nothing to boost the audio. The Farm wasn't going to hear much of this.

"Another thirty yards," said the one in the rear.

"Yeah," said the leader.

"This ain't good, man."

"Shut up."

"This ain't good, Gus."

"I said shut the fuck up," the leader stormed, waving his weapon in the direction of his partner.

In the cold cast of the lights over the track Blancanales saw the silhouette of a machine pistol. The follower was silenced by the provocative gesture, and the two men continued down the tracks. Blancanales had to take the chance. He slipped out of the bushes and followed after them, sprinting from shadow to shadow. The pair up ahead was high on anxiety but not too skilled at stealth.

They stopped on the tracks. Blancanales shrank into a weedy dark place. The leader, the one called Gus, faced away from the track, watching for trouble, while the follower crouched over it. Encizo saw him bend at a bulge alongside the central of the three-tracks set of railroad racks running side by side in this location. This was not the device Schwarz had located. The device was removed—no, just a cover lifted off. The man quickly extracted something from the device and slipped it into a camouflage backpack. Then he unzipped another section of the pack, removed another device and flipped it on. The screen blazed colorfully to life for a moment. The man was using his body to shield the screen, but wasn't counting on a voyeur in a nearby overhang of weeds. Blancanales clearly saw it was a cell phone swap.

The man on technical duty closed the device. The swap was made in less than a minute.

The two men moved on and the technical man crouched at the next device—and froze at the sight of Schwarz's steel wedge.

"What the hell is this?"

"What?" Gus demanded.

"Look at it!"

Gus shook his head. "I got no idea."

"Me, neither, but it wasn't there before! We're made! Let's get out of here."

"If they found them, they wouldn't have just left the igniters," Gus said, although he was obviously confused by the steel wedge. His head was oscillating, looking for signs of surveillance. The night remained still. "We gotta finish this job."

"Listen to me," his companion insisted. "It wasn't here before."

"You listen," Gus snapped. "They got us by the nuts. We don't do the job, we rot in federal prison. Forever. Understand?"

"Call 'em," the technical man said. "Tell them what we found."

Gus nodded swiftly. "Yeah."

"Don't let them make that call, Gadgets!" Blancanales snapped into his mike.

Schwarz did the first thing that came to mind—he

hit the detonator switch on the dedicated remote in his hand. The metal wedge reacted with a bang and rocketed into the device adhered to the railroad track with explosive force. The steel blade sliced through the adhesion of the device, just as it was intended to do, and kept going, into the technical man, who grunted and collapsed. The steel wedge clattered away over the track ballast. Gus bolted, made it four steps, then slammed into what felt like the front end of a diesel locomotive.

Blancanales's body blow took Gus down hard. A swift stomp broke several ribs and left him stunned. Blancanales snatched the Steyr SPP out of Gus's grip and in the same motion swung the butt of the weapon into Technical Man's skull as he tried to rise to his feet. The pistol was made of a composite polymer that the manufacturer had famously called "nearly indestructible." Sure enough, the composite didn't so much as crack.

Something in the Technical Man's skull, however, broke and he collapsed and was still.

Blancanales grabbed at one of Gus's wrists and twisted it, leveraging the man onto his face, then kept pulling the wrist until it was between his shoulder blades. Something cracked. Blancanales jerked a plastic cuff around it, then grabbed his other wrist and pulled it up, as well.

Gus screamed.

Blancanales landed both knees on either side of Gus's spine. All the air in Gus's body seemed to explode out of his mouth and he mustered no more noise or resistance.

"Need a hand?" Schwarz asked as he and Lyons arrived. Schwarz's unfired 93-R covered the lifeless technician.

"No, I got this." Blancanales gave Schwarz and Lyons a wicked grin. "Leave me in the car, will ya?"

"Able One?" Price said in the headsets. "What's the status?"

"How should I know?" Lyons growled. "I'm just Pol's sidekick."

"Able Three here," Blancanales said. "Listen, we have a backpack full of cell phones. These guys were going to swap them out. They're just changing out cell phones, for God's sake. This one was about to call somebody. If we make the call, we can trace it, right?"

"Yes," Kurtzman said. "Give me the serial number."

Schwarz snatched Gus's phone and pulled a miniature screwdriver out of a small leg pack. He spun the screws off and recited the serial number.

"Here's my thought," Blancanales said quickly. "We place the call, get the trace, then detonate some of the old phone devices. We take the new phones and the rest of the devices with us. Maybe whoever was in charge of having them placed, will think this pair screwed something up. Then we get these quick to the Farm and figure out whatever we can from them."

"It can't hurt," Price said.

"But I doubt they'll buy it," Schwarz said. He was now holding one of the devices—the one that the explosive chisel had sliced off the side of the railroad track. "They're using some kick-ass adhesive. Some sort of modified cyanoacrylate, I'd guess. Unless you're packing nail polish remover, we're not getting these things off the rails in a hurry."

"We can't risk it," Lyons said. "If these guys are expected to report in and don't—they might risk blowing these devices."

"No way," Schwarz said. "They're replacing the

phones for a reason. To avoid using the old, traceable signal."

"How sure are you of that, Gadgets?" Blancanales demanded. "Sure enough to stick around?"

"No way to that, either," Schwarz conceded.

"We've got the phone online," Kurtzman said. "When you make the call, we'll trace it."

Schwarz removed the old-system cell phone from the device in his hands. He jogged up the track and snatched out the new-system cell phone that the Technical Man had put there. He had the backpack over one shoulder.

"Dead," Lyons announced after a quick check of the technician with the cratered skull. He gave a bark of disbelief when he saw Blancanales about to hoist Gus onto his shoulders. "I'll get that one," Lyons said. "I think your nerve endings must've fried out, Pol. Your guts should be screaming at you by now."

"They're a little achy," Blancanales admitted.

In fact, the burn wound was throbbing. He could count the sutures by each individual needle of pain emanating from his side.

Lyons tossed groaning Gus over his shoulder and plodded with him up the steep berm. Schwarz had stayed behind to plant the phone in the ignition device adhered to the track, then he hustled after Lyons and Blancanales.

"I'm set," Schwarz said. "But I don't think this is gonna fool anybody."

A SMALLER GROUP had gathered in the War Room. Phoenix Force was absent, now en route to Europe. Able Team was on hand, as was Stony Man armorer John "Cowboy" Kissinger, a tall man with broad shoulders and narrow hips. Kissinger was well-known for his expertise with almost every type of weapon. He could dismantle and rebuild any firearms system put in front of him.

Kissinger was—like almost everyone at the Farm— a veteran of bigger, more public organizations in the outside world. He had spent years with the U.S. Bureau of Narcotics and Dangerous Drugs. When it was restructured as the Drug Enforcement Administration, or DEA, Kissinger went freelance for some time before finding a home at Stony Man Farm. He maintained the Farm armory, often upgrading and improving the standard-issue equipment.

"Explosives," Kissinger said, "are not my primary focus, but I read the research. Including the stuff the military researchers don't know I'm reading. So I know what the state of the art is in weaponized nanothermites." He set the device on the table, now in pieces, and waved a hand at it. "This is beyond what we thought of as state of the art."

Hal Brognola, sitting at his desk in Washington, edged forward in his seat and adjusted a camera on one of his displays to focus on the device. "Weaponized nanothermites aren't new."

"No way," Schwarz said. "They've been tested for years. They're looking at using MICs as primer in small arms. Not even for performance improvements. They want primers that won't release vaporized lead every time a round is fired."

"And this is an MIC?" Price asked.

Kissinger shook his head. "It's not."

"It's *not*?" Schwarz echoed.

"It's not a composite—not in the way everyone thinks of as an MIC, a Metastable Intermolecular Composite," Kissinger said. "The standard assumption is that MICs are *laminated* composites. It puts an ultra-thin, nanoscale layer of aluminum or some other metal fuel atop a layer of an oxidizer. The two materials are exothermically reactive, and the proximity is so close that the diffusion of the oxidizer and fuel happens much more quickly and energetically. The rate of reaction is much, much faster. We've been working on tuning nanolaminated pyrotechnics to achieve different results. Different metals used in the nanolayers, different fillers used to separate and encase the laminates, give you interesting results. And the reaction time is far superior to a simple mixture of the old powders used in more standard incendiaries."

"So how's this different?" Schwarz demanded.

"Particle size, for one. We're working with 100 to 200 nanometer-diameter particles when making the MICs. The particles in these devices are much, much smaller. They're in the range of one-quarter to one-half of one nanometer in size."

"They can do that?" Schwarz asked.

"Can we do that, you mean?" Kissinger asked. "Yeah. Maybe. Maybe in a lab. Or maybe not."

"So layers of particles that fine," Price said, "would be that much closer together. The reaction is that much faster."

"Much faster," Kissinger confirmed. "Here's where it gets interesting. There are no layers in this device. Instead of a layer of fuel and a layer of oxidizer, the particles are *conjoined*."

"Conjoined?" Price queried.

"No way!" Schwarz said. "They can do that?"

"Can *we* do that, you mean?" Kissinger repeated. "No way. They can, obviously. And they did."

"Conjoined—layers?" Kurtzman asked. "I think I'm a few steps back."

"You're not the only one," Brognola muttered loudly. "I've been lost for the past five minutes."

"Conjoined *particles*. Take one particle of fuel—at 0.5 nanometer in diameter. Take one particle of oxidizer, same size. Adhere them so they're conjoined. They're glued together. The reaction time is far faster than any incendiary device we've seen before."

"And this is not something that has been accomplished before?" Brognola challenged. "Not by the U.S.? Not by anybody?"

Kissinger shrugged. "Not by anybody as far as I know."

"This is good news, right?" Carl Lyons said, speaking for the first time. "Specialty item needs special people or special equipment to be made. Now we have something to go on. Right? So let's get going."

"You're right, Carl," Kissinger said. "This is indeed specialty technology. There are a few companies out there working on nanoparticles in this range, and a few university labs, as well. One of them is here in the United States. Company in Texas. Name is—get this—NanoPlasPulse LLC. Brains behind the operation is the CEO, Harry Envoi. They're using his patents."

"Ugh. This sounds like a familiar situation," Rosario Blancanales growled. "Like the Georgia lab."

"Yeah, I thought the same thing at first," Kissinger continued. "Then I checked the guy out. He's got the credibility that your friend in Georgia did not have." Kissinger tapped a stapled white stack of pages that lay in front of him.

Brognola tried to read the title through his video. "What is that?"

Schwarz raised the stack and read the cover sheet. "'Production Technique Studies on Conjoined Nanopowder Particulates for Metastable Intermolecular Composite Alternatives.'"

"Sorry I asked," Brognola said.

"Envoi wrote it. He's written several papers throughout the years. He's demonstrated long-term expertise and pioneering development in the creation of creating unagglomerated nanopowders."

"*Unagglomerated* means 'not glommed together,' I assume," Brognola said.

"Right," Kissinger said. "Think of it this way. The smaller the particle, and the closer a particle is to a complementary but different particle, the more the complementary effect will be—whether that effect is an incendiary reaction or, say, metal flexibility."

"So could Envoi be the guy who created the devices?" Lyons asked. "If so, what's his home address?"

"I'm not going to rule him out," Kissinger said. "I'll let you all do that. But here's the rub—at the same time we were doing a quick evaluation of this device, other devices were being evaluated in other parts of the world."

They had already received the news of other devices being discovered around the world. Tokaido's quick work had left many of the units in place and unactivated, and large-scale search efforts were turning them up.

"Twenty minutes before I came into this meeting, DARPA identified this material and set up a classified conference call with Harry Envoi. He's agreed to be a consultant on the investigation. I want to be in on that call."

"Absolutely," Price said, knowing the DOD's Defense Advanced Research Projects Agency would be thorough in its questioning of the CEO.

"The Japanese have ID'd the material, as well. As of ten minutes ago, there was a highly classified debate going on, among research and governmental offices in Japan. They're trying to decide whether to release their findings or not."

"Not anymore," Tokaido called from a desk away from the conference table, where he was monitoring, as far as Kissinger could tell, thirty windows on five computer monitors, shuffling through them at blinding speed. "They're going public in a few hours."

"Is that wise?" Brognola demanded.

"Are you going to try to stop them?" Price asked.

"No," the big Fed admitted.

"How can we know if it is a good idea or not?" Lyons demanded. "We don't know who we're dealing with."

"True," Brognola said.

"We don't know who is doing it or why they're doing it," Lyons added. "When the Oklahoma City bomb went off, we figured out why just by looking at the calendar—April 19, same day as Waco, must be somebody really pissed at the government. With 9-11 we knew right away it was Al Qaeda. This one? We don't know anything. We've got nothing." Lyons fumed, then waved at the cell phone from the Alexandria site. "Didn't that lead us anywhere?"

"The phone tells us nothing, I'm afraid," Price admitted. "They're off-the-shelf, pay-per-use phones. Other attack sites around the world have produced phones of various makes and models, all prepaid, using untraceable accounts. They've been purchased over at least the last twelve months, usually by the people who put them in the field."

"What can those people tell us?" Blancanales asked. "What about Groaning Gus—the guy we brought home from Alexandria?"

"He's at our safehouse. He's being questioned, but he doesn't know anything helpful yet. Recruited via telephone eight months ago, along with several acquaintances who all served time together at the penitentiary in Lewisburg, Pennsylvania. All convicted on pretty ugly crimes, all recidivists, all released within the past twenty-four months. They claimed they were paid twenty grand each in cash for placing the devices seven weeks ago. Half the cash came with the devices, the other half came afterward—and another twenty thousand was promised after the devices were employed." Price looked up at Brognola and the other faces. "That's the word used by their coordinator," Price said. "*Employed.* Yesterday they received more phone calls, directing them to return to the scene to switch out the phones with new phones, and our friend Gus—last name Balldis—found a box of fresh phones sitting at the front door. Along with a DVD showing a video of him placing the devices the first time. So they were essentially blackmailed into cooperating."

"What does all this tell us?" Brognola asked.

"That this is well planned and seriously, seriously well funded," Kurtzman said. "If the operation in Alexandria is exemplary of other operations worldwide, there must have been hundreds of hired hands to set those devices. The labor costs could be several million dollars. Plus more labor to surveil the first group and provide incriminating evidence against them."

"That doesn't take into account the cost of the devices," Schwarz said.

"Which may or may not have been significant," Kissinger added. "Without knowing how they were made, we don't know if it was expensive to make them. The materials themselves are not exceptional or terribly expensive. The housing is molded engineered plastic. High precision but also unexceptional. Thousands of plastics shops could have ordered the material and molded the parts without even knowing what they were for. The igniters? Specially made to create a small electrostatic spark but also unexceptional in terms of technology. These nanothermites were detonated by the very simple commands received by off-the-shelf, pay-per-use, mobile smartphones."

"What about the new cell phones?" Lyons probed. "They'll get a new phone signal."

"And we won't know how to identify it until the signal is sent," Kurtzman said.

"If Phoenix can get the box in Barcelona, we'll know sooner," Tokaido added from the sidelines. "Unless they blow the box first, we'll be able to trace any calls that come into it."

"Shit," Lyons said. "I don't want to wait on Phoenix. They're still over the damned Atlantic."

Hermann Schwarz was flipping through the pages of the white paper from the nanopowders firm in Texas. "If this stuff is as powerful as you say, Cowboy, then these devices are overkill. Way more powerful than required."

"Yes, absolutely, and that brings up something else we have to consider," Kissinger said, but he seemed uneasy about speaking his thoughts aloud. "This technology—it's fantastic. But it is not being used to its fullest potential."

"Let's hope to God they don't use it to its fullest potential," Brognola said.

"But, you see, it's obviously being used in a very

crude format right now," Kissinger continued. "Obvious to me, Gadgets, or anybody who knows how to work out the properties of an incendiary event from one of these devices."

"This one device will do way more than deform a railroad rail enough to cause a derailment," Schwarz agreed. "It'll melt the steel into soup. Whoever did this could have done the job with a device a quarter of the size. Even less."

"Which got me thinking, why'd they make the device so big? The answer I came up with is economy of scale," Kissinger said. "In other words, it's so easy and so cheap for them to make these big, powerful devices, why bother making smaller ones? Why not make them all monsters, like this. And I think whoever did this wanted it to be obvious. They *knew* the devices would be found and analyzed. They *know* what we have discovered. Now we know they can easily take down water towers. Suspension bridges. Burn craters in interstates just by driving down one at night and tossing these out the window. Destroy city water systems just by sticking them into the sewer drains."

Kissinger was clearly disturbed by the implications. "Somebody could go in and put a hundred of these on a hundred pleasure boats in one night and they'd all sink. Or on a thousand semis and cripple transport around the country. And every time one piece of the infrastructure becomes guarded they'll move on to the next. And we won't be able to stop them. Because this little mother can take down just about anything we can put up. And we can't put eyes on every square foot of the country all the time. This is the most extreme asymmetric vector I've ever seen—and whoever did this can almost certainly make them more effective. Smaller. More easily distributed."

Lyons was staring at him. "Jesus, Cowboy."

CHAPTER SEVEN

Midnight came. Everyone at Stony Man Farm nervously watched the clock in the War Room. They expected another attack at 12:03 a.m.

Tokaido's quick work had turned off the second series of attacks at 8:03. The scale had been miniscule compared to the first attacks, and only the Farm knew that there had been hundreds more signals attempting to transmit to numerous other locations within the United States and around the world.

The device obtained by Able Team in Alexandria, Virginia, was being intensively analyzed in the blast-proof lab at Stony Man Farm.

An encrypted, high-security alert originating from the Computer Room at the Farm had led to the retrieval of more devices. Some from the Alexandria site. Others from sites around the world. The second wave of attacks had been predominantly focused on railroads. At least fifteen sabotage sites had been identified in Australia alone.

China hinted that as many as 257 individual devices had ignited along Chinese railways. Russia, the other Central Asian nations, Europe and Brazil had all located and sanitized sites. Successful ignition had nevertheless caused widespread damage and even catastrophic derailments in fifteen countries. The scope of loss of life was staggering, and the potential of the catastrophe that might have been was the topic of widespread speculation in the media.

It was becoming clear that fewer than half of the devices that had been planted had successfully been ignited in the second wave of attack.

Tokaido and Kurtzman had been trying to establish a way to confuse or alter the signal that would leave the picocell without alerting the senders. But they needed the device to even start testing their ideas.

They also needed to know where the signal originated. They would begin working on that, too—once they had the device.

The 12:03 plan was a simple one—turn the picocell off. Tokaido had hacked aggressively into the power utilities in Barcelona and forced rolling blackouts. None of them widespread or long-lasting, but enough to establish a pattern. Maybe they'd fool the attackers.

But probably not.

Just before midnight, Eastern U.S. time, another blackout was scheduled to hit Barcelona. It would last ten minutes. The Barcelona picocell—assuming it had backup power—would remain functional, but there would be no operable cell systems to retransmit the calls.

It shouldn't have worked. The attackers should have known their picocell was under electronic surveillance. They should have known the rolling blackouts were a ruse. They should have known to simply delay the attacks until the power was restored.

And Tokaido was being locked out of the Barcelona power system. The IT staff had shut him out. They'd essentially turned off the computer control of the system, taking it all back to manual control—then flushed Tokaido's access by rebooting the entire system.

The power was restored at 12:19 a.m. Eastern time. The 12:03 attacks had been prevented simply by pulling the plug. The attackers could have chosen to launch the attacks late; inexplicably, they'd chosen not to launch the 12:03 attacks at all.

When it became clear that Phoenix Force would not have time to reach and shut down the picocell before the 4:03 a.m. EST attacks were scheduled, Stony Man Farm came up with alternative measures.

Barbara Price had taken it upon herself to make the decision. She had listened to Kurtzman and Tokaido describe what they believed would happen when those signals went out scrambled. There had been no indication that any of the devices could be detonated by anything except a specific signal.

But it was a risk. And Barbara Price had made it very clear that she alone would make the decision as to whether they would allow those signals to proceed to their destination, even in scrambled form. She and she alone would bear the brunt of the fallout.

And she had decided that the risk was worth the potential good that might come from identifying the targets.

Once she made her decision, she was on the phone to Hal Brognola. She explained their position and their options.

"Well, the only thing we have to do now is decide whether we are going to let this happen or not."

"The decision was made, Hal," Price said.

"By who?" Brognola said.

"By me," Price answered. "I have been following these events minutely. I listened to the expert opinions of Kurtzman and Tokaido. I'm in the best position to make this decision. I decided Stony Man Farm will intercept, scramble and allow the signals to go out to their targets."

Barbara Price heard Brognola chewing on something. It was an antacid tablet. As much as he tried to stay away from them, in certain situations he chewed them constantly.

"That is quite a risk," Brognola said. "If you are wrong…"

"Hal, I know what the repercussions will be if I'm wrong. And I know what the benefits will be if this works."

"I see," Brognola said. "I would make the same decision."

That had been at 3:49 a.m. The next set of signals was to be communicated via a proprietary cell signal to the picocell at 4:03 a.m. Eastern time. Right on time. The signals had come in through the picocell, been scrambled remotely by Stony Man Farm and allowed to continue on their way to their destinations around the world.

The applications put in place by the Farm cyberteam had worked perfectly. Their function was not in question. The question was whether or not the targets would react to the altered signals that they received.

At 4:10 a.m. Eastern time, Barbara Price finally let out the breath of air, as if she'd been holding it for the past seven long minutes. There had been no alerts.

But that in and of itself was confusing. Why had the signals even gone through the picocell again? What were the perpetrators thinking? Surely they must be aware by this time that their sole hub of communications distribution to their uncountable attack devices had been thoroughly compromised. How could they not know that?

IT WAS NOT YET FIVE o'clock in the morning. Fifty minutes ago, the next wave of attacks had been scheduled to occur—and they had, at precisely 4:03 a.m. Eastern U.S. time. They passed through the same electronic gateway, using the same codes and the same commands.

This time, Akira Tokaido could not hack his way into the Barcelona power grid control. He could not black out the city.

Stony Man Farm turned to its second option. Using its limited level of control to the box itself, it corrupted the outgoing signals. The attack calls were made, the call destinations were identified, but the transmitted signals were garbage.

None of the alert signals sounded in the Computer Room. Another wave of attacks had been prevented.

As much as they were relieved to have gained another respite, the fact that the signals continued to pass through the picocell at all refused to make sense.

The cyberteam scrambled to make sense of the incoming reams of data. They quickly realized the patterned similarity of the previous attacks. Targets included worldwide natural gas lines, oil pipelines and railroad tracks. Several refinery tanks had also been targeted, as were hundreds of commuter airport runways. These were small, sometimes unmonitored airports that served single-engine and private aircraft across the United States and around the world.

Price had recognized the potential of such a target immediately. How easy it would be to get onto a runway in an airport that was not even fenced. Not even manned during the overnight hours. How easy to walk onto such a property, maybe weeks in advance of the planned attack, wedge a device into a depression in the ground and leave it there until needed.

Then to ignite it in the middle of the night, and allow it to melt a ragged, gaping fissure into the surface of the runway. There might be no one present to see it happen. The damage might go unnoticed until it was too late—until some recreational pilot in a single-engine aircraft tried to land and found his landing gear sheared off by the damaged runway.

That, Barbara Price decided, was the most insidious element of these attacks. These devices were so small, so abundant, so easy to disperse, that they could create incidental havoc. They could be used to perpetrate off-hand murders. They could kill remotely and arbitrarily.

The large-scale attacks had already paralyzed many parts of the world. It was the potential of hundreds of small yet horribly effective attacks that would truly bring the planet to a standstill.

But the reality was that the focus of the attacks so far—successful and prevented—had been quite narrow in scope. Notably missing from the targets were large buildings. It was as if the terrorists were specifically avoiding such buildings. This despite the fact that the devices would have effectively melted through steel support beams on almost any city building.

It was almost as if the perpetrators were trying to be original. Although, if Barbara Price were to look ahead and allow her mind to accept the potential that the perpetrators could succeed wildly in a series of ongoing attacks, she could see them create in the minds of the people the impression that such buildings were actually safe places to be. It was easy to foresee a round of attacks that would then target city buildings and create an even greater sense of global insecurity.

That potential was skewed by the discovery by Carmen Delahunt of the first and only targeted skyscraper.

It was Cranston Tower in downtown Philadelphia. Construction had begun in April 2004 and was completed, after some financial delays, in December 2009. A highly secure, environmentally friendly and uniquely designed thirty-story high-rise with a unique domed top.

Cranston Tower was a multifunction building: offices, shops, a boutique hotel, exclusive condominiums. It was a destination residence for the wealthy and fashionable in Philadelphia, attracting a number of high-profile, high-price-tag retail outlets. The kinds of places that didn't welcome drop-in shoppers—you made an appointment.

It would also be an astoundingly easy place to sabotage using the nanothermite devices. Any resident or employee could have carried one in. Any hotel guest could have brought one. Any delivery person or maintenance worker could have stashed one in a pocket. Despite the high-profiled security of Cranston Tower, there were no measures that would have prevented a nanothermite device from being planted in hundreds of places within the structure.

Which didn't explain why this city building—of all the inhabited buildings in the world—was the first and only one to be targeted.

Philadelphia

HERMANN SCHWARZ DID NOT like their situation. He did not like not knowing what was going on. Or why. Or who was responsible.

Able Team penetrated Cranston Tower with almost no effort. Posing as a trio of well-to-do executives from a social media advertising firm, they freely entered the building. Carrying knapsacks packed with ordnance and gear, they made their way unnoticed to the fifteenth floor hotel and checked in. They wasted no time getting into their rooms and changing into clothing that would afford them better maneuverability.

A stairwell provided passage from the fifteenth to the nineteenth floor, where they found a maintenance elevator that responded to an electronically rigged key card.

On the twenty-fourth floor Able Team slipped into a dark, silent hallway. Only the overnight lighting was eliminated on this floor, home to an ultraexclusive shopping mall. The floor was ceramic tile, like something from the streets of a romanticized movie version of Tuscany. Engraved, matte-finished lettering identified the doors to the establishments along the hallway. The business names were nonspecific, as if identifying the nature of the business would be much too gauche. It was difficult to tell which business would sell rare artwork at a million dollars apiece or which was the corporate law firm that would handle a multibillion-dollar lawsuit.

Able Team found themselves standing in front of a jewelry store. The display windows were tiny and empty. The million-dollar necklaces and two-million-dollar tennis bracelets had been put away the previous evening. The stores were not expected to open for hours. Inside, security lighting highlighted more carefully emptied display cases and antique French furniture.

"What the hell?" Schwarz quipped.

"We knew this is what it would be," Blancanales pointed out. They had indeed expected the coordinates to take them to this exact location. They'd been debriefed to that extent, at least, before leaving the Farm. They hadn't taken the time to ask questions.

But it was a jewelry store.

"This does not make sense," Schwarz said. "What arc we missing?"

Carl Lyons touched his earpiece. "Can you get us in, Stony?"

Kurtzman responded. "Okay, Able, in about ten seconds you will break into one of the most expensive jewelry stores on the planet."

They watched the doors. It was a set of French doors, unexceptional and not even terribly sturdy, from appearances. There was no sign of an alarm system, let alone a door bolt.

"Try it now," Kurtzman said.

Blancanales put his hand on the door and pulled.

The door opened, and now that Schwarz could examine its edge, it was more than it appeared to be. The interlocks had moved under their own power as soon as Blancanales had set them in motion, exposing teeth that reciprocated to de-interlock. The door panels appeared to be composed of eight layers of laminated material. Several of the layers were dull metal, while others were gray layers of engineered ceramic plastics. Schwarz dropped to the ground to examine a small logo on the bottom of the inside of the door panel.

"It's rated like a very secure safe," Schwarz announced. He touched his earpiece. "Stony, we'd have got some serious armor protecting this jewelry shop. More than you might even expect for a place selling gaudy dinner plates at a quarter million a pop. Unless I totally miss my mark, this is titanium shielding inside the door panels. And in the ceiling and floor. I would be willing to guess that the titanium shielding extends around the entire structure of the store itself. It's a big, armored box. There is also some sort of an engineered ceramic substrate sandwiched in the layers of titanium. This is extreme."

Blancanales put his face right up against the interior surface of the wall inside the door and played with a tiny LED flashlight. When he finally got the holographic logo visible he nodded and tapped it. Schwarz examined it.

"Christ," Schwarz said, "this is a metallic glass." He stood in the middle of the small store and did a quick inspection of the walls. "Look at these seams. These wall panels are made to be detachable."

Schwarz jammed his fingers into one of the seams and yanked a wall panel back. It was a lightweight padded panel, and behind it was more of the solid laminated glass.

"This room is completely encased in metallic glass," Schwarz said. "I thought this stuff was only being used by the aircraft-design guys."

Blancanales frowned. "Stony, is there something you are not telling us about this place? I'm telling you, this damned store cost somebody one hundred million dollars to install."

"Metallic glass?" Lyons asked.

"It is a palladium alloy," Schwarz said. "Invented just a few years ago. They've just brought the first batches of it to market. Really strong stuff. Stronger than transparent aluminum."

"There's no such thing as transparent aluminum," Lyons said.

"It was a joke," Schwarz said. "Watch *Star Trek* much? There is a lot more going on here than just selling overpriced jewelry."

Blancanales scowled. "If there are nanothermite dcvices in here," he asked, "how are they getting activated? Stony?"

"They're not," replied Kurtzman. "Those phones wouldn't get the signals behind titanium and palladium shielding. Unless you've got something boosting the signal."

"These guys wouldn't take those measures," Blancanales said.

"Pol's right," Lyons said. "That doesn't match the methods we've seen these attackers use. They are not going to spend the time to install some sort of a mechanism to feed cell phone signals through the walls. They use the same devices they always use."

"Then the devices are behind the walls," Blancanales said.

"Underneath," Lyons said. "That would be the logical place to put it."

"Yeah," Schwarz said. "Remember, these guys aren't trying to steal anything. Whatever is stored in that safe, we have to assume they want to destroy it."

Lyons touched his earpiece. "Stony, do we still have no idea what's in this place? Have you guys turned up nothing?"

"We may have found something," Price said.

"No inventory for the store," Kurtzman added, "but we're piecing together high-security courier receipts. But it's just jewelry."

A moment later Kurtzman added, "Very, very expensive jewelry."

Aaron Kurtzman read the list aloud. "We have a handful of natural, high-grade red diamonds, valued at anywhere from half a million to one million dollars per carat. We also have one of the largest collections of cut painite gemstones and jewelry in the world."

"Bear, I am really missing something here," Lyons said.

"Were talking about some of the rarest and most valuable gemstones on the planet," Kurtzman said. "Some of these gems are worth twenty thousand, fifty thousand dollars a carat. There is at least one blue garnet in the mix with an estimated value 1.25 million dollars per carat."

"So what?" Lyons said. "What would be the point of burning them up?"

"They are assets," Kurtzman said. "The gems being stored in these vaults are not jewelry—they're net worth. Some of these gems are appreciating twenty percent per year. Unlike any sort of financial investment, their value is unlikely to drop. This makes them an extremely effective, secure, compact method of storing extremely large amounts of wealth in an extremely small footprint."

"Worth billions with a *b?*" Schwarz asked.

"Many billions."

"Oil profits?"

Kurtzman chuckled. "You're a sharp one, Mr. Schwarz. The names I'm getting are mostly in the petro industry."

"So the jewelry store shtick is a front. This is a fricking bank," Lyons said. "These are savings accounts."

"Worth billions with a *b,*" Kurtzman added. "The working capital of some of the biggest private oil concerns on the planet. Burn it up and you erase years of profits."

Philadelphia

SCHWARZ DESCENDED a proprietary stairwell, taking him under the jewelry store and below the vault. Above his head was several feet of concrete and reinforced steel plate, sandwiched together. This obstacle had been left in the building plans, even when the nature of the high-security room above it was not. This obstacle, Schwarz understood, was intended to dissuade anyone who knew about the value of the vault and thought he might find a way inside by burrowing up from below.

But the attack that was planned could exploit that layer of protection. Looking at the publicly available building plans, one would see quickly enough that it would be easy enough to remove that mass—with catastrophic results.

Schwarz used the key card provided by the Farm to open the door to this secure hold underneath the store. He lifted his MP5, pointing it into the face of the surprised security guard.

"Who the hell are you?" the guard demanded.

"Never mind," Schwarz said calmly. "You need to listen closely. I am not the bad guy. But I am sure you need to leave immediately. This place might be about to burn."

The man jumped to his feet. The quick action made Schwarz start, but he didn't fire. The guard was just startled.

Very startled.

"You know about it?" The guard looked terrified.

Schwarz sense of danger shot sky-high. "*You* know about it?" he demanded.

"I don't want to burn!" the guard begged. "They said we wouldn't burn!"

"Facedown, out here," Schwarz snapped.

Instead the guard dropped behind his security desk and dragged out his 9 mm handgun. When he reached over the desk to fire, Schwarz shot his arm to ribbons.

Another guard materialized from the opposite side. Schwarz triggered a blast but the man was already jumping for the emergency exit stairs.

The guard behind the desk got to his feet, eyes blazing, and hit his keyboard. An alarm activated and the guard ran for it—until Schwarz took his feet out from under him.

"We've been had," Schwarz radioed. "The guards are in on the attack. One of them just hit the alarm and made a run for it. He's afraid of burning."

"Pull out, Able," Price said. "We can't risk it."

"Can't do that, Stony," Lyons said. "We still have devices on-site."

Schwarz leaped onto the desk and put his whole head through the drop ceiling above him. There was a surprising lack of conduit, plumbing and insulation running in the ceiling. What was there was the underside of the massive block of reinforced concrete, seemingly precarious on the support beams on either side of the building.

He didn't even want to guess at the weight of the concrete. Schwarz could almost feel the mass pressing down on him from above. He walked along the desktop, ripping at the flimsy aluminum supports for the drop ceiling, feeling his way to one of the support columns, where a gigantic steel flange supported the concrete block. Take out one of these columns and the block might stay in place. Take out two adjacent columns—or maybe even just two adjacent flanges—and one end of the block would fold down, shear off the supports on the other side, and crash to the earth, twenty-odd stories below.

Once gravity took hold of it, nothing would halt the movement of that much mass. Not floors. Not support girders. Certainly not human bodies.

Cutting through the support columns would take no time for an adhered nanothermite device.

He pulled himself into the ceiling by one hand and explored the surface of the support column with the other.

The device was there, about as far up as he could reach. He yanked at the wallboard, ripping more of it free, and kicked a foothold in the wallboard below. The aluminum framing scratched and dug into his flesh. Schwarz did not even feel it. He fought his way up, burrowing into the wallboard and the wire and the cutting raw edges of aluminum supports until he could reach the device easily. Then he yanked at the plastic cover and wrenched out the cell phone inside. He snatched a spray bottle of acetone—standard SOG equipment for the foreseeable future. He sprayed a stream onto the column above the devices and winced against the fumes of the melting adhesive and acetone. The adhesive had been found to be a high-strength acrylic resin—Schwarz couldn't have muscled the device off the support beam if he hung on to it with his entire body weight. But in seconds, the acetone dissolved the cyanacrylate enough for him to pull it away from the column and he jumped to the floor.

"Stony, I found one," he radioed. "Its phone is disabled." He quickly reported on the location of the device. On the other side of the building, Lyons and Blancanales were also searching for the devices.

"Good work," Barbara Price said. "We see no signs of signals going into your location."

That was a little comfort. Who knew what sort of trigger was in these devices. It seemed ludicrous that they would be exactly the same easily removed devices that had been placed along hundreds of sections of railroad track and pipelines across the country and around the world. But it did look identical to the device they'd removed from the rail in Alexandria.

"Any luck on number two?" Schwarz asked.

"No luck yet," Lyons responded.

"I have to do this myself?" Schwarz quipped.

Schwarz raced around the circular hallway in the featureless, white-painted, undecorated section of the building. The floor was intended to be used for no other purpose than to guard the incredible wealth stored in the shops overhead. There were no doors to offices, and there was no entrance to public stairways or elevators.

But there was a piece of interior wallboard that had been recently disturbed. White powder coated the floor. Some of it still hung in the air. Schwarz was moving beyond it even as he noticed it. The next guard station room was as messed up as the one he had just left. Blancanales and Lyons were busily ripping out wallboard.

Schwarz gave a silent signal and jerked a thumb over one shoulder. He allowed the door to close behind him, then reopened it more quietly. Lyons and Blancanales joined him.

Lyons nodded, and with a movement of his fingers indicated the attack strategy. Schwarz would go low. They stepped into the open.

No less than four men had emerged from the hiding place in the wall, the place where Stony Man Farm's blueprint showed no access way. And yet here they were, their security guard uniforms augmented by ski masks.

When Lyons and Schwarz made their move, the four gunners brought automatic rifles to bear. Schwarz triggered a burst from his MP5 and cut their feet out from under them.

Lyons triggered the Auto Assault-12, blasting away the gunner on the right and blooding his neighbor. In full automatic, the AA-12 buckshot shells obliterated the targets in rapid succession. In seconds, there was one survivor of the original four, and he lived only because his feet had been shot out from under him before the shotgun blast reached him.

Blancanales never even fired his weapon.

There was movement inside the wall and Schwarz triggered a burst at the closing doorway. This was more than a convenient cavity in the wall; the wallboard was hinged and supported for more durable use as a hatch. Schwarz jammed the barrel of the MP5 through the gap as the wall section shut and felt the barrel jerk. Someone was trying to yank the door closed. Schwarz triggered into the unknown, hoping that the barrel had not been deformed enough to blow back. There was a heavy thump and the pressure on the door released.

The guard on the floor was a corpse. The hallway disappeared into the bowels of the unused floor.

"Forget it, Gadgets," Lyons said as he finished cuffing the survivor. "We gotta get that other device."

"Damn it," Schwarz said.

He jogged back to the room that Blancanales and Lyons had been searching. Blancanales was quickly crawling up into the wall along the support column.

"That's where mine was," Schwarz confirmed.

Blancanales ran his hands over every reachable inch of the column. "Not here."

"They didn't put the device farther than they could reach," Schwarz said.

"Makes sense," Lyons said. "Their handler would have given them those instructions, knowing they might need to return to change out the phones."

"We would have uncovered it already," Blancanales insisted.

"Maybe they placed it on a diagonal girder," Lyons said.

"Doesn't make sense," Schwarz said. "They're too stable and they spread the support too much. You'd have to take out several sections to destabilize the mass."

Schwarz was beginning to feel frantic. His eyes pulled to the floor and he knelt, reaching into the narrow gap where the support column descended, deeper into the building. He reached down as far as he could reach, feeling nothing except the rough concrete surface.

"Give me a hand," he barked.

"How'm I supposed to help? Shove you down the shaft?" Lyons said.

Schwarz had already inserted his head into the opening. "Just the opposite," he shouted back, and at that moment he had shimmied so far down that he began to slip headfirst into the channel.

Lyons snatched at his ankles and held on. "Damn it, Gadgets!"

"Don't worry. The drop's only about ten feet." Schwarz felt in darkness down the column. He turned on his headgear lamp but found he didn't have the space to raise his head enough to direct the beam, let alone see, so he flipped it off again. This had to be done in darkness.

His finger was sliced open. What was that? He felt the area. A metal plate. Conduit access panel or something. Why the curly shavings that sliced into skin?

"Turn me!" he shouted. "One-eighty!"

Lyons was grunting and complaining, then more hands were on Schwarz's ankles. With Blancanales's help, Lyons twisted Schwarz like a corkscrew, half a turn. Schwarz flipped on the LED again and craned his neck to see. It hurt like hell to get his head in that angle, but he saw the panel. Old steel. Fresh, gleaming metal shavings. The panel had been opened recently enough that the exposed shavings hadn't had time to gather dust or to oxidize. He used his thumbnail on the straight-edge screw—what the hell, it was bloodied already. And the screw turned easily. It was barely in there.

"It's here!" he called. A minute later he shouted, "Got it! Pull me up!"

But they dropped him.

THEY RELEASED Schwarz's ankles and dived in opposite directions when the burst of gunfire came at them from the entrance. Lyons spotted a gunner and blasted the open door with the AA-12, aiming outside the strike zone, but the gunner took buckshot and fell back, yelping.

Lyons touched his earpiece. "Stony, we have an entire damn army here. Tell me it is not law enforcement."

"Negative," Price answered. "Federal and city law enforcement have been informed that there is an operation at this location. They are hanging back. Those are not friendlies."

"Good to know," Lyons said. "But the funny get-ups gave them away, anyway." He put another 3-round blast into the opening, taking the walls down to the metal framing but driving the attackers farther away. He twisted out of the door. The injured gunner was staggering away and reached back when Lyons appeared, intent on tagging him with a handgun. Lyons blasted him with the shotgun, sending him to the floor in a heap and also scoring a hit on one of his fleeing companions.

BLANCANALES STUCK his face into the narrow framing space.

"You okay, Gadgets?"

"Oh, I'm great!"

"Can you climb the support column?"

"No." There was an exchange of gunfire, much of it from the AA-12. But not all of it. "Go help Ironman."

LYONS PULLED OUT a fragmentation grenade and sent it rolling after the gunners, then stepped back into the guard room in time to hold Blancanales back. The grenade burst and Lyons raced after it. Two severely wounded attackers were trying to flee but were forced to engage Lyons. It wasn't much of a fight. The AA-12 cut them down.

To his surprise, Blancanales was at his heels.

"Schwarz?"

"He said he would catch up with us downstairs," Blancanales said.

"Goddamned Gadgets!"

"You want a taste of your own medicine?" someone yelled from inside the door. Able Team had arrived at the first guard room. The gunners were inside.

A grenade rolled out the door toward Lyons and Blancanales. The attacker's timing was poor, and a good soldier wouldn't broadcast his moves so blatantly. Lyons and Blancanales had more than enough time to put wall between themselves and the grenade. When it detonated Lyons was on the move with shrapnel still rattling around his feet.

He unloaded his AA-12 into the guard room, then ducked for cover. Heavy fire filled the doorway, followed by running feet. Lyons and Blancanales filled the door aggressively, but the room was now empty. They were chasing the attackers in a circle. They were also cutting down their numbers rapidly. There were two more bodies in the room.

"We have them spooked," Blancanales said. "They're making a run for it."

The pair passed through the guard room and into the hall just in time to see the last attacker disappear through the hinged panel in the wallboard.

Lyons ducked through the opening, then slowed, moving carefully along the passage. He found a stair ladder. One of the attackers had just reached the bottom. There was a blast, and a rattle of gunfire, and two of his companions keeled over. The gunner observed something that horrified him, and reversed direction. He scrambled up the ladder, and too late looked up. The blast from the AA-12 nearly decapitated him. His body fell to the floor below.

"Gadgets!" Blancanales shouted. "That you?"

"Sort of," Schwarz said, coming into view below them. He was covered in dust, except where he was covered in blood. "Got it," he said, holding up a nano-thermite device in one hand, a cell phone in the other.

"Able," Price said with some urgency. "They are transmitting again. Get the hell out of there now."

"Good idea," Lyons snapped back. "We're coming down, Gadgets. Go, Pol!"

Blancanales stepped onto the ladder and dropped fast, barely using his feet to slow the descent, and hit the floor with a crunch.

"They're getting through, Able Team," Price said. "We're seeing calls into the building from different routes."

Lyons did not need to ask what the mission controller meant by that. The attacks were happening. The new phone system was in place on the two remaining devices. The terrorists had succeeded in activating the devices in this building. The massive concrete-and-steel security slab would soon lose two of its four supports.

It would swing open like a fifty-ton trapdoor, with Able Team underneath it.

Lyons heard the movement in the walls getting louder. It seemed to increase in volume like that of a hissing explosion. He knew the concrete slab was coming through the support column, both on the south side and north side of the building.

Lyons pictured the layout of the building in his head. He remembered service rooms and equipment rooms.

"This way."

There should be a primary stairwell ahead of them. Lyons didn't allow himself to be distracted by the odd sight of a burst-open hole in the wallboard. Apparently this was where Schwarz had made his exit.

The doors to the stairwell were to the right. He ran for them, counting on Blancanales to keep Schwarz moving. Lyons found the door and yanked it open.

The stairwell was empty. But from far below he could hear the screams and shouts of people crowding the stairs, desperate to evacuate. The alarms were screeching.

The building was vibrating.

"There is no way we are getting out anytime soon if we go down," Lyons reported to the Farm. "It sounds like there's a full-scale evacuation under way."

"To the roof," Schwarz said.

"So we have farther to fall when this building disintegrates underneath us?" Blancanales said.

"The building is not going to go down. If the security armor breaks free, it will pull through the center of the building. But it won't optimize the primary supports. If the security slab bends but doesn't break, the building will remain fairly intact."

"Are you certain of this?" Lyons asked.

"As certain as I can be," Schwarz said. "What I am certain of is this—if we go down, we are stuck with all the rest of them in the stairs. If that slab breaks free, we'll still be underneath it when it goes."

Lyons looked longingly down the stairs, feeling that he must do something to protect those people in case the slab did break free.

But sometimes there was just nothing to be done.

A billow of acrid fumes pulsed in their direction. Lyons slammed the door shut behind them, sealing them in the stairwell, but the gray toxic smoke began seeping through the seams. It was a burning, acrid stench. Something chemical was burning along with the concrete. It smelled unhealthy. They headed up.

It was as if the floors above them were deserted. There was no one coming down. The smoke filled the stairwell and rose with them, the air quickly becoming unbreathable. The building was shuddering and groaning.

Lyons wondered what it would feel like, exactly, if that slab did give way and tumbled and crashed through the floors all the way down to the ground level.

They still had one floor above them when they heard the clanking of a grenade bouncing off the hard stairs.

Lyons spotted the round and flung his body back into the others. They fell down the stairs together in a tangle of limbs as the round burst above them. Lyons pushed to his feet, scanned his teammates quickly for further damage, and ran up the stairs. He hacked at the fumes.

They couldn't stay here much longer. He spotted movement between the metal rails of the stairs, and perhaps it was his imagination, but it looked like the action of a man about to drop another grenade.

Lyons aimed through the bars of metal rails and triggered the AA-12. He ducked, but was still stung by buckshot that bounced back at him. He heard a groan above him, then the bursting of a grenade.

Lyons was afraid to breathe. If he took some of this stuff into his lungs, he might choke on it. He ran up to the next level, fired a blast at the closing doors, then fired another blast into the wounded, armless man who was still writhing on the landing. He was a dead man already; Lyons was doing him a favor by ending his suffering.

With Blancanales and Schwarz, Lyons burst into a penthouse apartment. It was deserted, with no furniture, and looked as if it had never been occupied.

The only indication of an inhabitant was a trail of blood heading across the hardwood floor.

They followed the trail and found a gunman in the same utility uniform as the others below. He was lying halfway through what would have been a living room in an unoccupied apartment.

The man was suffering from a massive wound to his lower leg. It looked as if he had caught part of the errant grenade blast.

He looked boldly up at Lyons as Blancanales relieved him of his weapon and put him in cuffs.

"I surrender," he said. "Get me to a damned hospital."

"We'll see what we can do," Lyons said. "Any more of you losers on the premises?"

"Two more. They just left me here. Sons of bitches."

Lyons headed for the exit to a courtyard. The wall here was glass and opened into what might have been a beautiful rooftop garden. But the planters were empty and the untended trees were dry and dead. The swimming pool was dry.

Lyons saw no one but spotted a rooftop equipment box. It was the only hiding place that immediately presented itself.

He directed Schwarz and Blancanales around the back, then Lyons hopped the rails, out of the garden and onto the rooftop proper. He waited momentarily, listening to a conversation on the far side of the ventilation equipment.

"We need a pickup! Answer me!"

"They ain't answering. They left us."

Underneath them, the building seemed to lurch. Lyons heard the screams of people on the streets of Philadelphia.

"That's right. They're not coming for you. You're not getting out of here," Lyons called out.

Lyons didn't really expect them to give it up that easily. There were footsteps. They were fleeing—who knew where they thought they were heading.

There was a rattle of gunfire. They had met up with Schwarz and Blancanales and had not survived the encounter.

JACK GRIMALDI PLUCKED Able Team off the rooftop and quickly out of Philadelphia, heading for a secure hangar.

Blancanales treated Schwarz's myriad wounds first.

"Nothing major," Blancanales said. "That which does not kill you makes you uglier."

"You think I look bad, you should see the wall," Schwarz said, almost smiling. "I broke outta that wall and those losers in the guard uniforms were screaming like punk teenagers in a horror movie. They thought I was some sort of zombie lord from hell come to eat their brains."

"How much morphine did you give him, Pol?" Lyons asked.

"Not a drop," Blancanales said. "He just talks that way sometimes."

"It's the Tylenol talking," Schwarz said, but in truth, he did look a little dazed. "Give me a break. You did drop me on my head."

It was a less gloomy trip than their recent chopper lift out of Atlanta. Grimaldi had reported that Cranston Tower was still standing, and people were still evacuating in large numbers, and there was no sign the slab had broken free.

"No thanks to you," Schwarz sneered at the wounded gunman, who had managed to survive the trip from Philadelphia despite screaming that if he didn't get some painkillers he was going to die. Blancanales finally got around to a quick suturing job.

By the time they unloaded him from the helicopter and propped him up in the corner of the empty hangar, in handcuffs and ankle cuffs, he had already provided as much information as he could possibly be expected to give. Blancanales had even held out a little long on the morphine, as an incentive, but finally decided the guy had no more intelligence to offer.

He knew nothing. Like all the others, he was a hireling, hired by other hirelings.

Now the man was heavily narcotized and sleeping like a baby. He would be picked up by some federal agency before he slept it off.

Able Team didn't really care what happened to him.

All they cared about was that they had escaped the Cranston Tower and maybe saved some lives—but once again they were coming away with almost no intelligence whatsoever.

CHAPTER EIGHT

Ramvik, Norway

The gaunt blond man watched the news out of Philadelphia. He was grinning. Skyn never saw him anymore without that cadaverous grin.

"Well, even if you don't get all your stuff back, you're certainly enjoying yourself," Skyn said.

"I certainly am. And I am going to get my stuff back. And my money. And my land. All of it."

"I guess I don't understand why you're not moving forward more quickly. What happened to your deadlines?"

Ramm seemed annoyed to be distracted from the news story and a video of billowing smoke over Philly. "I'm going with my gut, Skyn. I have to play this in the right way. I have to keep people guessing and off balance."

"I didn't know anything about this up in Philadelphia," Skyn said accusingly.

Ramm muted the TV and turned to Skyn. "My friend, you're my adviser and technical consultant. You are not my partner. I had not sought your advice on all phases of my operation. Maybe even on most of it."

Skyn nodded, but inside he felt those old fears again. That uncertainty he felt when he thought Ramm doubted his loyalty to the Ramm family cause.

Charles Skyn remembered the moment it had dawned on him that Olan Ramm would actually bring his plans to fruition.

Skyn had been intrigued when Ramm financed the construction of machinery needed to begin mass production of nanoparticles. When production began and Skyn had showed Ramm the first production devices, they'd gone together into some remote woods on Ramm lands, even more out in the middle of nowhere than his home.

Of course, Ramm consistently referred to his lands as the "remains of his lands." What he owned now was a fraction of what he claimed was rightfully his. And most of what he had today had come about through years of property buybacks. As much as it galled him, Ramm had paid real cash to take possession of lands that by all rights belonged to him and his family.

Olan Ramm could speak on this topic for hours at a time.

Ramm had been able to buy the vast sweep of acreage at a relatively low price. The land was close to nothing, usable for nothing. There was no one within miles, which had made it the ideal location for testing the first-produced nanothermite devices.

It was still summer in England, but biting cold where they were, deep in the woods on Ramm lands.

Ramm had constructed full-size replicas of the intended targets. There was a section of a crude oil pipeline, filled and pressurized. There were also several sections of different railroad gauges.

One device was placed on the exterior of the oil pipeline. It was rigged with a tiny detonator—essentially an electrostatic discharge device, USB-powered, controlled by a simple instruction relayed over an off-the-shelf smartphone. Olan Ramm made the call and sent the message, and the device functioned perfectly.

Ramm had insisted that the section of pressurized pipeline be filled with actual crude oil. He'd wanted this test to be realistic. The device sliced a white wound into the pipeline, and the oil gushed out and ignited. It became a burning river that flowed down an embankment into a shallow ravine, coating everything in oil, and everything coated in oil eventually burned.

The scale of the damage, from the oil and the fire, was impressive, and that was with one device and a limited amount of oil. Ramm was ecstatic at the thought of what thirty devices, planted on a half mile of oil pipeline, would accomplish.

Further tests were conducted on sections of railroad. Ramm had purchased actual rail, of different gauges, and he had old and new rail. Charles Skyn didn't think the age or the gauge of the rail was going to make a bit of difference in terms of the performance of the device—and he was correct. Eight devices were tested, and eight sections of rail warped and liquefied and melted into the ground. Each burn left a gap in the rail of a yard or more, and the metal rail that remained was brittle from the heat. There was no way a locomotive could stay on that track.

This tract of Ramm land was also useful for its roadways. It included paved surfaces, unused for many years. They served to test the devices on pavement. Ramm intended to scatter devices on roadways around the world, burning impassable potholes. A few dozen devices, scattered from a moving vehicle, could transform a one-hundred-million-dollar stretch of interstate highway in the United States into just so much rubble.

The old, faded strip of paved road on the Ramm lands burned and crumbled when the device went off.

Ramm had also had a section of concrete poured on land, three yards square, using highly tensile concrete. He was replicating the surfaces of major commercial airport runways.

The nanothermite devices burned the surface and ate their way through the concrete and weakened it with intense heat from the inside out. The damage looked small, but when Ramm hit the brittle surface with a rubber hammer it shattered like glass.

Just think what would happen when an airliner taxied over it at one hundred miles per hour and the concrete actually crumbled under one wheel.

Charles Skyn had been wearing a sort of patronizing smile on his face when he'd said to Ramm, "You really mean to go through with this!"

"Of course I do," Ramm had told him. "I did not know you doubted my intentions."

"I never dreamed that you could get to this point so quickly."

Ramm's disappointment had been evident. "You never had faith in this plan."

Charles Skyn had felt for the first time as if he might be endangered. For the first time he'd been certain this emotionally stunted child-man was capable of committing the crimes he was planning, which certainly made him capable of less extreme crimes, such as disposing of Charles Skyn.

Skyn realized at that moment that his position with Ramm was worse than tenuous.

He'd needed to salvage credibility with Ramm, and he knew just how to do so.

"Ramm," he'd asked, "is this all you are planning? Railroads and pipelines? Is that the extent of it?"

Ramm, standing in the burned wood with the stench of black oil smoke drifting around his blond head, had narrowed his eyes at Skyn and asked, "What are you saying?"

Skyn had assumed a thoughtful look. "My friend, your focus is on oil. Land-based transportation and infrastructure. I believe you are missing another big opportunity here. I'm talking ships."

Skyn explained how easily one of his devices could penetrate the reinforced double hull of a modern oil tanker. He explained how easy it would be to equip one of the devices to adhere firmly to the hull of a tanker, even in salt water. He explained how many millions of gallons of oil could be removed permanently from market availability by targeting oil tankers on the sea at the same time as targeting oil pipelines across the continents. Skyn explained how it would be even easier to sabotage and destroy hundreds of oil tankers that no longer transported oil, but nevertheless sat at docks and were used to store oil by the millions of gallons.

And then Charles Skyn, still improvising, painted the picture for Ramm of what would happen to an oil tanker that was opened up and ignited in a harbor. He described a flaming lake of crude oil that would expand to cover the bay, until it reached the shores and flames jumped to buildings on the land.

Ramm's suspicion of Skyn's loyalty eased. Skyn had redeemed himself to Ramm.

More than that, he'd found himself interested in playing along.

And always, in the back of his head, Skyn was planning on getting out before this thing really got serious.

CHAPTER NINE

Barcelona

David McCarter had seen slums in a hundred cites. London's were the worst, maybe because England was where he had come from and he still felt some sort of personal responsibility for the place. But the truth was London slums stank as bad as any slum anywhere in the world. And worse than most.

Barcelona slums were downright clean by comparison.

Thankfully the street was mostly empty. Many of the buildings on this block were vacant and awaiting restoration.

"Smell that salty breeze?"

"Sea air? *That's* what you smell?" Rafael Encizo said.

McCarter tapped the Land Rover steering wheel impatiently and glared out the window. It was late morning, after seven hours of transport from the East Coast of the United States to the east coast of the Iberian Peninsula. The Stony Man trace had led them into the El Raval neighborhood in the Old City section of Barcelona. Some of the structures here dated back hundreds of years—and some had suffered from a century or more of neglect. Only because they were constructed using heavy stone and brick had they survived at all.

Now many city blocks in this area had been cleaned up. Others hadn't.

They were parked in the street in front of a five-story walk-up, partially under renovation, with a view through the overgrown edging of the second building— the one that was their target. It was only four stories, and in serious disrepair.

Stony Man Farm was convinced this location was the relay point of the phone calls that had ignited the terror around the globe.

McCarter glared up the building side. "He could have scaled the side of the bleeding building by now. Where is he?"

At that moment Gary Manning's voice came on the line through his earpiece. "I'm in position. I've got a view of the apartment. They left the curtains open. Isn't that convenient."

"So? Anything to see?"

MANNING POSITIONED himself in the empty room with direct line of sight to the target apartment across the street. "Nobody's in. But the other apartments are pretty well occupied. Lots of men."

"Say again?" McCarter demanded.

"Men. Lots of men standing around in at least three of the apartments that I can see from here. More men than I would expect to see at an apartment building— and no women or kids. We're not about to raid the Barcelona YMCA by mistake, right?"

"We've got the right place," McCarter said.

"Stupid me," Manning said. "They don't let you bring guns into the YMCA. And these guys have guns. Several handguns. Make that two AKs. There's an hombre in the apartment below with some sort of old-fashioned side-by-side shotgun, maybe a 10-gauge."

"I think they're waiting for us to coming visiting," McCarter responded. "T.J.? Cal?"

Calvin James responded. "We noticed the same thing. A lot of guys around. No ladies. No children. No toys in the yards," he reported. "Not a very family-oriented place. Just a bunch of guys looking bored and surly. What time does the workday start in Spain? Shouldn't they be at the office?"

"I think they do freelance work out of their homes, mate," McCarter offered. "Namely waiting around for bastards like us to show up and stick our noses into their business." Then McCarter added, "But we cannot assume there are no civilians in the building. Got it?"

"Got it," James answered.

"Understood," Manning confirmed. "Want me to get their attention?"

There was a pause. "Go ahead," McCarter said.

GARY MANNING was whistling as he dropped the binoculars onto their neck strap and lifted the M16, mounted with an M203 grenade launcher. He'd been waiting for the chance to try out the new sighting system that he—and Kissinger—had tested in the blast-proof armory lab at Stony Man Farm.

He took aim at the window of the apartment directly below the one that was their target. The man with the old Spanish side-by-side shotgun was rummaging in the fridge in the kitchen, visible in one window. The front room of the apartment, through another window, was empty.

Manning aimed for the empty front room and pulled the trigger. The grenade flew through the open space between the buildings and put a hole through the glass window, then dropped out of sight.

Then came a gunshot. And another. Then a series of quick fires.

The hungry guy in the kitchen straightened when he heard the glass break but dropped to the floor when the shooting started.

Not bad, Manning thought. The grenade was composed of a series of explosive blanks, fused to burst at irregular intervals over several seconds to imitate the sound of shots. He and Kissinger had also tested several variations in the lab before the detonations sounded like convincing small-arms fire. It sounded pretty realistic out in the field, too.

Manning could hear the hungry guy shouting in Spanish.

McCARTER AND ENCIZO, still unnoticed in their vehicle in front of the next building, watched through their field glasses as the few visible occupants reacted to the sounds from above. A trio had been sitting on the front steps of the place, smoking cigarettes and trying to keep their shirts draped over their handguns.

They didn't bother trying to hide them anymore when Manning commenced with the fake gun battle upstairs. They yanked their weapons out in broad daylight and hurried inside.

McCarter gave the word as he and Encizo stepped from the SUV and headed inside. "They've cleared out of the front," he informed James.

"We have at least one guard sticking to his post at the back door," James advised.

"Understood." McCarter and Encizo slipped across the street. They watched the last stray pedestrian leave the area before McCarter gave the okay to Manning. Who knew how long their luck would hold? A broad-daylight hard probe in an urban theater was not something Phoenix Force undertook lightly.

But waiting until nightfall was out of the question.

McCarter led the way inside, finding a dirty lower-level small space at the stairs and a hallway to the left. With a nod he put Encizo on-station at the bottom of the stairs and headed into the hallway himself.

An apartment door stood open and he ducked inside, scanned it, took two more steps and scanned the room. Cigarettes burned in an ashtray. Filth was piled high in the kitchenette. The occupants had left in a hurry.

McCarter stepped back into the hall and found another door a few paces down. Nobody home except the stench. These guys were slobs. No bachelor cred.

Down the hall was a corner, and when he peered around it he found a gunner tucked in a corner and fiddling with the safety on a handgun while watching out the window. He swore mildly and stuffed the Glock into his pocket, bringing to bear the old hunting rifle and pointing at the door.

The gunner may have felt more secure with his familiar old gun but it didn't last. He'd been too distracted to notice the large English gent stepping around the corner or the two commandos who had entered the building via the door in front of him.

He was staring down no less than three well-equipped soldiers. They were everything he was not: trained, skilled, well-armed and confident. McCarter snatched the rifle and knocked the butt into the gunner's forehead, outfitting the falling body with plastic cuffs before it had hit the ground. McCarter yanked the Glock 17 out of the man's pocket.

Silently, McCarter led James and Hawkins to the front.

"One down," he informed Encizo. "Real amateur. But they won't all be. Stay focused."

They nodded and ascended to the second level. Another empty hallway. Several closed doors. They didn't have time to scour the place. They were reasonably certain the picocell and the other hardware would be bunched together in the top-floor apartment. Above they heard the thumping of feet and shouting in Spanish.

"Give us another distraction, Gary," McCarter said quietly.

"Maybe not," Manning responded. There was a sudden exclamation from the floor above. Something had changed.

Encizo managed to understand enough of the muffled rapid-fire Spanish. "They just figured out there's nobody in the apartment."

MANNING WATCHED the occupant of the apartment finally get up the nerve to look into his front room—which he found empty.

"They just made me," Manning relayed as the occupant jumped into the front room and pointed his side-by-side into all four corners looking for an intruder. There was no place a man could have hidden in the tiny space. The man shouted angrily to the others in the hall, then turned his attention to the window, and his gaze focused on Manning. Manning waited until the man raised his old side-by-side shotgun, then triggered the M16. A burst of 5.56 mm NATO rounds stitched across his chest and dropped him to the floor.

"Now those were real bullets," Manning said.

The apartment door opened with a kick and a gunner with an AK-47 shot wildly toward the window until Manning triggered another burst that chopped at his arm and shoulder. Manning heard the scream and the AK was dropped.

A wild-looking figure planted himself in plain sight just long enough to fire a small black handgun, but Manning spoiled the shot by stitching through his stomach with two of the four rounds in his next burst.

Were they just going to keep presenting themselves for him to shoot like plywood bandits in an old West shooting gallery?

No, they weren't. They were going to come and get him.

"BLOODY HELL," McCarter said as a thunder of footsteps clapped across the ceiling above them and headed for the stairs—putting the herd of gunners and Phoenix Force on an intercept course. One of them appeared ahead of the pack, and cried out at the quartet of commandos waiting for him with submachine guns. He made the worst sort of battlefield decision and raised his handgun to fire. Rafael Encizo chopped the gun out of his hand with a round from his Heckler & Koch MP5. Calvin James put three rounds in his abdomen. T. J. Hawkins cut through the man's sternum.

McCarter held his fire. It had been, quite literally, overkill. The man was dead on his feet, and a pair of his friends following from above watched through the rails as the ruined body seemed to hang in the air for a moment, then collapse as a corpse.

A black Glock handgun bounced down the steps and landed at McCarter's feet.

A hail of wild gunfire rained down the stairs along with challenges in Spanish.

"Manning," McCarter said into his radio. "Give them some gas on the third floor."

"Understood." It wasn't an ideal strategy. Gassing the third floor might send the gunners up to the fourth. But Manning was there to protect the room where the picocell was thought to be.

"Masks," McCarter ordered, pulling his gas mask over his face as the CS grenade punctured a window and streamed through an open door above Phoenix Force. The tear gas billowed out. There were shouts of alarm, then hacking and choking. A few of the gunners stumbled down the stairs with their hands in the air.

Then it got ugly. There was a cry of rage from the floor above and a rattle of automatic fire came down the stairs, cutting down the men trying to surrender.

RAFAEL ENCIZO, born in Cuba, understood the Spanish gunners perfectly. One voice rose above the others. "Upstairs, you idiots! We can seal it off."

"They're heading up to the fourth floor, Gary," Encizo advised Manning.

"I can't reach them on the fourth floor unless they open the door to the target apartment," Manning said. "You don't want me blowing that door open from here."

"You are correct," McCarter stated, very clearly, so there would be no mistake. "We can*not* risk collateral damage to the cell equipment."

"Understood," Manning said.

McCarter took point up the stairs, through the dissipating gas. There were bodies. A man with a mangled shoulder was bleeding his life away and James quickly cuffed his good arm to his ankle. The man would almost certainly die of blood loss within minutes—but it couldn't hurt to make sure he was not going to shoot one of them in the back before he did. The stairs to the next floor were offset, at the end of the hall, unattached to the primary stairwell. McCarter leaped up to the landing and saw a door being pushed shut. He triggered a burst that wormed its way through the open space and the door stopped moving. McCarter snatched an M-84 hand grenade from his belt. Encizo was now at his side and sent a burst through the gap in the door as an insurance policy, allowing McCarter to step quickly up the steps, toss in the grenade and yank the door closed. With just over two seconds to get to cover; McCarter sailed down the steps and fell into a crouch with his fingers in his ears and his eyes squeezed tight.

A million candlepower was the old-fashioned estimation of the amount of light emitted by a flash-bang, and McCarter was acutely aware of how much damage that could do to his vision if he happened to be looking at it when it went off. Enough of the light sliced through the tiny gaps around the door that he saw it through his closed eyelids. The bang was loud, even with his fingers in his ears.

He jumped to his feet and kicked through the door, sweeping the room left as Encizo went right. Moaning men sprawled at the far end of the narrow hall, holding their heads. They were all blinded and/or deafened to some extent and would be for hours—if they lived that long.

A door to an apartment on the right was yanked open. McCarter and Encizo fell back to allow the passage of a burst of machine-gun fire. McCarter charged in as the burst came to an end, facing a dazed-looking figure with an AK-47. He was gunned down even as McCarter spun to another gunner emerging from behind a sofa. The man wasn't even fully on his feet before he was dead and slumped over onto the couch.

Encizo saw a door open at the far end of the hall. Automatic gunfire erupted, tearing into the ceiling and walls and splitting open the head of one of the moaning men—although it didn't come within ten feet of Encizo. Encizo stepped into the apartment with Mc-Carter. Hawkins and James were retreating to the stairs.

Another burst of gunfire came down the hall where Encizo had been standing, and there were screams from the fallen men, followed by shouts of terror.

"Covas!" one of them screeched in Spanish. "You're shooting us!"

"Go to hell!" There was another burst. More screams. One of the screams was cut off.

Covas, Encizo decided, was one heartless son of a bitch. He moved out for a view of the hallway. The stunned men on the floor were nearly all bloodied—all shot by their own man. A small, dark, bald figure popped into the hallway, with a long burst of gunfire extruding from a submachine gun. He thought he'd give himself safe passage with a solid wall of flying rounds, but it just didn't work that way. His ammo was used up in a flash—long before he could clear the path of Rafael Encizo, who delivered a short burst into his exposed torso. The man yelped but managed to pull back without taking a serious hit and Encizo heard the quick change-out of a magazine.

"Covas!" another voice shouted. "Get your fucking hands off me!"

Encizo was surprised to see a new gunner emerge into the hallway—shoved by Covas. The man saw himself perfectly targeted by Encizo and raised both hands, his weapon falling to the floor. But then his attention snapped to the hallway he'd just come from and his body clenched in terror. He held out his hands as if to protect himself. Covas—who else could it have been?—gunned the man down himself.

Then Covas emerged airborne, leaping across Encizo's target zone to get to the safety of the adjoining hallway. Encizo triggered a burst and followed the flying body, puncturing the man up the side. Covas collapsed out of sight and Encizo followed after him. He heard McCarter at his heels. Encizo went left.

There was a live gunner crouched in the hall to the left, and Encizo took him down with a quick no-nonsense burst to the chest.

Covas sprawled on the floor, still alive. Encizo snatched the AK away and cuffed him, wrists and ankles.

"Clear," McCarter announced behind Encizo. He'd checked the apartment and found it empty. James and Hawkins had finished checking the other third-floor rooms, which apparently left just one apartment. "Gary, did any of them make it into the target?" McCarter asked through his headset.

"Manning?" he repeated a moment later.

MANNING WAS FLAT behind a pile of plaster rubble and rotted wood framing that probably dated to the nineteenth century. In the five-story walk-up where he was positioned, the fourth-floor interior was almost completely demolished, leaving a large open space and precious few hiding places. When he heard the approaching footsteps they were almost upon him and he made a lunge across the floor and crawled into the pile of debris.

The intruders were in a hurry, and they stopped behind the cover of a wall just long enough to scan the open space of the big room. Somebody shouted a command and they jogged out of hiding to the next set of stairs.

Manning decided they must have been called to the scene by the men whom McCarter and the others were engaging. Maybe they assumed he was on the roof.

But one of them wasn't convinced the fourth floor was empty. The last man in the line walked more slowly, not turning his back on the room, his combat shotgun low in his hands but ready to trigger. He wore some sort of a floppy leather hat that was pulled low over his eyes. The exposed skin of his face and neck were crisscrossed with a tattoo of woven barbed wire.

Manning could see him through the rubble, which meant the gunner could see Manning, if he was sharp-eyed enough. But his vision didn't rest on the pile of old plasterboard and wooden studs. Or did it, briefly? The man gave a sort of shrug and headed up the stairs.

Manning did not like this son of a bitch. His gut told him Barbed Wire Face was a pro. A master. Maybe trained. Maybe just intuitive. Which meant the shrug had been for Manning's benefit.

Manning knew this kind of man. He had encountered him in the past, maybe a hundred times. You didn't underestimate an enemy like this.

But the guy had underestimated Manning. The stupid shrug was out of character, along with the suddenly loud tromping of his feet on the stairs. If not for that, Manning wouldn't have known him for the dangerous expert that he was. Barbed Wire Face would be coming back momentarily with reinforcements.

Manning sprinted into another hiding place—a cavity in the wall that had been ripped out as a part of the demolition. It even gave him several narrow gaps in the remaining wall to watch the room.

"I have company," he said through his mike quietly.

He could hear the racket from the adjoining building. He wondered if the others would even hear the message. It didn't matter now because the intruders were coming back. Barbed Wire Face had sent four men to do the dirty work and take the risk.

They were armed with old AK-47s and they began firing at once, three of them directly into the debris pile where Manning had been hiding. One of them, just in case, triggered a burst into an even smaller stack of old, twisted lumber in the farthest corner of the room. They unloaded enough firepower to ensure a kill—not enough to waste rounds, then quickly investigated the results.

The debris pile was directly in Manning's line of sight—as he was in theirs—and he wasn't going to let them see him first. When they were facing away from him he stepped into the open and triggered the M16, delivering a 5.56 mm round at their legs before stepping back to avoid any return fire that might come his way. Then he stepped right back out again and fired the M16 into the two blood-covered men who were still standing. They were cut down hard. Manning spun on the man who'd gone to search the lumber pile. The man's face was seeping blood, but he was trying to get his AK-47 lined up on Manning.

His burst was way off the mark; Manning's was not. The Canadian commando started the burst low and stitched up the enemy's torso until the gunner fell and the AK-47 clattered across the floor.

Manning returned to his closetlike hiding space. Nice little spot, he thought. He could see them—coming from upstairs or downstairs—but they couldn't see him. Like the perfect blind for hunting feral pigs in Alabama. Let the little porkers walk right up and get shot.

Maybe not very sporting…

But this wasn't about sport, Manning reminded himself as one of the news images popped into his head. The one from that little town in Wyoming where those stupid reporters had been driving like maniacs to get out alive and then the video guy yelled, "Get 'em!" And those two idiot reporters had stopped to pick up three young men. It was the right thing to do. But they all died. And if those reporters hadn't stopped they could have driven through that wall of fire a half minute earlier and maybe the fire wouldn't have been so intense and maybe they would have made it through, instead of burning up.

After the first, traumatic live broadcast the news media hadn't replayed the sounds of those five innocent guys from Backwater, Wyoming, burning up. Not many people had heard it. But Gary Manning had.

That's what this was about, Gary Manning thought.

When it came to the people responsible for the carnage, Manning didn't care about being sporting or fair. He cared about eradicating them from this earth.

More of them were coming down the stairs. Manning stepped into the open and gave them a high-velocity round. The blast ripped them to pieces and sent another pair screaming to the floor. A burst of 5.56 mm shockers ripped up their struggling bodies and Manning laid on the trigger, allowing the hail of rounds to travel into the second pair who blundered into their path. More footsteps retreated back the way they'd come.

According to Manning's count, there were two of them left up there, and one of them was Barbed Wire Face.

He heard a door slam. He heard a crash. It sounded as if they were barricading themselves in. He raced up the steps and tried the wooden door. Locked tight. Maybe we could blast his way through it. But they'd surely be waiting for him.

Gunfire. Manning returned to his floor and saw rounds being triggered at the building where the pico-cell was set up.

"Manning!" It was McCarter.

"Here," he said. "Sorry. I've been busy. We've got reinforcements in my building."

"You secure?"

"I took care of most of them, but the diehards on the fifth floor are shooting into the target apartment." Even as he said it, the windows of the empty front room took a barrage and the glass fell to the street below.

Manning stuck his head out of the window—just a little—and saw the tip of an AK muzzle firing from a window just above him.

"Maybe I can take care of this in a hurry," Manning related. "Hold on."

He searched the street below. No sign of life. Anybody in the vicinity would have been smart to get to cover. Then he extracted an M-67 from his pack, stuck his entire upper torso out the window and lobbed the grenade into the window directly above him. It arced inside. There was a gasp, but Manning was pulling himself back inside quickly. The fragmentation grenade detonated, filling the space above with high-velocity shrapnel.

Manning was already running for the door to the upper level and he kicked it twice before the wood splintered and the furniture behind it scraped out of the way. He ran into the room, firing before he had a target. One man was a bloody pile near the window. The M-67 must have gone off almost at his feet and what was left of him may or may not have been Barbed Wire Face. The face was too messed up to tell.

But there was a bloody trail heading across the room, to a ladder to the roof. Manning turned to see a leg being pulled through an open hatchway. He jogged to it, sent a burst up through the hatch, then followed quickly and poked his head out. There was a man on the roof, staggering across a flat, littered surface, his combat shotgun still held in a low-slung firing position. It was Barbed Wire Face. He spun toward Manning and blasted, but Manning withdrew inside. When he stuck his head out again, Barbed Wire Face was at the edge of the roof.

Manning approached at a trot. His adversary turned and tossed the combat shotgun away. He gave Manning a smile that did not make him look like a man about to surrender, then stepped onto the building ledge.

Manning continued to stalk toward Barbed Wire Face. He didn't believe that this man was about to jump. But jump he did. Manning raced to the ledge.

Down the side of the building was a bright orange heavy-duty trash tunnel. Barbed Wire Face had tossed himself into it and was clawing his way down the inside of the tunnel, using the metal tunnel ribbing as hand holds. He was descending fast and Manning judged he would make it to the bottom without serious injury.

Unless Manning could do something about it. He snatched out an M-67 and did a quick scan of the streets for nearby civilians. He was happy to find none. He tossed the grenade into the trash tunnel.

Barbed Wire Face hit the bottom inside a freshly emptied Dumpster container, his feet landing with a hollow metal thump. A hard landing, but the man was still functional.

He raised his gaze up the building side, saw Manning and flattened against the building to avoid any gunshots Manning might try to send at him.

Then the grenade clanged as it hit inside the container, joining Barbed Wire Face and a few other scraps of trash.

Manning had already pulled back to avoid catching any of the shrapnel when the fragmentation grenade went off. He heard the burst with great satisfaction, followed by a brief rain-shower sound of shrapnel ricocheting wildly inside the bin.

The container was now a wading pool of blood and gore—a fitting end for Barbed Wire Face, as far as Manning was concerned.

"Manning here," he said into his mike.

"You need backup?" McCarter asked.

"That problem is resolved," Manning said. He quickly retreated down the stairs to his former position, with its bird's-eye view of the target apartment. "I've got the target covered. You can enter."

"ABOUT TIME," Encizo muttered.

"Move back, Rafe. Hawkins, this is your baby," McCarter snapped.

Hawkins moved to the front in the bloody hallway, to the damaged but still closed door to the target apartment. He put his weapons away and pulled out the tool kit, along with a vacuum-packaged fire suit. He quickly slid the suit over his BDUs. It was some protection but not much, not against incendiary shrapnel. If one or more of those nanothermite devices went off when he was inside, there would be little hope that he would escape serious injury, at best. He glanced over his shoulder. "Back. You guys have got to move back."

McCarter did not like watching Hawkins go into that apartment alone. On the other hand, this was not a conflict situation. If there was trouble, there was nothing McCarter or any of them would be able to do to help Hawkins.

Calvin James was at the rear, keeping a guard on the stairs from below, just in case more reinforcements showed up. For now the building was quiet.

"Stony here," said the voice of Barbara Price. "What is your situation?"

McCarter quickly updated her on their insertion. The Farm had been monitoring the radio traffic during the insertion. Still, there had been little time to keep the mission controller up-to-date on their precise activities.

"We are ready to enter and remove the equipment," Hawkins said.

"Go ahead, T.J." Aaron Kurtzman said.

Hawkins walked into the room without further consideration. The room was empty. He saw nothing out of the ordinary. He examined the configuration of electronics equipment staged on the kitchen counter.

All the devices were plugged into a single, laboratory-grade surge protection device. Whoever had set this equipment up had counted on a heavy population of hired gunmen to protect it. There were no alarms in evidence.

There was still the chance that the electronics—or the very walls of the apartment—were rigged with incendiary devices to burn the place to the ground if the electronics were tampered with.

Hawkins stepped up to the power supply and yanked the plug from the wall. The systems lights turned briefly from green to yellow, and then a small LCD screen notified Hawkins that the unit had sensed a power outage. The backup power had came into play. The display estimated a power supply time of 7.6 hours.

Hawkins quickly removed the cover of the power supply and saw nothing he had not expected to see.

He pulled out wire cutters and cut the cable from the power supply to the other electronics.

No fire. No booby trap. He grabbed the tiny pico-cell device itself, along with the OMC—Operations and Management Center—device. Without bothering to disconnect them from each other, he lugged them off the counter in the kitchen and stuffed the individual components into many-layered fireproof bags. Like the fire suit he was wearing, the bags might or might not offer protection in case an incendiary explosive went off within one of those pieces of electronics.

Hawkins sealed the bags, leaving only enough of an opening to allow the cables to snake from one to the other. Then he tucked one bag under each arm and left the apartment.

Guarded fore and aft by his teammates in Phoenix Force, Hawkins descended through the death-filled building at a near run, all the while wondering what it would feel like if one of the devices abruptly burst into flames, and he suddenly had a package full of 1500°F tucked into each armpit.

In the street were the sounds of the Barcelona police getting closer. Hawkins jogged to the SUV. McCarter remotely opened the rear. Hawkins stuffed his packages into the heavy round blast-containment chamber that weighed down the back end of the SUV. He slammed the hatch shut and spun the wheel to lock it—and was somewhat surprised to realize that he had made it out alive.

Then Hawkins was yanked into the backseat of the SUV by Calvin James as McCarter slammed on the accelerator, taking them up the street and around the corner. He slowed the vehicle as a city police car with lights and siren passed them going in the other direction, turning into the street they had just left.

The team headed for Moll Nou, driving fast but within the speed limit. David McCarter slipped the SUV between a pair of buildings that led them to open water. On one side of the dock inlet was the Barcelona Aquarium. He followed the road on the other side for another three hundred yards, then yanked the car right onto the dock. A hybrid cargo-and-pleasure boat was the only watercraft at this end of the wharf, and there was a gangplank in place, allowing for the movement of supplies via forklift. At the moment, the forklift was loading a pallet of boxed vegetables on board.

The forklift driver saw the SUV coming. He veered out of the way. McCarter pulled the SUV up the gangplank and into the cargo hold.

The interior storage compartment was longer than it probably should have been. The SUV slotted into a rear section and Encizo jumped out and yanked down on an overhead sliding door that sealed off the excess space.

Outside, the forklift operator spun his pallet of fresh vegetables in a one-eighty and pulled into the storage compartments of the boat again. He put the pallet of celery, tomatoes, potatoes, onions and white asparagus directly in front of the door that had just closed.

"We are on board," McCarter announced into his mike.

"Got it, Phoenix," Barbara Price said. Almost immediately the cargo hold was closed and the boat left port. It was thirty minutes before it was out of the harbor and into the open waters of the Balearic Sea.

CHAPTER TEN

Balearic Sea

Phoenix Force spent the time nervously in the blastproof compartment of the Navy SEALs black ops cruising vessel. Stony Man Farm had appropriated the use of the hydro boat for Phoenix Force. There was no way they were going to risk taking the devices onto an aircraft.

"Okay, T.J.," Price said finally. "Let's do this."

The door to their compartment was opened, the pallet of produce having been repositioned to allow Hawkins plenty of room to work with the blast containment chamber in the rear of the Land Rover. The blast box had rudimentary controls on the outside. Rudimentary was all that was needed to tell if there had been a high-temperature event inside the chamber. So far, there had been nothing.

Hawkins spun the lock wheel control and pulled open the hatch. James wielded a chemical sniff device over the open blast container and adjusted the controls. Finally he switched it off and pulled the device back.

"Nothing," he said.

"How sure can you be with that thing?" McCarter asked.

"With standard explosives, if it is not encapsulated, you can be reasonably certain of getting some sort of a reading," James said. "With this stuff, though?" He shrugged.

"We've done everything we can do to ensure it won't blow up in my face," Hawkins said. "So we might as well get at it."

The ship was outfitted with sophisticated electronics useful for espionage and special forces missions in the Mediterranean. Hawkins opened the blast packages, withdrew the equipment and reassembled them on the test table. He plugged each into a power supply, then into the transmitter that would give Stony Man Farm complete control and access to whatever was inside.

Stony Man Farm, Virginia

"No BULLSHIT TODAY, gentlemen," said the voice of a head researcher from the United States Defense Advanced Research Projects Agency. "You're not going to win or lose any military contracts out of this. You're going to help us pin down the shits behind these attacks. Understand?"

"I understand perfectly," said the man named Envoi, who was CEO of the awkwardly named NanoPlasPulse LLC.

"Here's the big question to start you out with, then," the DARPA scientist said. "I've read your website. I've read your white papers. I know your technology. I know what you claim you can do. Is it true?"

Kissinger rolled his eyes. The DARPA researcher who had been put in charge of the teleconference was throwing his weight around—treating it like an interrogation rather than an intelligence-sharing interview. On the one hand, it absolutely was a time for a no-bullshit discussion. On the other hand, he was putting NanoPlas-Pulse LLC's CEO on the defensive for no good reason.

"They don't teach effective people skills over at DARPA, do they?" Price said. She was in no danger of being heard. Stony Man Farm did not officially exist as far as the U.S. government was concerned, so how could Stony Man Farm be on a high-security conference call? The Farm was only listening in—for now.

CEO Envoi answered coolly, "Sir, I'm not sure what you're challenging me on. We have a patented technology for creating unagglomerated nanopowders. That's true. We can control particle size with a high degree of precision. I don't regard these as claims but rather as fact that has been accepted by the industry. Our standard products are 80-nanometer nanoaluminum and 25-nanometer nanosilver. It's pretty easy for our customers to measure. I think we would have been called out on it by now if our claims weren't correct."

"Fine," the DARPA scientist retorted. "What about smaller particles?"

"Smaller as in the 10-nanometer particles we claim on our website," the CEO said, an edge to his voice. He didn't like the DARPA scientist-cum-bureaucrat any better than Barbara Price did. "You're not going to get us on any deceptive advertising charges there, either."

Kurtzman raised his eyebrows.

"What I mean—" the DARPA scientist started to say.

"Every batch of nanopowders is audited for particle size and consistency in-house, as well as by our customers when they take delivery. We've also had numerous customers demand third-party verification. We've had production glitches here and there in the beginning but none of the deliveries failed to meet spec."

"Thank you," the DARPA scientist responded. "What about smaller sizes?"

"We don't advertise smaller sizes. No claims to refute on that score. Are you asking if we're capable of producing nanopowders at less than 10 nanometers? If you've read my white papers you know we are. Have you really read my white papers?"

"Yes," the DARPA scientist said.

"I thought you started this call by saying there would be no bullshit," said Envoi.

Despite all the horrors of the past few hours, Aaron Kurtzman felt a grin on his face. Kissinger was nodding, too. Envoi wasn't backing down.

"So why the bullshit?" Envoi demanded. "If you want me to answer a question, I'll answer it honestly. Have you or have you not read the white papers about our capabilities to control nanopowder sizes?"

"I have," the DARPA scientist replied, "but "

"So what are you really trying to ask me? If the company lied in its published results?"

"No. You misunderstood my question."

"Then so did I," Barbara Price said, hitting a key to allow Stony Man participatory access to the call. "You're wasting time, DARPA, and we do not have time to waste."

"Who is this?" the DARPA scientist demanded.

"Have you not been briefed on secure conference call protocols?" Price demanded. "My access clearance is now visible on the call security log monitor."

Kissinger took over before the DARPA scientist could get in again. "Hello, Mr. Envoi, I've also read the NanoPlasPulse LLC white papers. Your paper, Production Technique Studies on Conjoined Nanopowder Particulates for Metastable Intermolecular Composite

Alternatives, indicates you've been able to produce particles at 1 nm with a great deal of consistency. It also says you can create 100-nanometer conjoined particles and 200-nanometer agglomerated matched particles. What we're extremely interested in knowing is the potential for conjoined, matched, nonagglomerated particles in the 0.25- to 0.5-nanometer range."

There was a moment of silence.

"Is *that* what the terrorists are using?" the CEO of NanoPlasPulse LLC asked in amazement.

"You're not allowed to ask that question!" the DARPA scientist snapped.

"CNN's asking it as of ninety seconds ago," Kissinger retorted. "The Japanese figured all this out not long after we did and they're not trying to keep it quiet. They've released what they know to the media."

"That's incredible—the technology you described," Envoi said. "Conjoining at that scale is not possible using any method I know. The answer to the question is no, my company cannot do that. None of our competitors are even close to doing it, as far as I know. No university lab that I know of can do it."

"What's the potential for taking your method and optimizing it to drive down the size of the particles?" Kissinger asked.

"We think we could go a little further, but even when we conjoined 100-nanometer particles—the technique we used is probably not applicable to conjoined particulates much smaller than 100 nanometers. Our process was to create almost microscopic batches of nanopowders as crystalline solids with impurities to create vacancy defects, then used various methods to return the crystals to nanopowder sizes. Our entire output of conjoined 100-nanometer particles was less than a gram."

"Considering the number of devices deployed in the attacks, and assuming they all used the materials found in the recovered devices, at least five hundred kilograms of this material was produced."

"Five hundred—!"

"That's top-secret information!" the DARPA scientist interrupted.

"Anderson Cooper's in big trouble then," Price said. "He's talking about it now. Mr. Envoi, I for one have no educational background in weaponized nanopowders. But the devices obtained by the U.S. and other governments, as far as we can tell, are composed of these extremely tiny particles, the biggest at approximately half a nanometer. In each case there is a high density of matched, conjoined pairs—up to eighty percent."

"At eighty percent density, there's not much room for impurities so I'll assume they're not using the decrystallization approach we used," Envoi said, his voice clearly shaky. "Here's the truth. And this is not bullshit. I *am* one of the top guys in the world in terms of nanopowder research. There's me, Ken Saitou in Tokyo, Anne Sankt in the UK. We're the only real experts left when it comes to nanopowder conjoining. Talk to them. They may know something I don't know. But I'm telling you this—what you're describing can*not* be done with the methods I have ever heard of."

KISSINGER STARED AT THE phone when the call ended. "Shit," he said.

"What about the others he mentioned."

"They seem to be a close-knit group of scientists," Price said. "If he doesn't know what made this material, then they won't know it—unless they developed it and sold it to the perpetrators. In that case, they won't have reason to say so when our obnoxious friend at DARPA calls to chat. We've already begun background checks on these three, as well as every other scientist and researcher who's been involved in nanopowders research—especially research into conjoining."

"That is the key," Kissinger said. "Think about it— take an oxidizer particle, one two-billionths of a meter in diameter, and a fuel particle of the same size, and glue them together. When they ignite, they ignite with a level of efficiency like nothing we know. You pack them together in a block of plastic and ignite them all at once—the heat is incredible. The efficiency is like nothing you've ever seen. No wonder they need so little of the stuff. It's going to burn close to the theoretical maximum of the two components it is made of. No matter what, I guarantee you it will always be hot enough to get through anything it is adhered to."

Ramvik, Norway

CHARLES SKYN WAS FORCED to turn sideways to make it through some of the narrow passageways in the great hall of the Ramm family mansion. A small rodent scampered from a pile of cardboard boxes on one side and skittered into a hole that had been chewed years ago into a cardboard box on the other side of the passageway.

Skyn had been making his home at the mansion in Ramvik for more than two years. Some of the boxes that turned this large dining hall into a narrow warren of passages predated him by at least a decade. On arrival he had been astounded to find the historic family home filled, some places to the rafters, with cardboard boxes, plastic crates and, in some cases, simply mounds of trash.

Olan Ramm had claimed that every item stored in the mansion was of personal value. He claimed, in fact, that he had been collecting the lost and stolen and sold-off belongings of his family for all of his life. He told the story of finding one of the families in the town in possession of a decorative finial that once stood atop a post on the entrance gates to the Ramm family home. The gate had been torn down in the 1930s. The iron was sold off. Apparently some of the decorative pieces had been given away or simply taken from the scrap heaps before it was hauled off.

But as far as Ramm was concerned, anything that had belonged to the Ramm family once, belonged to the Ramm family forever. He recognized the finial, with the Ramm crest, being used as a knocker on one of the homes in town and he had pounded on that door with his fist. He demanded the return of the finial and he demanded an apology for the insult that such a use implied.

The owner of the home had refused, even when Ramm insisted that the man should do so for no other reason than because he was of the Ramm family—and the Ramm family had jurisdiction in his part of the country. The man had laughed in his face.

Ramm—all of thirteen years old at the time—came back in the night, used an ax to remove the finial from the door and used a bottle of burning gasoline on the front door of the house as a way of ensuring that the family inside was duly rewarded for the injury and insult they had perpetrated.

Of course that anecdote had been a perfect addition to a case that Charles Skyn was building against Olan Ramm, a case that would prove Olan Ramm was insane. The case would free Charles Skyn from any obligation to share his profits with Olan Ramm after he fled Norway to commercialize the technology that he had developed in the mansion just outside the town of Ramvik.

Charles Skyn was British and he knew a thing or two about royalty—and he knew that Olan Ramm, last of the Ramm line, had no idea how royalty should behave. Not that Skyn had ever said anything even remotely insulting to Ramm.

Ramm was his bread and butter.

Ramm had financed Skyn's research for a year in the UK. The success he achieved had led to Ramm offering an even better and longer-term funding commitment. This time, Skyn was obliged to relocate his research to Ramm's home in this cold, unpleasant little town in Norway. The research results would be the proprietary commercial property of Ramm and Skyn. They'd share in the profits.

When Skyn began to learn more of Ramm's plans for generating those profits, he almost laughed in the man's face. What Ramm was proposing was preposterous. But the methods by which he intended to pull it off would certainly work.

Skyn was interested in sharing those profits, ambivalent to Ramm's methods, and doubtful of Ramm's capacity to actually carry out the scheme.

But that did not mean that Skyn was uninterested in joining Ramm. Ramm had a source of funds that seemed inexhaustible. Such funding would help Skyn perfect his technology in secret. When the time came, he would distance himself from Ramm and dissolve their partnership. After the funding, before the profit sharing.

Skyn knew how to ensure the propagation of his research results to secure digital sites as development progressed. He kept regular updates in digital vaults around the world. When the time came to part ways with Ramm   even if Ramm kicked him out without a scrap of hard data or a single sample—Skyn's research would still be waiting for him in cyberspace. He would be able to access it, and, at that stage of development, he would be able to sell it.

When the time came, Ramm would have to be exposed to the world for the lunatic he was. That would preclude any of Ramm's claims to Skyn's technology being taken seriously.

Skyn watched Ramm start out crazy and go downhill from there. His schemes manipulating the world oil markets were as preposterous as his rationale for doing so.

But it was so fascinating to be a part of it. And when Ramm actually started putting the pieces in place, Skyn found he couldn't seem to tear himself away. It was all too grand and exhilarating.

He still considered Ramm to be insane. And nobody out in the real world ever had to know that Skyn was a willing accomplice. Along with the remote research data storage that Skyn updated frequently was a quasi-factual journal describing his day-to-day life as essentially that of an indentured servant to Olan Ramm—and how that servitude had turned to slavery. Skyn—he claimed in his own journal—was now a prisoner to Olan Ramm. Ramm was forcing him to create the weapons he was using. He described Ramm as homicidal. Power mad. Schizophrenic, probably. Obsessive-compulsive on a grand scale, certainly.

And he was a hoarder. To reinforce just how crazy Ramm was, Skyn had included quite a few photographs of the interior of the Ramm mansion. It was like something out of two horrible reality television shows put together: *Compulsive Norse Hoarders* meets *Lifestyles of the Richest Norwegians*.

Skyn had seen the shows where miserable old women spent all their time collecting trash in the streets and stored it in ever-growing piles in their homes, until getting across the living room meant clambering upon piles of garbage. They kept bringing in more until there was no floor space visible. Then every surface was covered. Then the appliances became storage places and stopped functioning. The plumbing would no longer work and soon the poor idiots had nothing left except a single chair in which to eat and sleep and live their lives amid mountains of refuse.

Those television shows always depicted the arrival of a mental health professional, come to cure the hoarder over a weekend of sound-bite therapy. It never worked. Almost every episode ended with the hoarder's house still filled with filth.

What Skyn had come to appreciate most about the hoarders was the tenacity with which they held on to their precious trash. They could rationalize keeping a sodden newspaper from two years back, or a broken badminton racket or a cage containing several dead budgies.

Skyn had secretly recorded conversations with Olan Ramm that could have been written for one of those shows. He would pause to admire some cast-off garbage in the pile and he would ask Ramm about it. Once Ramm had explained, in precise detail, how a great-great-uncle had sold nine costumes that had been used by the family for masquerade parties when they visited friends in mainland Europe. The costumes had gone to a local group that put on free theater productions in the town.

"They were on my inventory of missing property," Ramm had told Skyn. "We were all great keepers of records. My great-great-uncle was among them. I went through his diary page by page as part of assembling my inventory. Most of the things he owned that were of value and many of the things that he owned that he did not consider to be of value are recorded in his diary. He considered the costumes to be worthless but valuable to the theater in town. I consider them valuable to the Ramm family because they belonged to the Ramm family."

Olan Ramm had ended that anecdote with the line that was his mantra. "Once it belongs to the Ramm family, it always belongs to the Ramm family."

He was certainly insane.

But he was very focused in his insanity, wasn't he? Skyn found his way up the back stairs, to the bedroom that was less trash-filled than the rest of the house. From here, using an analog phone, Ramm issued his orders and watched his televisions.

Skyn placed a box on the floor. Inside were twenty-four prepaid-use smartphones—all of different designs. Skyn began to wearily unbox the units one by one and plug them in to charge on the big surge protector.

"Somebody took my picocell," Ramm said.

Which was disturbing news to Charles Skyn. He knew what a picocell was—but he didn't know Ramm did. He didn't know Ramm had acquired or used a picocell. He didn't know how Ramm could have put it in place and used it without Skyn knowing.

Skyn really should stop underestimating Olan Ramm.

Stony Man Farm

KISSINGER SHOWED UP in the War Room and was uncharacteristically subdued.

Barbara Price looked up with tired eyes, surprised to see the man standing next to her desk. "Something on your mind, John?"

"I need to make a phone call," he said. "I need you and Bear in on it."

It was an odd request. "To Envoi," Kissinger said. "I think I'd like to consult with him further."

Barbara Price frowned. Did Kissinger think the head of NanoPlasPulse LLC was hiding something? She'd judged Envoi as sincere, although she never put her faith in uncorroborated intuition.

"This could be important?" she asked.

"Maybe…"

"Bear." Barbara waved Kurtzman over and got a secure line out to the nanopowders company in Texas. She went the pedestrian route—through his secretary.

"May I ask who's calling?"

"No."

"Mr. Envoi is not doing interviews."

"Tell Mr. Envoi we spoke earlier today. We were on the same conference call."

The secretary was clearly doubtful. Price thought she should have just spearheaded through the company system and rung Envoi's line directly. But she didn't want to come across as just another obstinate Fed.

"Hello?" Harry Envoi said cautiously.

"Mr. Envoi, you may recall…"

"I recognize you, young lady," Mr. Envoi said.

"You may recognize me, as well," Kissinger said.

"Yes, I do. You're the one who actually read my

paper. I appreciate your efforts to keep the previous call from deteriorating further than it did. How can I help you?"

Kissinger looked at Price, almost as if he were embarrassed. "Mr. Envoi, you said something that I should have followed up on at the time. It only occurred to me when the call was done."

Price was expecting Kissinger to ask some technical question. Instead he said, "You said there were three nanoparticles-conjoining experts left—yourself, Sankt and Saitou."

"Yes?"

"*Left* means somebody else was there and now is gone," Kissinger said.

"Yes?"

"The reason I called you back was to ask who else *was* there?"

Ramvik

CHARLES SKYN clearly remembered sitting in the folding chairs in this very room on the day Ramm finally took him into his confidence.

"Oil lines," Ramm said. "Your devices can render a twenty-foot section of oil pipeline useless. And we can take them out by the thousands."

"But replacing them isn't difficult."

"To a point. Replacing one hundred of them is still a big undertaking, but spread that effort across the world and it can be accomplished fairly quickly," Ramm allowed. "Replacing several thousand around the world would be impossible to do quickly. There is simply not that much oil pipeline in readiness to install—and every day that goes by that a pipeline is nonfunctional, it costs the owners millions and the nations they serve hundreds of millions."

Olan Ramm described a similar effect on the railroad systems. Sections of rail were much easier to manufacture and could be installed much more quickly.

"But once they see the ease with which the rails can be sabotaged, who'll ride them? No one. The commuter rails will be unused. Who'll ship their goods by rail when the risk becomes so great? What carrier will insure any shipment by rail when the risk is sky-high? I tell you, it will hurt their economies nearly as badly as the loss of oil—and the nations will pay to free themselves of that risk."

Olan Ramm described how the economy of each nation would wither—and how such nations would pay any cost to escape the oppression.

"The genius of the plan is this," Ramm said. "The ease with which each nation will escape the disaster. I am not going to ask them to give up their wealth or their oil. I'm not looking for a ransom. I only want returned to me what is rightfully mine."

That's where the skewed genius of Ramm's plan shone through. His claims were absurd. Preposterous. But Skyn was very interested in seeing him push those claims upon the world—just to see what might happen when he did.

And just so long as Skyn didn't stand to take any of the blame for Ramm's insanity.

There had never been any reason for him to be loyal to Ramm's cause. It was not his cause. Truth be told, he was loyal to the payoff, and the excitement, and he loved being the perpetrator of mystery. He loved being the one who played the sides against each other. Ramm's cause was the preposterous fantasy of a man whose emotional development stopped at age twelve.

It had been Skyn's idea to fake his own death in the first place. Too late he had seen the weak position this put him in. He had already disappeared, and if Ramm decided that he was disposable, there was nothing to stop him from making Skyn disappear for real.

For that reason, Skyn had gone to great lengths to maintain his usefulness in Ramm's eyes. This included his plans to expand the initial wave of attacks to include maritime oil storage and transport. Adding oil tankers to the initial attacks had given them the extra punch needed to get the attention of the world. The perfectly executed sabotage in China, and the brilliant footage that came of it, had riveted the attention of the world in ways that undocumented disasters could not.

Skyn had been the one to argue for the development of a special device to take out aircraft during the initial rounds of attacks. These devices cost one hundred times as much as the standard nanothermite device that they were utilizing. Those things could be made for several dollars each. The devices that were disguised as functional laptop computers had cost thousands.

He and Ramm had argued over the need for this special exception. Skyn had been very insistent. He'd maintained that the success of the initial attacks would be enhanced by specific attacks on passenger aircraft.

"The world needs to know that no mode of transport is off-limits to us," Skyn insisted. "You can't allow this gaping hole in your coverage. Consider how nervous the world is with airline travel. When 9/11 happened the world was amazed that so many aircraft could be controlled and brought down. Think about this, Ramm—if you bring down more aircraft than 9/11, and do it as a part of a bigger, more broad-based series of attacks, it'll make 9/11 look like a bank robbery."

In truth, Skyn saw no special reason to target the airlines in the initial attacks. But his insistence on doing so, for the good of the cause, had helped convince Ramm that he was fully on board with the cause. That he was dedicated to the cause.

It also convinced Ramm that Skyn had an ongoing value as a consultant. If he had more value to contribute, Ramm wouldn't have him killed. Right?

His most recent move as Ramm's idea man had showed him just how much his star was diminished.

"I think it is time that we begin manufacturing a new generation of devices," Skyn said.

"Why?"

"The devices that we've been making are beginning to be found too easily. All around the world, people are discovering them on railroad tracks, bridge trestles, water towers, everywhere."

"But there are hundreds still in place. And we can put more in place on whatever we like."

"Can we?" Skyn asked. "How? We are losing our ability to hire people in the field. Our recruiters are bringing no new people on board. Half our recruiters have cut ties. No offense, Ramm, but your methods have alienated almost everyone who worked for us. We need devices that can be deployed more quickly and easily, and can be actuated without these convoluted communication systems. I've come up with several designs that will work for us, and have great potential."

Skyn withdrew a series of handmade diagrams and laid them on the table in front of Ramm. Ramm looked at them, clearly unenthusiastic.

"Can I show you?"

Ramm shrugged. Skyn, uneasily, proceeded. He explained the top drawing.

"This is a flat device, actuated by timer. This unit is designed especially for roadways. See how the shape is hexagonal but flat. It could be tossed onto a roadway and remain there until the timer activates it. It could even be driven over unnoticed during the wait period. These could be deployed by a single person, driving down the road and tossing them from a car window, particularly during low-traffic nighttime hours. I estimate that two hundred units could be dispersed along a major interstate highway over the course of three hours. Timers could be set for four hours. Once they started going off, no one would try to stop them. You could decimate a stretch of interstate highway, making it unusable for months, at least. Take a big city such as New York or London, hit all the major roadways that head into the city, knock them all out of commission simultaneously, and you have a city that will almost cease to function."

Ramm nodded. "Skyn, the truth is, I don't know if we need these. I do not know that the attacks are going to need to continue. I believe what we have in place now will be more than adequate to achieve my aims."

"But your options are decreasing by the day. By the hour. Your devices are being discovered and removed. You are completely dependent on the battery lifetime of the communication devices. Even if your current sending system remains uncompromised, you have a month at best before all of your devices become incommunicado. What will you do when you've got no devices left to actuate? You'll have no leverage. You'll have no weapon of enforcement. You will not be able to enforce your will."

Ramm shook his head and said that this was not

strictly true. "There are several carefully staged device sets that are not dependent on phone actuation. They're not dependent on device battery life. They will remain in place, and controllable, indefinitely. They will almost certainly not be found."

Skyn was shocked. "Where?"

"Places you don't need to know about," Ramm said.

"But what methods have you used?"

"Skyn, you do not need to know."

Skyn stared at him. "I see."

"May I remind you, again, we are not partners. You are my technical consultant. As it turns out, I do not need your consultation on all my technical enterprises."

Skyn nodded, then smiled slightly. "I see. No problem. Should we then even be continuing manufacturing? We are still putting out these devices on the order of hundreds a day."

Ramm agreed it was time to scale back manufacturing. "Not that we will not need them again. And we may even someday need to use your new designs, Skyn," Ramm said, tapping the pages. "But if all goes as planned, and I think it will, the attacks will cease. Once I have attained my position, and retrieved all my property, and retrieved my stolen wealth, there's nothing more I will need."

Skyn nodded. His thoughts were swirling. It sounded very much as if Ramm was on the verge of letting Skyn go. And Skyn was certain that he would not be allowed to go anywhere. If this was the end of his employment, it would be the end of his life. Which meant it was time for Skyn to begin the next phase of his own personal strategy. That included getting the hell away from Ramm, and to begin exploiting the reams of data and the evidence and the photos and the video that he'd collected during his time with Ramm.

But that would require an opportune moment to escape. In the meantime, he needed to keep Ramm intrigued with his capabilities. He needed to create a perception that he could still be of value to Ramm.

That would give him the time he needed to organize his flight.

"I would like to stay in consultation with you, just in case we need to resume broad-based efforts. If the world doesn't respond exactly as you planned, there may be need for more escalation. Don't you agree that is a possibility?"

Ramm nodded, then shrugged slightly.

"Just in case, I think it would be a good idea to complete production on the current run. We have the materials. The line is in operation. Why not finish it up? It will take another four days before our current materials store runs dry. It can't hurt to have a well-stocked armory. Don't you agree?"

Ramm considered that, then nodded. "Fine. Continue production until our materials run out. Then shut down the facility in the manner we planned."

Dalsfjorden

HE HAD TRAVELED that morning from the Ramm estate to more lands, far north of Ramvik. There was a remote stretch of land owned by Ramm where no person lived for thirty miles in any direction. In the midst of this wasteland, hidden in pine woods, was the Ramm factory.

It was down a long dirt road, inaccessible by wheeled vehicle for half of the year. There was an old steel structure set in the woods. It'd probably been some old farmer's feed storage building. Now it was where the world's most sophisticated weaponized nanothermite devices were produced.

The grounds also contained material storage bins, a large generator and fuel oil tank, and a large camper that housed the five men hired as manufacturing workers.

Skyn traveled in the company of two of Ramm's bodyguards. Ramm had hired this pair when he was in his early twenties. They had grown rich in his employment. They were loyal to him absolutely. Skyn knew he had to kill them along with the manufacturing crew to make his escape foolproof.

Ramm had never sent two bodyguards with Skyn on his trips to the plant. Ramm claimed that the danger was worse, now that the operation was under way. He was doing this for Skyn's protection.

Skyn knew better. The bodyguards were there to make sure that Skyn did not run.

But the bodyguards seemed unaware that Skyn knew their real task.

Skyn entered the factory. The interior was dominated at one end by the thing called the Oven. It was not an oven, although the cabinets of an industrial ceramic oven had been used to house its workings. Inside were sifters, electrostatic generators, crystallization bins and electromagnetic separators. This was Skyn's contribution. This made the devices special.

All the rest of it was manual labor, and it took only five people to run this factory. They had been hired from a little fishing village 250 miles to the northeast, and they had made more money doing this job for a year than they had made in their entire lifetimes. They were illiterate, simple, probably mentally stunted. But they were trainable. They were happy to have the work. They could stand living out here in the middle of nowhere. The satellite television that Ramm paid for in the trailer was endlessly exciting and entertaining.

They were happy. Everybody was happy.

Ramm's bodyguards stood around the interior of the plant watching him work with the production crew for a full hour before they got fed up.

"How long are you going to be?" one of them demanded.

"Three or four hours," Skyn said.

The bodyguards became agitated. No one had told them they would have to wait around this place for three or four hours.

"We're ending production in the next few days," Skyn said. "We need to finish this run. We need to finish it correctly. Sorry if you have a problem with that, but that is what I've been instructed to do. You don't like it? Call Olan."

The bodyguards were certainly not about to call Ramm to complain.

"What the hell are we supposed to do here for three or four hours?" one of them demanded.

"Go and watch TV. They have satellite in the camper."

It took them ten minutes, but finally the bodyguards decided they had no other choice but to go watch television in the camper.

Skyn worked with his crew, going through the motions of checking out the latest production run, pretending to adjust the operation of the Oven. He gave the bodyguards plenty of opportunity to get settled in the camper.

He left the plant and entered the camper to use the

washroom, grabbed a bottle of beer from the fridge and left again. It was a reconnoiter and he'd found the bodyguards just where he wanted them to be: in front of the TV. One of them was flipping through the channels. The other one was snoring in his chair.

Just before Skyn reentered the factory he pressed the button on his remote control. Twelve nanothermite devices had been placed underneath the camper, tied in to its electrical system, and could be activated only by Skyn's remote control. He'd put them there months ago.

He closed the door to the plant and watched through the plastic window of the door as the camper sizzled, collapsed and melted. The intense heat reduced it to a warped pile of plastic and blackened metal that bore no resemblance to a camper trailer.

As soon as he was certain that the nanothermites had finished their mission, and anything in the camper that was going to explode had exploded, it was time for him to go. He turned to his production crew and gave a wave to the head man. He quickly counted the staff, making sure that his full crew was in place. He wanted to solve this problem in one fell swoop.

Everybody was present. A couple of the workers were sniffing the air. The fumes from the burning camper were starting to make their way inside.

Skyn left quickly, shut the door behind him and jogged to the car, where the spare key was where it should be above the visor. He pulled away from the site and triggered the remaining nanothermites.

Ten of them had been placed in and around the production building itself. There was also the added fuel of the devices that were in the process of being produced, as well as the raw materials. The result was a fire that burned white-hot. Watching it from a half mile away,

Skyn was certain that the light would be visible from orbit; it was that bright.

When he returned to the site, after some of the intensity had died down, he was delighted at the result. The fuel tanks, the entire production building, everything had vanished. The ground where they had been was a lumpy, steaming pool in the woods. All the metal, all the plastic, maybe even the ground itself had been liquefied in the heat. The equivalent of eighty-seven of the devices had ignited in the small area. The red-hot lake might take days to cool.

With that, Charles Skyn drove away. He headed south and caught the E6. For four hours he drove, with his eyes in the rearview mirror as much as they were on the road in front of him.

In Oslo he had a car waiting. Skyn parked the vehicle belonging to Olan Ramm's bodyguard and walked four blocks to a mechanic's shop. A year ago, Skyn had paid the mechanic ten thousand euros, cash, to store his VW, and to drive it once a month and generally keep it in readiness. There was a promise of ten thousand more if and when Skyn picked up the car.

The mechanic had done a good job. The battery was charged and the tank was full and the VW started without hesitation. He handed the ten thousand euros to the mechanic and left Oslo minutes later.

Skyn was tempted to burn the bodyguard's car and burn the mechanic in his shop—but that would be like waving a flag to show Ramm the route he was taking.

Four hours later he was in Kristiansand. The twice-daily Fjord Line ferry wasn't running, but there were private craft to charter.

Thirteen hours after burning Ramm's production

facility to the ground, Charles Skyn debarked in Hirt-shals, Denmark.

In Hirtshals, also many months ago, Skyn had left himself an emergency package: money and a change of clothing. He'd paid an exorbitant sum to charter a private jet. But what the hell? It was Ramm's money. Cash, in fact, stolen from a box on a shelf in an old bedroom. Ramm had forgotten it was there.

It was a white-knuckle flight. He had the executive jet all to himself and finally had to yell at the flight attendant to stop asking him if he wanted a drink. He couldn't drink. He had to stay clearheaded.

Security was the tightest he had ever seen it. It didn't help that they were the only flight into St. John, New Brunswick, in nine hours. The entire security crew seemed to want to get in on the act.

Skyn had expected this. He had nothing even remotely suspicious on his person. It still took half an hour to get through screening.

He had another stash in St. John—a safe-deposit box with new identities, credit cards and a hundred thousand U.S. dollars. He rented a Tahoe.

He turned it in at the Hertz in Bangor and rented an Avis Mustang convertible under a different name. He bought an Infiniti G25 in Boston. He'd always wanted one of those.

He drove the Infiniti to his new hometown.

Olan Ramm would never find him among the millions of people in New York City.

Stony Man Farm

IN THE FIELD of nanoparticle conjoining there had been four recognized superstars. "One, to be perfectly honest, is me," said Harry Envoi, CEO of NanoPlas-Pulse LLC.

Another was a Japanese intellectual and researcher named Saitou. "Sad story. He lost his wife in the tsunami in 2011," Envoi explained to Barbara Price, John Kissinger and Aaron Kurtzman. "Ever since then his work has been feverish. I think the poor guy is working himself to death. But he was always a pacifist. He's steered away from work on weaponized nanoparticles. He won't even experiment with nanothermites, let alone develop them. He's always looked at conjoined particles for industrial and medical applications."

The third name on the list was Anne Sankt, in the UK. Another scholar and researcher on the staff of University College London. "She spends half her time in London, the other half at the UCL School of Energy and Resources in Adelaide. She's become a less important figure in the field in recent years," Envoi said. "I don't like to spread rumors, but I hear Anne spends a lot of unnecessary time at the Asian nightclubs in Adelaide."

Or pretending to, Price thought. The same thought occurred to Kissinger and Kurtzman. Making the world think she had a drinking problem would be good cover for some clandestine work.

"Anne's blonde," Envoi added uncomfortably. "Chinese and Japanese businessmen or tourists in Adelaide—they're always interested in meeting blondes. I think she thrives on the attention."

And then Envoi gave the name Charles Skyn, who fell into the "who else was there" category.

"He was a student of Anne's several years ago, but he went off on his own about 2007. He was some kind of a savant. A genius. He seemed to ramp up from student to world-class expert on the topic of nanoparticulate conjoining at incredible speed. Was doing some sort of independent research. Grant-funded at first. Wasn't putting out many papers. Then he ran out of cash and got a corporate sponsor. Did that for a year. Wrote one interesting paper, purely theoretical, about using a particle accelerator as a way of creating ultrasmall particles. I peer reviewed it. It was interesting, as I said, and worth publishing simply because Skyn had shown such insight in his early years and everybody felt there could be a genius in there, ready to emerge one of these days. But his knowledge was mostly learned by rote and his new theories—like the one about the particle accelerators— were fanciful. Kind of useless unless you have a particle accelerator to test it out on and even then you'd come up with so few ultrasmall particles you could count them on your fingers and toes. He was already ahead of his mentor—Anne Sankt. She'd started going downhill academically by this stage, but he may have been ahead of all of us. But we'll never know. He died before the paper was even published."

"Died?"

"Went out on his boat and never came back. Wreckage washed up a few days later. That's pretty dead, isn't it?"

There was silence.

"You think he faked his death?"

"Maybe," Price said.

"Why would he do that?"

"It sounds like a long shot. On the other hand, we have this technology that couldn't have come from many people. We do not know where it came from. The world's foremost expert on the technology cannot explain where it came from. We have to start somewhere."

"Who's 'we,' by the way?" Envoi asked from the

phone speaker. "Oh, wait. Forget it. Don't tell me. You'd have to kill me."

Price smiled. She liked Dr. Envoi. "We won't tell you or kill you—how's that?"

"Fine."

"But I think we'll stay in touch, Dr. Envoi."

"Then call me Harry. I'll call you Agent 99."

Price smiled. "Just call me Barb."

CHAPTER ELEVEN

Stony Man Farm

The voice of David McCarter came over the speakers. "Stony, if we have targets in the vicinity, we have to go get them."

Price was bent over Kurtzman's shoulder assessing the targets they had identified. "Phoenix, I don't think they could be closer to you. These targets were specifically chosen for you. Somebody knows you have that box, and they may even know your location. And they're setting you up. They want to take you out."

In fact, there was just one series of signals that came through the picocell at that time, and they were to the targets in close proximity to Phoenix Force. There were no reports of attacks anywhere, worldwide, at that time.

The only attacks even attempted on the planet were on the closest piece of land to the black ops boat containing the members of Phoenix Force.

It was impossible that it was a coincidence. Whoever the perpetrators were, they specifically wanted to draw in whoever had taken possession of their picocell.

And Stony Man Farm understood that it was being manipulated. They knew that the terrorists had the capability to perpetrate other attacks. They were not dependent on the one picocell that Phoenix Force had appropriated.

The terrorists had drawn Able Team into the tower in Philadelphia and then used alternative means of communication to ignite those devices. They had almost taken out the tower with Able Team inside.

In exactly the same way, the signals in Santa Ponsa were bait.

The issue now was whether Stony Man Farm should take it.

But there really was little debate. The Farm had profiled these terrorists. To call them ruthless was an understatement. Their strategy was to use terror and violence as tools of manipulation. If they set bait and nobody bit, they would be offended. They would certainly take their retribution by triggering the devices.

Stony Man was damned no matter what they did.

"Bloody right they want to take us out," McCarter said. "That doesn't mean we can't go and take care of those targets."

"They may not even be legitimate targets," Price said. "Their entire purpose is to draw in whoever is on the trail. It is too dangerous. I am not sending you into booby traps."

"What are the targets?" McCarter asked.

"Santa Ponsa," Price said. "On Majorca."

"I've been to Santa Ponsa," said Rafael Encizo. "Went there with a girlfriend once. Nice views, but I can't think of anything there that our friend would get satisfaction from destroying. It's just a tourist place."

Kurtzman zoomed in on something on the screen. "That's not all that is in Santa Ponsa," he said. "It's the Majorca endpoint of an undersea power system bringing electricity between mainland Spain and the island. There's a pair of HV DC cables laid in the waters. They have a capacity of 200 MW. Each. Total capacity 400

MW. It's a five-hundred-million-dollar project. And it starts in Santa Ponsa."

"I still don't think I'm getting it," said McCarter. "It doesn't seem like our friend's style. Sure, he could cause some real headaches for the guys at the utility company. But he's not exactly going to kill off a lot of innocent people just because he burns up some wire. It won't even be a major repair job."

Barbara Price took a few quick steps. "Phoenix, I do not think that this is about killing civilians or destroying infrastructure—not this time. This is about sucking us in and taking us down. I do not know how we are going to be able to engage these targets. The risks are fantastic. We simply don't know what is in store for us—we only know that there is something in store for us."

"Understood," McCarter said. "But the alternative is not dealing with those targets. Or even worse, letting the Parma police move in and handle the situation. No offense to the Spaniards, but I don't think they are prepared any better than we are."

Price couldn't seem to think of a good argument.

"We are on our way, Stony," McCarter said. "Unless you directly order us not to go."

Barbara Price closed her eyes briefly. "I'm saying nothing of the kind, Phoenix. We'll see if we can't evacuate the site."

Balearic Sea

THERE WAS NOTHING David McCarter hated worse than leading his men into a known trap—but it wasn't as if they had a choice. If they did not go in, who would?

Besides, these traps were set specifically for Phoenix. It was almost personal. And David McCarter was not going to allow some poor Spanish cop to get taken out by a trap meant for him and for the others in Phoenix Force.

The black ops cruising vessel was already heading south over the section of water called the Balearic Sea, with the island of Majorca coming into view. They would dock within ninety minutes.

Gary Manning took the pages out of the oversize printer and slapped them on the table.

Calvin James winced and said, "What in the hell is that?"

"That's our target," Manning said.

James shook his head. "I don't know why," he said, "but I was expecting a big old davit on the shore with an electrical cable wrapped around it and heading up into a high-tension tower. Call me stupid, but what the hell is all that?"

"The sea line comes out at the site of an existing power station," Aaron Kurtzman explained over the speakers. "What you are looking at is no less than three power plants. You have a coal-fired power plant that dates back to the 1940s—it's nonfunctional and probably not a target. Also an oil-powered plant, made up of modular generators. Eighteen small generators, which are turned on only as needed. Alongside it is a highly advanced solid-oxide fuel cell power plant. A hybrid plant, with high temperature fuel cells and gas turbines. It uses the fuel cells to store and release energy, accommodating higher levels of demand. That section of the plant has been open for less than six months. It's fully operational. All these power sources feed the grid."

McCarter tried to assess the chaos of buildings, fuel storage tanks, cooling towers and transmission towers on the sheet in front of them. "Stony, I think the sea line should be at the bottom of the priority list, along with the coal plant. The oil generators and the hybrid plant are the real vulnerable targets. That's what can't be fixed."

Island of Majorca, Spain

THOMAS JACKSON HAWKINS stood against the fence bordering the property. It was ten feet tall, chain link and laced with ugly orange strips of plastic. Apparently the fence was designed to give some privacy to the huge electric generation plant.

The building was six stories tall and two blocks in length, and the external walls were entirely glass. Inside were rows of generation machinery that normally chugged constantly, turning fuel oil into electricity and feeding it into the grid for consumption by the people on the island of Majorca.

But today the big parking lot out front was empty. Hundreds of spaces but zero cars. The machinery inside was silent. It had been shut down, an emergency procedure required when the place was evacuated.

Supposedly the entire staff was gone. Supposedly the only people on this entire vast site were the five men of Phoenix Force.

T. J. Hawkins knew that was not the case. He didn't know how he knew it. Sometimes you just felt this stuff in your saddle sores.

"Move in, T.J.," said the voice of Calvin James.

Hawkins followed these instructions. He was an excellent soldier. As a Ranger, he'd worked with some of the best. He'd also worked with some of the worst. There were bad apples, even in the Special Forces of the

United States. Even at the top levels of command in the United States military. There were always bad apples.

Well, not always. In a small, tight, effectively led organization of professionals who depended upon one another to get a dangerous job done, the bad apples were weeded out quickly. And right now, to his relief and satisfaction, T. J. Hawkins was in such an organization. Phoenix Force was the most capable group of men he had ever known, and the commander of Phoenix Force, David McCarter—the one that everybody said used to be a hothead—was today an extremely competent commander.

He could still lose his cool from time to time, but who the hell didn't?

T. J. Hawkins was satisfied with where he was, with what he was doing with his life and with the difference he was making in the world. And maybe one day this work would kill him, but he would leave the world a better place for his efforts. Of that he had no doubt.

And today, maybe he could do a little more good before a bunch more people got killed.

When bad things happened in the world, Hawkins could usually figure it out. The things that people did usually made some sort of twisted sense. Taking drugs out of desperation. Robbing a liquor store to pay for the drugs. Setting fire to your house to collect the insurance money. Those kinds of crimes had some sort of excuse behind them, at the very least. Even these deplorable acts were done for a reason.

Even desperate, selfish power grabs had reason behind them. Wanting power was something that motivated many men. He'd seen it a thousand times. It was something that had a place in the logical working of the world, even if it was entirely selfish.

But people did not kill globally and indiscriminately for *no* reason. Why the hell were these people not at least issuing demands?

Not knowing what they were after, these mass-murdering terrorists of unknown origin, helped the terror grow—which, Hawkins understood, was exactly what the terrorists wanted right now.

Eventually, they would make themselves known. They would issue their demands and their agenda would be made known to the world.

No matter what that agenda turned out to be, it would be vastly insufficient to excuse what had been done to the people of the world. These acts could never be justified.

Hawkins checked his line of thought. He was only getting himself agitated when he most needed to be cool. They were walking into a huge glass box, filled with machinery, filled with weapons that could melt that machinery to the ground and filled with an unknown number of men who were willing to shoot down Phoenix Force rather than let them remove those weapons.

Hawkins stepped across the open lawns surrounding the vast glass building until he came to the shelter of a low line of decorative grasses. It wasn't much cover, and he had a feeling that anyone watching from any of the windows on this far end of the power plant building would be able to spot him pretty easily. But Calvin James was approaching the building from an even more vulnerable path, with less cover—as in fewer decorative grasses. As much as he was watching for gunners intent on shooting him down, T. J. Hawkins watched for a gunner who had already spotted Calvin James.

They were surprised when a gunman stepped through the rear doorway, oblivious to the Phoenix

Force warriors, and fished in his pants with his weapon under one arm. He was well into his piss when he realized he was not alone. James and Hawkins had closed to within twenty paces. The man did a double take and snatched up the AK-47 hanging from one shoulder, but Hawkins and James cut him down where he stood.

A second man appeared at the moment of the gunshots—just in time to see his companion collapse.

Hawkins and James turned their weapons on the newcomer the instant they saw the man. Caught in the middle was the tempered-glass door. But the impact of rounds from the M16 reduced it to pebbles that rained over the gunner. He was still triggering his own AK-47 into the ceiling before he fell.

"Got a couple," Hawkins reported, "but I think they know we're here."

Without waiting for a response, James and Hawkins stepped over the carpet of glass pebbles and inside the building. They went through a short walkway and found themselves in the suite of offices. James quickly snap-kicked open the first door and covered low and to the left as Hawkins covered high and to the right. The office was empty. Three more doors were opened and found to be empty.

"They're going to be waiting for us just outside that door I'm guessing," Hawkins said.

The front office section ended with a pair of double doors that led onto the generator floor. They were heavy, steel fire-safe doors, intended to insulate the offices not only from potential generator fires but also from the noise of the huge engines. James nudged the door open an inch with his foot and gunfire slammed into the metal on the other side.

"I was right," Hawkins pointed out.

"Never doubted you," James said. He nudged the door again, just enough to see a small section of the generator floor and the huge glass walls looking out onto the fuel tanks that fed the generators. He slipped a flash-bang through the opening, then pulled the door shut. James and Hawkins crouched, facing away from the door, with their fingers in their ears, and rode out the shriek of noise. Then they kicked through the door and found themselves face-to-face with a large switch gearbox controlling the eighteen generators inside the massive glass building.

The generators were laid out in two rows down the length of the interior. There was a narrow walkway between each generator and the glass wall, and where James and Hawkins emerged they faced a pair of gunmen, blinking frantically, trying to see through their temporary blindness. They never would. Hawkins stitched them both across the chest and sent them sprawling on their backs. Another figure, another hundred feet beyond, stepped into view long enough to fire a burst that rattled against the glass and sent James and Hawkins for cover behind the nearest generator, labeled in bright yellow paint: G01.

Hawkins peered around the corner of the generator, down the center aisle of the building. He pulled back sharply, a burst of machine-gun fire chasing after him. He glanced over at the next row, where the first generator was labeled G09.

Hawkins hatched a quick strategy: he would circle around the wide switch gearbox, allowing him to come out on the far side behind the cover of the G09 generator. James nodded and glanced skyward himself. He patted the black steel casing of the generator. The casing was only warm to touch, and Calvin James intended to go up top.

Hawkins darted behind the switch gearbox, which filled almost the entire width of the building at the far end. He came out the other side and found himself behind generator G09. He glanced to the right of the G09 generator, and again pulled back quickly as a burst of fire came at him.

The gunner guffawed and yelled. It was in Spanish—but Hawkins was a Texan and if he knew any Spanish it was the profanity being hurtled at him by the Spaniard with the AK. Hawkins muttered angrily and spun around the corner of the G09 generator long enough to send a burst back at the gunner with the filthy mouth.

"You don't say such things to a Texan about his mom," Hawkins growled and had the satisfaction of seeing the Spaniard fall to the floor.

Hawkins crept around the generator to take him between the G09 and the G08. Calvin James was now lying atop the G01. The aisle between the G01 and the G02 was also empty. Hawkins felt uneasy with James being up top—it seemed too vulnerable a position. He would likely be a target from far across the massive interior.

James was feeling a little uneasy himself. It was, indeed, a vulnerable spot. On the other hand, it gave him a wide-open view of the entire wing of the power plant. He rose slowly into a crouch, the two rows of generators stretched out like beds in a garden. He saw the heads of several gunmen huddled together at a spot behind a generator labeled G15. He sank back down, primed a fragmentation round into the M203 grenade launcher mounted on his M16 and gave a nod to Hawkins.

Calvin James was a skilled marksman, even with a

weapon as imprecise as a grenade launcher. But it was a significant distance between him and the G15 generator. He had to place the round precisely between the G15 and the G16 generators to take out the group of gunmen. If he put it on the far side of the G15 or too close, in front of the G15, the massive generators themselves would shield the gunmen from damage.

He just had to get it right the first time.

He rose to his feet, steadied his grip on the M16/M203 and triggered the round.

"Nice," Calvin James congratulated himself.

The frag grenade settled almost directly on top of the gathered gunmen. In fact, Calvin James could've sworn he heard the thing hit a head instead of the floor in the fraction of a second before it went off.

He clambered to the floor on the far side of the G01 and he and Hawkins raced down the center aisle, looking for targets in the spaces between each of the generators, until they came to the G15. Hawkins and James pulled up fast, before the open space was revealed. Someone staggered out from behind the G15, his face mangled and bloodied but his torso more or less intact—protected by some sort of body armor beneath his clothing.

His tattered hands waved a 9 mm handgun across the center aisle and he fired blindly, sending the bullet into the far glass wall. Calvin James squeezed a single round from his M16, puncturing the man's skull. He staggered backward three steps, then draped himself on the corner of a generator. The handgun flopped the ground.

The open floor between the G15 and the G16 was splashed with blood. None of the other gunmen had survived.

The far end of the vast interior space was empty.

"Look for it," Calvin James said, nodding at the G04 generator across the aisle from the G15. James covered the center aisle as Hawkins shouldered his weapon and began a manual search of the G04.

The power plant staff had done him a big favor by shutting the plant down before they evacuated. The power modules were warm and cooling fast, which made a manual search without gloves possible. He felt inside the painted nooks and crannies, trying to find a hiding place for the nanothermite device that he knew was there. It made sense that a device would have been placed on each and every one of the eighteen generators.

If the nanothermite devices had a single limitation, it was their range. No matter how hot they could burn, they couldn't burn far. They needed direct contact. One nanothermite device would essentially eat its way through the guts of a piece of machinery like an 1880 kV oil-powered generator, but it wouldn't singe the paint on a second generator just ten feet away.

Whoever was planting these devices seemed to have no shortage of the things. He could throw them away like candy. If he was going to take down this plant, he would do a thorough job of it, by having a device rigged on each and every one of the generators.

Hawkins tried to think of the most effective spot to stage a device for completely ruining each generator. The way to do it was to completely destroy the integrity of the engine block. He crawled on top of the G04 unit, his hands probing into the deep crevices of the metal, trying to find the device by feel.

But he wasn't finding it.

Calvin James was in the middle of the aisle, eyes and ears open for any sound of an approaching enemy.

He glanced at Hawkins, who was frowning at the blue-and-black machinery.

"Try the next one," James suggested.

Hawkins turned his search to the G03 unit.

But he didn't think it mattered which unit he searched. They'd all have one of the devices. He just hadn't figured out where yet. He'd missed it on the G04.

But why had he missed it? He had searched deep in the crevices of the unit, in the places where a device such as a nanothermite ignition would cause the most damage. That would be the logical place to stage the device to cause the most destruction.

The vast, glass-enclosed wing of the power plant felt foreign. This was a place that should be filled with the vibration and noise of machinery, with the fumes of the burning fuel, and the heat radiating from machines. It was as if the building itself felt uncomfortable in the cool stillness.

T. J. Hawkins had an image in his head of what this place was like at any other time. The noise and heat. The heat. The radiant heat from each unit would be constant. Touching the blue sections of the power module would likely earn you a good burn. Whoever had been hired to plant these devices—probably employees of the plant—would know better than to go sticking an arm down in the crevices between two pieces of 270-degree metal.

Right. He was looking in the wrong places. He had to look in a place that would not be dangerously hot, even when the power module was in full operation. He returned to the far end of the G03 unit, to the black casing around the alternator itself. He stepped onto the integrated ladder and found himself on the roof of the alternator unit, ten feet off the floor. There was an access panel here, and he quickly untwisted the easy-open screw latches. He lifted off the panel.

The inside surface of the hatch had a big yellow decal warning of extreme danger. It showed a vivid image of the stick figure suffering electrocution.

Hawkins stuck his hand inside and felt around the underside of the top of the cabinet. Good place for a nanothermite device, he thought. The device would almost instantly burn itself free of the top of the cabinet, drop onto the insulated coil of the alternator and eat its way through. Even if the power module block continued to function, there would be no electricity generated out of this modular unit. Not without complete replacement of the alternator.

And there it was. He felt the block in his hand. He removed the plastic lid, and the communication device preferred by the enemy: the cheap, off-the-shelf, convenience-store mobile phone—dropped into his hand. He sprayed the device with acetone, let it eat up the adhesive foam for a few seconds, then freed the nanothermite device itself with a jerk.

"Got one," Hawkins said in a quiet voice as he dropped to the ground.

"Good work," James said. "Seventeen more to go."

"Stony, do we really need all of them?" Hawkins asked into his headset.

"Best to get them all," Barbara Price said. "Are you secure?"

"At the moment," James said.

The two of them walked back to their entrance point, to generators G01 and 09, and as Calvin James stood guard Hawkins began going through each power module, removing the communication devices, one by one.

"SEE ANYTHING UNIQUE about these devices, T.J.?" Aaron Kurtzman asked.

"Only thing different is that the cell phone's in Spanish," Hawkins responded. "The device itself is the same configuration. There's a foam adhesion layer, securing it to the metal underside of the cowling. There's a plastic lid, holding in a cheap-ass cell phone, connected using a short USB. The phone is pretty well charged."

"Give us a call, would you, T.J.?" Kurtzman asked.

Hawkins thumbed a phone number that Stony Man Farm had dedicated to testing the devices. He heard a half ring before the line was picked up at the other end, and a squeal of computer talk came from the speaker. Hawkins lowered the volume, and stuck the phone into a pouch of his pack. In Virginia, Akira Tokaido was already running his tests and traces on the signal from the unit.

Hawkins was hoping Tokaido would get some useful intelligence out of his testing—this time.

"Did you get a strange vibe from Akira when we were at the Farm?" Hawkins asked Calvin James.

"I got a strange vibe from everybody at that particular time," James said. "But, yeah, Akira wasn't himself."

"Way more agitated than I'm used to seeing."

"Too personally involved," James said. "He's beating himself up."

It was something Hawkins didn't think much about. Hawkins knew that the cyberteam at Stony Man Farm worked tirelessly to cull the global networks for electronic intelligence. They were an invaluable component of the Sensitive Operations Group's overall mission.

But Hawkins also didn't think of the Farm hands as having involvement that was as personal as that of the commando teams that went to the field.

Tokaido, in particular, hardly ever communicated with commando teams in the field. So, more than most, Tokaido seemed detached from the human element of the mission.

But Hawkins knew he had been mistaken about that. Tokaido felt personally responsible for the lack of the software system that could have detected and prevented some of the initial attacks.

Hawkins knew better. If Tokaido couldn't program it, then it probably couldn't be programmed. No good would come from Tokaido blaming himself for not being able to accomplish a miracle.

But people had died and Tokaido blamed himself for not being able to prevent it. Hawkins didn't think he had ever seen Tokaido so angry.

The cool Japanese dude certainly had a heart, Hawkins thought.

And the cool Japanese dude, Hawkins had heard, was killing himself to find some kind of usable, actionable intelligence from the bits and bytes that were coming in from the thousand attack sites around the world. So the very least that T. J. Hawkins could do was to provide Tokaido with all the evidence he could use.

CHAPTER TWELVE

Majorca

The General Atomics MQ-1C Grey Eagle hovered in the sky over the island of Majorca, unseen by the civilians below. Unseen by the skeleton crew in the air traffic control towers in the city of Parma. Unseen, but seeing. The third-generation Predator aircraft had the sky virtually to itself, with aircraft grounded throughout Europe and the Mediterranean.

The drone was nine yards in length, eighteen yards from wingtip to wingtip and had a takeoff weight of 3200 pounds. It was powered by a Theilert Centurion 1.7 heavy fuel engine that gave it a relatively small output of 135 horsepower. It could fly only 155 miles per hour, under ideal conditions, and had a service ceiling of 29,000 feet, although at the moment it was much closer to the ground in a near-hover. It could stay in the air for more than a day, and had a crew of zero human beings. Its operation was controlled from miles away or even— as in this case—from a continent away.

Santa Ponsa, Majorca

McCarter stepped between the large painted tanks, watchful for signs of movement. The tanks were fuel cells, not the propane tanks that they resembled. The

Farm had assured him that small-arms gunfire would not penetrate the steel skins.

The idea was to keep anything else from breaking the shells. McCarter had not had sufficient time to come to understand what would happen if those shells were broken. From his understanding, it would not be an environmental catastrophe—just a major setback for the power plant.

But McCarter wasn't worried about the utility budgets of Spain at the moment. He was more concerned with keeping his men alive. He did not like this setup. He did not like the fact that he was obliged to lead his men into it. And he did not like the fact that he had no idea what they were going to encounter here.

"Not a thing," Manning said into his mike.

At the south end of this new, hybrid power plant installation, with its fuel cells and its sophisticated distribution equipment, Rafael Encizo stepped across the gravel and peered behind the next cell, the size of a fuel tank on a railcar. He scanned and turned back to McCarter, then shook his head negative. Nothing to see.

Well there was something to see here, somewhere. There was something here. Something waiting just for Phoenix. A trap laid for whoever it was that had located and stolen the terrorists' communication hub.

McCarter started down the aisle, eyes peeled for any sign of the sabotage devices. It should be easy to spot them. This new, shiny facility was composed of almost twenty buildings, transformer stations and fuel-cell structures, and they had all been painted matte white.

The place was humming gently, but there were no sounds of voices. There should be no one here. The staff had been quietly removed. The Spanish government had wanted an explanation when the request came from the United States for evacuation of the plant, but when no explanation was forthcoming, Spain agreed to the evacuation anyway.

"Well," said Gary Manning, "I don't think everybody got the message about the mandatory time off. I have two bad-asses in berets."

McCarter didn't answer. At that moment, Encizo raised his hand and gave a swift poke to the north. McCarter and Encizo flattened against the concrete foundations of the huge fuel cells. They watched as a pair of gunmen slunk around the corner, watching behind them and never noticing the pair of gunners who were in their path. They looked around the side of the building, and one of them nervously checked the magazine on his AK-47. When he happened to glance in the direction of David McCarter, McCarter had already closed to within a few paces and was facing him down with the Beretta combat shotgun.

The gunner made the same last bad decision of his life that other men had made—thinking he was a faster shot than David McCarter. The moment the man pulled up the AK-47, McCarter triggered the blast that nearly severed his trigger hand from his body and cut into his vital organs. The AK-47 flopped to the ground and the would-be gunmen dropped on top of it.

His companion spun, his weapon at the ready, triggering before he found his target, and Encizo placed a burst in his side before the trail of AK rounds could complete half of the circle needed to reach McCarter.

McCarter and Encizo checked around the corner—looking for whatever it was that the gunners had been so worried about. There was nothing there.

They moved ahead, down the next unchecked aisle, and Encizo poked the nose of his weapon barrel around the corner. It was enough to call up a hail of rounds from between the fuel cells.

The barrel of Encizo's MP5 did not appear to be wounded.

McCarter stepped out and fired once, taking one of the gunners directly in the chest, and sending him sprawling into the legs of his partner. The second man staggered backward even as he raised his own assault rifle and attempted to fire it. The second blast from McCarter's combat shotgun turned his chest and face it into a massive spray of blood.

Manassas, Virginia

JERRY SCOPE WOKE when his wife's phone began to shrill in the darkness. It was the middle of the night. Who was calling his wife at this time of the night? At first he was irritated, but then he realized it could not be good news.

Then it was his phone ringing. His wife's phone stopped, and started ringing again. His phone kept shrieking at him from the living room, and then his son's cell phone began to squawk from the hall closet, where the phone was perpetually forgotten in a coat pocket. Scope made it to the living room when the home phone began to ring, as well. He grabbed the landline phone.

"Jerry Scope?"

"Who is this?"

"Is this Jerry Scope? You are being contacted by an agency of the federal government."

"Yeah, right."

Jerry Scope hung up the phone. Only then did it occur to him that a practical joker would probably not have the capability of dialing into all of his phones simultaneously. Maybe he should have been less quick to dismiss. The landline phone rang again. He wondered if whoever it was had the capability to make the phone ring louder than it typically did. He knew that was unreasonable, but it certainly sounded like it.

He snatched up the phone again.

"Jerry Scope?"

"Yes. This is Jerry Scope. Who is this really?"

"I am calling from an agency of the federal government. Our people will be arriving at your house within five minutes. Please be dressed and ready to go. This is an international emergency."

"What?"

"Do you understand, Mr. Scope? This is a matter of international security. Your expertise is needed."

"Oh. Okay."

His wife was standing behind him, looking concerned.

"Jerry?"

"I've got to go somewhere."

"Who was that?"

"I'm not quite sure," he said.

"Does this have to do with work?"

"I guess it does."

Then, before he even started to get dressed, there was someone pounding on his front door. And ringing the doorbell at the same time.

Scope was dressed and at the front door in three minutes. There were two men standing on his front step, having refused his wife's invitation to step inside.

"I should really ask for some identification," he said.

"They showed it to me already," his wife said hesitantly. "They really are Air Force."

"Uh-huh," Scope said. "I'll call you as soon as I can, honey."

Jerry Scope left with the men. He wasn't all that certain that this was the right thing to do. Not at first. The one man did indeed look pure military. He was an Air Force colonel, according to his uniform and stripes. The other man looked like he should be playing the part of a stuffed-shirt high-school principal in some sitcom about poor kids at a rich kids' private school. The man was tall, black, professorial. And when he spoke he sounded like a professor, as well.

"Mr. Scope, I know that this is sudden. You are needed." The black man held the door for Jerry Scope. Scope got into the back of the black car and the professor slid in beside him and shut the door. The colonel got behind the wheel and drove.

A United States Air Force colonel was serving as their chauffeur. If this was legit, this was pretty damn important. Scope did not think that Air Force colonels did a lot of chauffeuring duty.

The tall professor did something unexpected. He pulled a piece of paper out of his blazer inside pocket, unfolded it and began to read. It was a statement of security. It was brief, and to the point.

"I am sorry, Mr. Scope, but I need you to sign off on this. It is an oath of secrecy."

"It sounds pretty general," Scope said. "No promise of court-martial or jail time if I violate it."

"You can't be court-martialed because you are not military. We would not be coming to you if we thought that you were anything except a loyal U.S. citizen. It's probably not an enforceable document. I request, however, that you take this oath."

Scope shrugged. He had not had any inclination not to take the oath.

By the time the oath was made Scope found that the car was pulling into a local hotel. It was one of those all-suites hotels with the huge atrium. The colonel stopped the car at the front door, where two men in dark suits were milling around and making the doorman extremely nervous.

The black man jumped out of the car, and Jerry Scope followed him. As they made their way to the elevators and ascended to the top floor of the hotel, they had a full view of the atrium. And Scope could see at least five men in dark suits on-station throughout the interior of the hotel. When they got to a room, there were two young men in jeans and turtleneck sweatshirts hanging around the door. They were playing cards, using an old trash bin lid as their playing surface. Scope could not see a trace of the weapons that he knew lay underneath their outerwear.

The professor opened the door to the suite and ushered Smith inside. A large pot of coffee was steaming and a worktable was set up, and on it was a diagram.

The tall, black professor waved at the table. "You can call me Henry," Huntington Wethers said to Jerry Scope. "I will not insult you by pretending that it's my real name. I will not tell you what agency of the government I come from. I will only tell you that this is a matter of international security. There is a terrorist attack ongoing as we speak. Thus the reason for urgency. There are American soldiers on the ground at this location—" Wethers tapped the huge diagram "—fighting the enemy, and you are in a position to help us."

"I will," Scope said. "Of course I will. That's Santa Ponsa."

Wethers smiled. "You recognize it by sight?"

"Well, sure, it's pretty big news among we power plant aficionados." Scope leaned over the diagram. It was the diagram he had seen before. Nothing secret or highly secure about it. In fact, it had been touted as the blueprint of future hybrid power plants. On the same site as an antique coal-powered plant, once responsible for spewing huge amounts of emissions into the atmosphere over the beautiful island of Majorca, now stood a combination of an advanced power-sharing system, with power cables that went from the island to mainland Spain, as well as one of the latest fuel cell power logistics systems.

"Okay, Mr. Scope," Wethers said. "If you were a terrorist, and you were attacking this facility with the intent of harming a large number of people, what specifically would you do?"

Scope was, of course, aware of the attacks going on around the world. There had been several train derailments. Aircraft had been brought down out of the sky. The loss of life had been catastrophic. And there had been the pipeline fires. There had been the town in Wyoming....

"Mr. Scope?"

"I am thinking," Scope said quietly. "I am not sure I can even answer that question."

"If the power cables were compromised," Wethers said. "My understanding is..."

"It would flip a circuit breaker." Scope shook his head. "Simply put, that's what would happen. It's not like the waters off the coast of Majorca would suddenly become deadly. The electricity would be shut off virtually instantly. The cost of repair would not even be substantial. Not compared to the three-hundred-million cost of the system in the first place."

"The oil-fueled power generation system?" Henry asked.

"They could disable the generator modules, for sure," Scope said. "They could do all kinds of things to destroy them, neutralize them, make the plant unusable. What they could do at this plant that would affect the civilians—I can't even guess."

"My understanding of the fuel cell system is that it is largely nontoxic," Wethers probed.

"Pretty much. There's no way you could turn it into a WMD."

Huntington Wethers nodded, pulled an acetate image out of his briefcase and set it on the table, over the diagram.

Scope leaned over it and, at a glance, found something out of place. He pointed to one section of it, and looked at Henry. "What's that?"

"Mr. Scope," Wethers said, "we are hoping you can tell us."

"It looks like some sort of a drainage pipe. Maybe just flood mitigation drainage. I don't know."

Now the man called Henry was pulling some sort of a tablet computer from the briefcase on the bed, and he slid it to Scope. It was the same image, and the legend in the lower right-hand corner told him that it was live. The image was shifting even as he looked at it. Scope knew he was looking at an aerial shot of the facility. Maybe, he thought, it was one of those drones. It was certainly moving slowly enough. He dragged his eyes away from the mishmash of code letters and symbols in the lower right-hand corner and followed the image on the screen. It was following the enigmatic line of the piping that seemed to be leading away from the center post power plant and into the town.

That long, light-colored line traveled all the way from the power plant into the town, then vanished. He put his fingers on the screen and tried to enlarge the image, only to find that it was already as tight as he could get it. He tried to backtrack. He found that the image obeyed his commands and took him back to the power plant.

He followed it directly into the small facility that housed the many components of the solid oxide fuel-cell-based hybrid power plant.

"Henry?" He looked up and realized the man had been watching him carefully. "Can you get me performance records for this plant?"

Wethers put down the tablet and moved to where a computer workstation was set up on the table. He tapped at the keyboard, and spoke into a headpiece. His words were low but urgent. The monitor came to life, and a series of documents sprawled onto the screen. He pushed back his chair.

"Here they are," he said.

Scope moved to join him at the computer and perused the records for a minute. He began to understand what he was seeing. The text was in Spanish, which he barely read, but it was clear from the performance report numbers that the solid oxide fuel-cell plant had been underperforming for at least a month. He looked at the numbers on the display.

"Henry," he said, "see this? The hybrid section of the plant has been doing a lousy job for at least a month. See the drop-off in efficiency?"

"I see it," Huntington Wethers said.

"This line seems to indicate daily testing," Scope said. "If I'm reading this correctly, then the fuel cells themselves are functioning to spec. However, the gas turbine is essentially nonoperational."

"A gas turbine in a solid oxide hybrid power plant?"

"Gas as in hydrogen gas. One of the reasons this plant works so well, and so efficiently, is that residual hydrogen is fed into a gas turbine and burned for additional power generation. But the gas turbine in this hybrid facility is not functional, and has not been for a month. The residual hydrogen is not being burned. And nobody seems to have noticed it—or cared."

Wethers was nodding. "The hydrogen could be channeled off-site. That could be the purpose of flexible tubing that goes from the facility into the town."

Scope shrugged. "That's where my expertise runs out. From what I know, and from what I can see in these records, the hydrogen has not been used. Someone at the facility has gone to the effort of not addressing the situation for some reason. If I was going to use this facility in any way to harm the town of Santa Ponsa, the only way that I could think to do so would be to channel some sort of dangerous material from the plant to the town. The only dangerous material would be hydrogen. If that hydrogen is being pumped through flexible tubing from the solid oxide cells into the town, and stored somewhere in the town, and that hydrogen can be released and ignited, then you have a weapon."

As unlikely as it would seem, the color drained from the dark brown skin of Henry's face. He leaned forward in the seat behind the display and began pulling up— of all things—architectural and archeological records from Santa Ponsa. Scope did not know if he was seeing something he should or should not be seeing, but he leaned over Henry's shoulder and stared at the images as they flashed by. He saw catacombs. There were, in fact, large, ancient wells, channels, even what appeared to be caverns underneath the ancient city of Santa Ponsa.

"What are those? Roman?"

"Roman, Moorish, Byzantine. There have been recent discoveries of a significant well and sewage and drainage systems under the town. More extensive than was once thought. There's even a Roman catacombs section. It's all off-limits. None of it has been developed as tourist attractions. In fact most of it—" the man who called himself Henry was reading the fine print on the screen "—looks as 'if it is archaeologically inconsequential.' Look at this. The air inside is 'stale and unbreathable.' There is little natural ventilation. Due to the danger of suffocation by explorers, recent ventilation shafts have been drilled at five different locations in Santa Ponsa."

Scope stood straight. "Henry, what would happen if a few million cubic feet of hydrogen was channeled underneath the city over a period of several weeks, and suddenly ignited. Would the explosion carry aboveground?"

Wethers looked at him. "Not exactly my area of expertise," he said. "But if I was a terrorist..."

Scope nodded. "Exactly." The engineer was quickly tracing the lines of the different systems in the hybrid plant. "Look, Henry, if you can get an engineer on-site, you can reroute this tubing into the diesel generator. An override feed controls the diesel generator. There's a fan there—it's a gas pumping system to keep the hydrogen flowing. You can override the speed controls, and start sucking that hydrogen out. It can't explode if it's not there. Send it through the generator, turn off the safety overrides and the venting safety overrides. It will suck the hydrogen out from under the city as fast as it can. You'll burn out the gas pump motor eventually. The trick is to keep the pump going as long as possible to vent as much hydrogen as possible. You'll need to nurse it along."

Huntington Wethers—the man calling himself Henry—nodded. "Jerry, if we got the pipeline in place and we gave you control over that system, could you operate it?"

"It's in Spanish," Scope said.

"You'll have a translator," Wethers said.

Scope nodded. "I'll do my best."

Santa Ponsa, Majorca, Spain

GARY MANNING STOPPED behind the large gray switching station box that fronted acres of other large gray boxes of the hybrid power plant.

Manning glanced down the aisle and took in the sight of a trio of gunmen hugging a fuel-cell tank as they attempted to sneak up on the aisle where, Manning assumed, they thought they'd find McCarter or Encizo. Like all the mercenary hirelings whom the Stony Man Farm commando teams had encountered since this series of attacks began, the enforcers were a mishmash of amateurs, local hoods and even guys who had never used a gun before.

Manning assumed that the sabotage work done here at the power plant had been perpetrated by plant employees, bought off by the terrorists. There was some serious funding behind the scenes. Hand out twenty thousand dollars here, thirty-five thousand euros there, and you could convince a lot of people to do some very horrible things.

Of course, when they took the cash and they did the deed, these people thought their work was done. But another whole class of hirelings had been on the job, making video footage of the sabotage as it happened. That video had been leveraged against the saboteurs. They were then forced to do jobs they had not originally signed on for.

Around the world, these people were coming out of the woodwork. Many were turning themselves in rather than continuing to cooperate with terrorists.

There were dozens cooperating with investigators around the world, helping investigators locate nano-thermite devices by the hundreds.

But no one knew what percentage of the saboteurs was coming clean. A tenth of them? A quarter of them? Even if it was as many as half, and that meant they were finding half the devices still staged to carry out their attacks, there were hundreds more attack sites still undiscovered.

Of course, a lot of the saboteurs were not turning themselves in. They were doing what they were being told to do by the terrorists. It seemed too easy not to. They were going out to their planted devices and making the cell phone switch. Easy work and better than jail—if you didn't have a conscience. If you weren't worried about being haunted by the spirits of your victims.

The fact that there were so many people out there who would do despicable things for a wad of cash sickened Gary Manning. And he didn't really care if the guy he was shooting down was an amateur with a firearm.

If he was a part of this terror, then there was no reason not to exterminate him.

Manning's weapon today was an old favorite. The SA-80 assault rifle shot a 5.56 mm NATO round. He liked the pistol grip; it gave him a feel of precise control. Not that he needed it with the three stooges in front of him. One of them accidentally knocked his hunting rifle against the side of the fuel cell. His companion hissed at him savagely. His companion was no better soldier. He had his own submachine gun held pointing at the ground. Number three had a big .45-caliber revolver, which was held loosely, way too far out in front of his face. If he triggered that thing, Manning thought, it would fly back and give him a concussion.

They were idiots. As far as Manning was concerned, they were evil idiots.

The one with the submachine gun finally saw Manning standing there. He looked up at him, and Manning's casual stance and his amused smirk put the man off his guard. But not the guy with the .45. He gave a whining cry and spun like a top, the .45 stiff in front of him. As inexperienced as the man was, he was firing from close range, and Manning was not about to let that happen. He triggered the SA-80. The gunner took a burst to the high chest, and fell with the .45 unfired. Manning took out the other two before they could bring their weapons to bear.

Somebody on the far side of the fuel cell tank fled, his feet noisy on the gravel, and Manning followed his location by sound. The man reached the end of the aisle, at the far end of the hybrid power plant, and turned, and for a second Manning saw him run across the end of the aisle. Manning stepped across to where the man would come out.

The man ducked around the little shack at the southwest corner of the power plant. He grabbed the door and
slipped inside. A second later another enforcer emerged
from the rear and ducked into the building. Maybe it
was some sort of rendezvous point.

Manning crept across the gravel to use the concrete
sidewalk that had been installed as part of the power
plant. The concrete made far less noise when walked
upon than the gravel. They taught you these kinds of
things in soldier school.

He made it to the shack unheard and unseen. The
building was meant for infrequent use, and in the mild
Mediterranean climate, so the construction was thin
aluminum over a bolted steel frame. Manning didn't
know the gauge of the aluminum, and wasn't certain
that his 5.56 mm rounds would penetrate it. But it didn't
matter. All he wanted to do was drive those gunners out.

In fact, he specifically did not want to kill them.

He put a burst in the lower right-hand corner of the
building, and the racket was incredible. He could only
imagine what it was like inside the building. There was
panic inside. A gunner slammed out the door, searching for a target for his 9 mm handgun, and looking a lot
more competent than the bozo with the .45. Manning
cut him down and observed that the man fell without re-
leasing his weapon. He struggled on his back, and Manning gave him a shot to the chest. His struggles stopped.

The second man simply tried to run for it. He bolted
from the shack without even glancing to the side, almost
tripped over his fallen companion and took two steps
before Manning's weapon of choice ended his escape.
He fell hard on his face. He turned over, pushing himself up with a hand that gripped a machine pistol and

swung it wildly, and Manning fired a burst that nearly took off the man's forearm.

McCarter and Encizo joined Manning at the shack. Still being stealthy, Manning gestured them to silence, then gagged his prisoner.

McCarter hand-signaled the others brief instructions, then stepped through the narrow spaces where three of the short tanks abutted the longer tanks of one of the fuel cells. Manning thought briefly that he was glad he was at the front, not trying to squeeze through the space that McCarter took, between the three short tanks. Manning didn't know if he'd even fit. He gave McCarter and Encizo a fifteen count to get into position.

As he waited, he found himself eyeball-to-eyeball with a warning label and the word *Danger* in English, Spanish, Italian and French, with a bright orange background. The illustration showed a stick figure in peril of being melted, another being electrocuted and still another being crushed. Manning idly considered the fact that, although he considered himself to be a reasonably smart guy, he couldn't figure out how he would get crushed from any of these pieces of equipment. They all weighed tons. As his mental count reached thirteen he heard the scuff of feet on the gravel and then on the walkway that surrounded the hybrid power plant. The man was coming closer.

When he stepped into the open his eyes landed on Manning, who promptly cratered his skull with the butt of the SA-80.

There was a rattle of gunfire from out of sight. A companion who had witnessed his colleague being disabled fired wildly at the altercation—killing the unconscious man as he dropped. Manning waited for the

burst and then slipped around the corner for a fraction
of a second and directed a burst at the gunner. The man
took it in the pelvis, squealed and sank to the ground.
A third gunner appeared to Manning's far right and
fired a shotgun. The pellets spread far before a handful stung his flank.

Manning rushed across the front of another gray box
with more stupid stick-figure warning labels. Manning
didn't feel in any danger of being crushed, electrocuted
or burned with acid. Where was the label that showed
a stick figure taking buckshot in the ass?

Another man appeared from between the gray structures and thought he was fast enough to take advantage
of Manning, but Manning fired on the run and at the
same instant a bullet flew from the old carbine. The
gunner's round flew into the sky. Manning's rounds, on
the other hand, gutted the gunner in three places. The
gunner dropped. As he did, Manning spotted movement behind him.

He relayed his position to McCarter and Encizo and
trailed the new gunner— heading back toward the little
shack. Manning took the front route, where he could
move faster on solid concrete than on noisy gravel, then
crept across a strip of grass to position himself behind
the nearby marble sign that advertised, in foot-tall letters, the name of the company that built the hybrid facility.

He could hear the gunner's footsteps coming around
the far side. He didn't spend any time with the prisoner
Manning had cuffed and gagged there but came around
the corner and took a burst that amputated the man's
right foot at the ankle. He flopped to the ground screaming, the blood puddling under him rapidly. Manning
closed in and spotted the source. The man had taken a

shot to the thigh. His femoral artery was pumping his lifeblood into the gravel.

Best to put him out of his misery now. Manning delivered a mercy shot to the head, and silenced the screaming, and heard a gasp around the corner.

Manning poked his head around the corner, where an unscathed gunner with an AK was backing away from the grisly sight of his dead friend. When he saw Manning, he opened his hands to drop the AK. He raised his hands in the air, his eyes wide as beer cans, and made a sobbing sound. "No!"

Then he began to jabber and stutter in what even Manning could tell was very poor Spanish.

"You can grovel in English," Manning said.

The humor was lost on the surrendering gunman, who did indeed begin to beg for his life in London-accented English. His hands went to the top of his head, and his eyes were red and rheumy.

"All right," Manning said. "Shut up, walk over here slowly, stand right there."

The man did as he was told, and Manning trussed him up using plastic cuffs. Ankles. Wrists. His wrists were secured with one extra tie to an exposed steel support beam for the roof of the little shack. The man wasn't going anywhere, but he kept moaning and whimpering.

Manning glared at him and said, "Shut the hell up."

The prisoner took orders well.

Rafael Encizo came back with a prisoner of his own, in a black jogging suit and a black ski mask. He flopped him next to the bloody corpse at the feet of Manning's Englishman. Encizo's prisoner came to and went through a spasm when he saw what he was lying next to, then rolled his eyes up at Encizo.

Encizo poked the man in the belly with his weapon. "You're not a commando. You're not a soldier. You don't even have street smarts."

The man was trying to wriggle sideways to put distance between himself and the headshot corpse.

"Who hired you?"

The man responded in rapid-fire Spanish. Encizo engaged him for a few minutes, then shook his head. "He doesn't know anything."

"Of course he bloody doesn't," McCarter responded, returning with James and Hawkins. "Nobody knows a bloody goddamned thing." McCarter turned his gaze on the man who was hanging from the roof support.

Manning's prisoner said something unintelligible.

"You're a Brit," McCarter said accusingly

The man nodded glumly.

"So am I," McCarter said. "You're making me look bad in front of my friends. I don't like running into stupid bloody Brits. I'd just as soon have every stupid idiot Brit like you dead. Makes the world a better place, if you ask me. If you've got anything to say that might help redeem yourself, now is the time to say it."

He shook his head frantically. "I don't know anything. We were hired to plant a bunch of those bombs, you know? Then we get this call what says we got to go back now, because there's been some sort of a bloody screwup. That's all I know. They showed us the video they took of us planting the bombs and then bloody blackmailed us to come back. The videos had all our information. They had names and identification numbers and our bloody passport numbers. Right there on the video. They said they would release it to the authorities if we didn't do the follow-up job. That's all I know, mate."

"I'm not your mate," McCarter snapped. "Now there's something really unusual about this situation. Why is there a Brit in this team, on Spanish soil? You want to explain that to me?"

The fidgety Brit looked terrified.

"I think you have got something more you can tell us," McCarter said. "This is good news for you and good news for me. I get some answers. You don't get shot in the head."

"You wouldn't shoot me in the head," the man gasped. "Not a fellow Brit!"

"I'm Canadian," Gary Manning announced, raising his SA-80 in the air as if raising his hand in class. "I'd have no problem shooting you in the head. I had no problem shooting this guy in the head. Remember? You watched me do it."

The Brit glanced at the body on the ground with the exploded skull, then looked away.

"I can handle this," McCarter said, raising his weapon and pressing it against the forehead of the hanging Brit.

"No," Manning said, "let me." He put his own weapon against the forehead of the man.

McCarter shrugged. "Let's do it together."

"Jesus Christ, no!" the Brit wailed. "I'll tell you. Bloody goddamned hell, I'll tell you whatever you want to know."

McCarter didn't lower his weapon, but pressed it in harder, forcing the man's head backward. It looked painful. "Okay, mate," McCarter said, "start right now."

CHAPTER THIRTEEN

Manassas, Virginia

Huntington Wethers stuck his head out the door of the hotel suite. The pair of Special Forces agents in civilian clothing, pretending to play cards on the fifth floor of a hotel in the middle of the night, looked at him curiously.

"Either of you speak Spanish?"

"I'm Puerto Rican," said one of the guys.

"Get in here. We got a slight change of your responsibilities tonight."

He was an Army Ranger, pulled out of rotation temporarily to serve as a blacksuit with the Justice Department's SOG. It was a thankless assignment. He would never be able to talk about it, to his friends or family, or even to his comrades in the Rangers. As a condition of taking this assignment he had undergone Justice Department security clearance. It was a level of security clearance that several top-ranked generals in the U.S. military would have been flabbergasted to know even existed.

For this Army Ranger, his blacksuit rotation in the secret Sensitive Operations Group had consisted of more than one highly dangerous field operation. Tonight, however, was not going to be one of those.

He was instructed to take one of the hotel chairs, watch the screen and translate the Spanish instructions that were displayed for the scientist who was running the computer.

This Army Ranger knew that, as mundane as the work might be, the operation involved the mitigation of the terrorist attacks that had been ongoing. He knew that the primary field teams of the SOG were on the ground somewhere, trying to stop another attack, or perhaps even trying to track down the source of the attacks. This blacksuit might never know precisely what his role tonight had to do with the whole operation—but he would know that he had assisted in saving lives.

Majorca

DAVID MCCARTER DIDN'T LIKE this idea at all. He wanted to get into the town, and he wanted to go there now. Their British friend had confirmed the existence of devices in the town's catacomb vents. He was a researcher who'd been in the catacombs and helped map them out—and helped plant a high-explosive device in one of the chambers to drive out the hydrogen. Massive volumes of burning hydrogen would be ejected from five vents into the middle of inhabited Santa Ponsa.

"Stony, I don't think we want to waste our time on HVAC repair. We should be disarming the damned town!"

"I intend for you to do both things," Barbara Price said.

They jogged to the rear of the hybrid power plant.

"Is this it?" McCarter asked.

"It's gotta be," Hawkins said. "It sure doesn't look like a part of the original installation."

McCarter had to agree with that. The flexible tubing was like some heavy-duty dryer hose that had been screwed into an emergency exhaust vent from the hydrogen pipeline. The hydrogen pipeline was intended to take the excess hydrogen into an auxiliary generator, where it could be burned to produce additional power. It was one of those features that gave this plant such a high degree of efficiency. The fact that the hydrogen had been channeled away for the past five weeks explained the drop-off in the plant's overall efficiency. The flexible tubing was in an out-of-the-way spot at the rear of the hybrid plant, where it sat alongside the original piping into the ground.

"We got it, Stony," McCarter announced. Already Calvin James was spinning the large-diameter screw connection and had the flexible tubing disconnected in a matter of seconds. Hawkins and Encizo were scraping away the gravel with their hands. The flexible tubing was under less than an inch of gravel, and soon they had it unearthed all the way to the chain-link fence. McCarter scrambled over the fence, where he found the tubing sprawled down the rocky hillside. The tubing seemed to wander down the rocky hillside and disappear among the stones and undergrowth. McCarter could only assume that it ran all the way to the town and down into the catacombs under the residential resort area.

"Okay," McCarter shouted over the fence. "There is plenty of slack on the line. Start pulling it through."

McCarter babied the flexible tube as it was threaded through the narrow gap underneath the chain-link fence. His primary fear was that the rough ends of the chain links themselves would rip through the wall of the tube. But it seemed to be a tough flexible plastic, made to withstand exposure and rough treatment. Within minutes, an extra fifty feet of tubing had been threaded through the opening under the fence, and McCarter clambered back over.

The flexible tubing was dragged to the far back corner of the hybrid plant, where Hawkins was removing a section of the cabinet.

They were all hurried. They had more immediate dangers to erase. Hawkins reached under the edge of the metal panel and wrenched it off, leaving patches of bare metal that were still screwed into the box itself. He dropped the bent steel cabinet door to the ground and said, "Now what?"

Calvin James was staring at the revealed contents. They could see the fan of the gas pump, designed to keep feeding the hydrogen into the generator, where it was burned to generate extra electricity. James looked between the venting inside the cabinet and the flexible tubing in their hand, and shook his head.

"I don't know how we can do this," he said.

"What do you mean?" Encizo asked. "We just push it in. It'll stick."

"No way it'll stay in place," Hawkins said. "When we turn this pump on, we're turning it on full blast. We're trying to vent all the hydrogen from under that damned city. The tube has got to be secure. Duct tape ain't gonna do it."

McCarter's ire was rising. "We need to weld the thing in place. Or bolt it down. Or something. But we don't have anything to do that with." He touched his headset. "Stony, you got any bright ideas as to how we can actually attach the vent pipe?"

"There is no screw connection," Price asked, "such as at the ventilation point?"

"It wouldn't matter if there was," McCarter snapped. "That's not a robust connector. That connector and this flexible tubing were made for a slow, low-pressure ventilation of hydrogen gas. What you are asking us to do is to use the same piping for a high-velocity extraction of the gas. I just don't think it's going to work."

"But it might work," Price said. "And if it does work, it reduces the danger to those people. It just might save lives. Now you need to figure out a way to get that piping connected to the pump. I don't care how it happens—it just needs to happen. And it needs to happen right now, because there are also five igniters ready to go off in that city. If our control over their signals isn't as good as we would like to think it is, then there's going to be a lot of dead tourists in Santa Ponsa. You'll just have to figure it out."

"Understood, Stony," David McCarter said.

Then he turned off the headset and kicked savagely at the nearest metal box, creating a six-inch-deep dent in the metal, and shouted, "Bloody hell!"

At any other time, under any other circumstances, Calvin James would have laughed out loud to see David McCarter lose his cool. There was the good old hotheaded McCarter he had known for years. But right now, Calvin James felt just the same way. He wanted to hit something, or to kick something, or to destroy something. He didn't want to be standing here trying to figure out how to make a round pipe stick in a square hole.

"Stony," James said, "I'm going to read you the numbers off of this tubing. I need somebody to figure out what it is made of. What its properties are. I think the name of the company is Angel FP. There's a number here—687 EFP. Tell me what I've got."

"One second, Cal," Aaron Kurtzman answered him. "Angel FP is the name of the company and 687 EFP is a grade of flexible pipeline manufactured in the UK.

They use a technology of high-tensile synthetic yarns. These yarns are circular woven, and the materials are encapsulated on both sides with elastomeric material. The specifications for the elastomerics are not on the website. They claim a high degree of flexibility, resistance to kinking, resistance to environmental compromise."

"What about thermal resistance?" James demanded.

"It says highly thermal resistant," Kurtzman said.

"That means nothing," James said. "What the hell is high thermal resistance? Two hundred degrees? A thousand degrees?"

"Elastomerics could be almost anything," Kurtzman agreed. "Why do you want to know?"

"I'm trying to figure out if there is a way to heat seal this thing."

"Heat seal it to what?" McCarter asked.

James held the connection end of the flexible tubing to the exposed gap in the venting that channeled the hydrogen into the generator.

"Look. We could weld this connector directly to the metal plate if we had a welding torch. And if we could have any assurance that the tubing itself won't simply disintegrate under the heat."

"Cal, are you suggesting we go rummaging around in that goddamned building looking for a blowtorch?"

James didn't appear to hear him. He reached inside of the open cabinet and dragged out a sheet of thick insulation material. He read numbers off the paper backing into his headset.

David McCarter was beside himself. "Cal, what the hell good is this doing us?"

"Hold on," James said. "Stony, can you find that material type?"

"Affirmative, Cal," Kurtzman said. "I found the manufacturer. Looking it up."

"What I really need to know is if it's a ceramic fiber," James said.

Kurtzman responded, "Yes, it's a ceramic fiber. High-temp thermal insulation. You could use it in a blast furnace."

"Who cares what kind of insulation it is?" McCarter said.

"Ceramic fiber won't melt," Hawkins explained. "It can protect the flexible pipeline from heat. We wrap it around the line. As much of it as we can find. On the end that goes inside the pump."

"What for?" McCarter demanded.

"To protect the damned tubing," James said. "Break open any of those boxes. Anything that has working parts should have high-temp insulation inside. Just drag out as much as you can find."

"Jesus, mate, whatever you say," McCarter complained, grabbing at the access panel of an adjacent switch-gear cabinet. The insubstantial-locking mechanism was no match for McCarter's frustration. He gave a heave and the access panel sprang open. Pieces of the lock fell at his feet.

He thrust his arm inside the cabinet and pulled out several long strips of spun-fiber insulation. He read the numbers printed directly on the fiber. "PCW 36—"

"Perfect," James said.

"How do you know?"

"PCW is polycrystalline wool. Made for real high-temp applications. That's exactly what we need. Find more."

Calvin James and T. J. Hawkins began to carefully wrap the high-temperature insulation wool around the exterior of the flexible tubing. Manning and Encizo returned with a pile of the stuff big enough to make a mattress.

"Good," James said. "This ought to do it."

"I'm not going to ask where you're going to fit it," McCarter said. "Because I'm afraid you'll tell me."

"Wrap the end of the tubing with as much of the stuff as you can," James said. "Hopefully with this much of the high-temp insulation around it, the pipeline will be protected. Then we jam the whole thing into the box, so that the open end is flush with the gas pump intake."

McCarter frowned at them as they wrapped the last long strand of insulation around the tubing. It was an awkward-looking arrangement. They wiggled and stuffed it into the open cabinet. McCarter could see that the open end of the flexible tube was indeed pushed flush up against the gas pump intake vent. He could also see that the vent was only loosely settled into place.

"I know there's more to this than I've figured out yet," he said. "I'm also hoping that one of these days you'll fill me in as to what it is exactly they are doing."

"We have to get a tight strong seal on this line to withstand the pressures of the pump. It's got to be a tight lock," James said. "And as you said we don't have time to go looking for a blowtorch. So we're going to melt it in place."

"Melt it."

Calvin James nodded. "Melt the box around it."

"Using…"

"Now you're getting it," Hawkins said. He pulled a microthermite device from his the heavy black bag, which was now full of them. He tossed the device to Calvin James, who caught it deftly and placed it on the top right corner of the cabinet of the hydrogen pump.

A second device was placed on the opposite edge of the cabinet. James and Hawkins assessed the placement.

"It's obvious what they're trying to do," Manning said. McCarter glared at him. "What's not so obvious is how it's going to work. If it's going to work at all. That's one of the ugliest monkey-rigged contraptions I've ever seen."

"With the devices on the far edges of the cabinet, it'll melt through there, and hopefully create enough heat to deform the entire cabinet around the tube," James explained.

"I can see that," Manning said. "But we don't know the specs on the microthermites or the cabinet. It burns too hot, the entire cabinet will disintegrate. If it comes in contact with that wool, even if it is PCW, it might burn right through it and through the tube inside it."

"We know," James said. "You got a better idea, now's the time to speak up."

"No, I don't have a better idea," Manning said. "If it works you look like geniuses."

"And whether it works or doesn't work, we're done with it, and we can get the hell out of here, and get into the damned town where we can do some actual good," McCarter said. "And where I actually have a clue about what my team is doing."

"STONY, LET ME HAVE Akira," James said.

"Tokaido here."

It didn't sound like the Tokaido that Calvin James knew. The man was under a lot of pressure. And he was carrying around a lot of guilt. It was undeserved, but Calvin James understood it. They had all, every member of the Sensitive Operations Group, been in that place, where logic didn't matter and all that did matter was the failure that resulted in people dying. Tokaido was going to be haunted by the ghosts from the aircraft over Europe and Southeast Asia for a long time.

But he couldn't afford to let his own issues get in the way of the mission.

"Tokaido, we need you to send activation signals to two of the devices. We're actually going to try to make use of them. I don't really have time to explain it. What we need to do is melt down a pretty heavy-gauge steel cabinet and encapsulate a pipeline."

"Interesting. And how are you accounting for the high temps of the devices themselves?" Tokaido asked. "I assume you have some way of keeping the devices from just burning the entire thing up."

"Yeah, I assume we do, too. You can do it, right?"

"Sure. You got the devices staged?"

"The nanothermite devices are in place. T.J. has the phones."

"Okay, I need to ID the specific phones you are going to use."

"Serial numbers?" James asked.

"No need. Just dial in on them. One at a time. When the call comes in, I will ID it. Then, after you have them both in place, I can send the commands to fire."

Hawkins dialed in to the special test number that Tokaido had set up at Stony Man Farm. He heard the screech of a computer response, and then heard Tokaido respond on the headset. "Okay, I got that one. Put it somewhere. Carefully. Don't get it mixed up with the others. Now dial in on the second phone."

Hawkins dialed in on phone number two, got the same screech and Tokaido responded, "Good. Number two is locked in. Now plug them in to the devices. I have disconnected both phones. I won't do anything more until I hear that you are completely set up at that end."

Hawkins carefully connected the USB plug on the first phone and tucked it into the nanothermite unit on the left.

Then he connected the USB plug on the second phone, tucked into its nanothermite box and snapped on the cover, as if he was snapping on the plastic battery cover on the underside of a toy. The devices looked like toys, cheaply made toys.

He followed the other members of Phoenix Force to the far end of the power plant, where they were using one of the large generator housings as shelter from the devices when they were activated. Although, if he had his preference, Hawkins would've liked to stay and watch the thing do its work.

But he knew better.

When he was huddled with the other members of his team, Calvin James gave the go-ahead to Tokaido.

"Done," Tokaido said.

They looked at each other. James frowned deeply, and cocked his head, as if trying to hear something. For a second, maybe, he thought he heard a sizzle. Then, they all heard a loud ting, like heat-stressed metal.

"Well?" Tokaido asked.

James said, "Hold on a second."

He walked carefully out from behind the protection of the metal cabinet, with the others following him, none of them eager to get near an uncontrolled burn that might be throwing off fragments of liquid metal. They could see the rising smoke from the generator housing, and they could see that the generator itself was deformed and looked as if it had collapsed upon itself. The burning seemed to have ceased. The cabinet had turned to slag.

"It looks like this thing might've actually worked," James declared. He and Hawkins got close enough to inspect the integrity of the flexible tubing. It seemed partially crushed, but at least seventy percent of the width remained open. It should still provide for sufficient volume when they turned the pump on. The cabinet of the unit had indeed collapsed and deformed around the tubing, and when the molten steel had solidified again, it had formed a steel grip on the flexible pipeline. Because of the protection offered by the ceramic insulation, the tubing had not burned through.

What was left after the operation was not pretty, but it appeared it had actually worked the way they had intended.

There was only one way to know for sure. And that was to turn the thing on. Only then would they know if the high-temperature destruction of the steel cabinet had in fact allowed for the venting of hydrogen.

"Okay, Stony, start her up," Calvin James said into his headset.

Manassas

"DID YOU GET THAT?" Barbara Price asked.

Huntington Wethers, standing in the hotel room, nodded and said, "Got it. Okay, Mr. Scope. Give it a try."

Jerry Scope, with his Spanish-speaking Ranger interpreter sitting by his side, began the deceptively simple steps that would start up the fan on the hydrogen generator. The display showed him multiple outages. The generator itself seem to be frozen. A safety mechanism was attempting to block all its functions. Jerry Scope disabled the safety and told the fan to start working.

On the screen, the display for the fan operation turned from red to yellow, and then to green. It appeared the fan had started.

Santa Ponsa

"IT'S STARTING, Stony," James said. The five of them were standing around the flexible tubing watching it vibrate as the fan began to create a vacuum that pulled gas through it. Hawkins had raced to the far side of the generator unit, where the vent was expelling air. He pulled at the hatchway lock, which gave way without too much effort, and yanked off the vent cover. The air flowed out more easily. McCarter was watching him.

"How will you know when it starts venting hydrogen?" he asked.

"My voice will get really funny, like Donald Duck," Hawkins said.

"You and I both know that's helium," McCarter snapped. "I think I'm writing up every damned one of you for insubordination."

He touched his headset. "Stony, we're done here. We're leaving now."

Manassas

JERRY SCOPE WAS PLAYING with the controls, watching the sensors that continued to work. He didn't know how accurately they continued to provide information. He could see pressure, fan speed, fan temperature, but that was about it. He had no visual on the site on the Spanish island of Majorca. He had no way of knowing if the flexible piping remained intact. All he had were simple readouts and a scroll of textual information from an on-site computer monitoring system that had so far been irrelevant to what he was trying to do.

The young man from the Rangers diligently translated every message that was displayed, and Scope was attempting to judge their meaning, even as he carefully accelerated the speed of the fan, without overstressing the pressure readings.

The tall, dignified black man, the one he was supposed to call Henry, did not seem like the kind of man to become excited or even urgent. But now he was growing visibly agitated.

"You understand what I'm trying to do here, don't you?" Scope asked.

"I understand," Huntington Wethers said. "And I see you keeping that thing from going into the red. I know you're doing your best, Mr. Scope, but I also know that the amount of gas you're moving out of that system right now is a drop in the bucket. We need to ramp this up to some pretty significant air volume."

"Hydrogen volume movement," said the seconded translator, who then winced and said, "Sorry."

"Hydrogen volume movement," Wethers agreed. "We're talking about many hundreds of thousands of cubic feet of hydrogen—at least. It is all just sitting there, underneath all those people. I don't need to tell you what might happen if that gas is vented into the town and ignites."

"No, you don't," Scope said. "But if I overheat the thing, we're done. If we keep the pressure steady, then there is no reason for the hydrogen to seek out those vents, right?"

"There's no reason for that hydrogen to seek out the vents at all," Wethers reminded the engineer. "Whoever has planned these attacks has also planned on creating the positive pressure needed to force the hydrogen into the open vents, if and when they decide to ignite it."

Scope caught the eyes of the translator. They both got the feeling this man Henry was hinting that he knew more than he was telling. Such as, maybe he knew that there was already some method in place for forcing the hydrogen out at the right time.

"So, do I push it hard and risk burning out the fan or do I bring it up slowly, and try to settle for a sustained drop-off of that hydrogen?" Scope asked.

Hunt stared at the control panel, routed in from the system halfway around the world, with the flowing lines of text that he didn't understand, and with row after row of blinking red indicators that showed sections of the site were disabled or nonfunctional. He didn't know the best answer to Scope's question.

Then Scope helped him decide. "Okay, let's think about it in these terms. If the hydrogen is going to be passively directed to the existing vents, then our steady extraction pressure from the pipeline might be enough to counteract the passive flow. If the attack depends upon some sort of sudden displacement of hydrogen, and that attack happens within the next day or so—before an alternative method can be put in place on Santa Ponsa to vent the hydrogen—then nothing we do is going to mitigate the attack. Not by much. If there is that much hydrogen, really all we can do is counteract a passive flow. Look."

Scope indicated a series of numbers. "This is our current rate of flow. If I push this thing hard, I might be able to double that. If there is so much gas underneath that city that it would make for an effective attack, our top extraction rate is going to be on the order of maybe one percent an hour. If I push it really hard, maybe I'll get to 1.5."

"In other words," Wethers said, "we're not going to drain that hydrogen. Not this way."

"Correct."

"So our goal here is to simply keep the pressure steady," Wethers affirmed with a nod. "That is all we can really do."

"And although I have no idea who you are, my friend, I have a feeling that you will be sure that a more robust system is put in place in the city to clear out that hydrogen, as soon as the immediate danger has passed."

Wethers nodded again. "Absolutely we will. As soon as it is feasible. As soon as—as you say—the immediate danger has passed."

"I'd like to make an observation," said the blacksuit, who was supposed to be doing nothing but translating Spanish.

"Yes?" Wethers asked.

The young man nodded at the image on Wethers's tablet. It was the aerial shot of Santa Ponsa. "I know I don't know what's going on. And I don't know what you guys are planning, exactly—"

"Yes?" Wethers said.

The blacksuit tapped the tablet screen.

"I'd want to turn those two off *first*."

CHAPTER FOURTEEN

Santa Ponsa

With a revamped priority list, the men of Phoenix Force headed into the Santa Ponsa tourist region. Well-manicured lawns surrounded expensive vacation villas and hotels. There were shops and golf courses and smartly dressed Europeans spending idle days in this idyllic setting. The series of global attacks that had brought scheduled air travel to a virtual standstill had trapped some vacationers on the island—but there were worse places to be trapped.

Or so the tourists must be thinking. They didn't know about the potential conflagration that could come. McCarter was behind the wheel of the Land Rover, cursing at the loss of the twenty minutes it had taken to rig the exhaust system at the power plant. He understood the reason for it, but it was twenty minutes that they could have spent disarming the actual ignition devices in this area.

He stomped on the brakes when they approached a private drive protected by an automatic gate. The coordinates for the vent put it inside the grounds of the villa. Manning and Hawkins left the vehicle, and McCarter stomped on the gas again before their doors closed. He pulled around the long, twisting road that followed the rocky shoreline, and stopped it at a barked instruction from James, who was watching his GPS.

"Twenty yards," James announced. "That way." He pointed out the right front passenger-door window. McCarter spotted the place where the vent must be. It was bricked up like a well, with a heavy steel grate and a warning sign to keep anyone from trying to get inside.

McCarter also saw that Phoenix Force was not the first to arrive.

GARY MANNING WAS BACK against the brick alongside the entrance to the private villa. Hawkins glanced at the display on his GPS and nodded. They were on the right track. Manning grabbed at the top of the gate and hoisted himself up and over in a single leap. Hawkins landed beside him. A brick retaining wall protected this section of the drive, and Manning jogged along it, toward the front of the villa. There was a fountain playing in the center of the circular drive. He could hear the ocean down on the rocks beyond the villa. There was no sign of life.

Manning stopped at the end of the brick wall and peered around it. On the far side of a manicured lawn a few wooden chairs surrounded some tropical trees. Hawkins glanced at his display again and pointed to the far end of the lawn, where the brick wall of the estate continued. There was a noticeable bulge, as if it was made to accommodate a circular room. But there was no roof. Manning and Hawkins headed across the lawn.

"We've been noticed," Hawkins observed, pointing out the tiny motion detectors stationed on one of the shade trees. The residential security system was the kind that a lot of people didn't even turn on during the daylight hours. Manning thought it highly unlikely that the residents of the house were a part of the attacks. They were just unlucky enough to have one of the vents adjoining their property.

To his surprise, the door of the villa burst open and a middle-aged man in expensive but casual resort wear stormed out, shouting at them and waving a rolled-up magazine.

Manning turned, without slowing, to display the fact that he was carrying an automatic rifle mounted with a grenade launcher. Manning gave him a quick gesture that told him in no uncertain terms that the best place for him to be was inside.

The owner of the villa, as taken aback as he was by the sight of two heavily armed commandos in his front yard, did not get the message. He stood there, gaping at the two of them—and that got him killed. Something moved in the vegetation atop the brick wall next to the vent. Manning and Hawkins spotted it immediately and both of them dropped and rolled, getting themselves out of the line of fire. A rifle blast kicked up dust at about the place where Manning had been standing, while a machine pistol chugged angrily. The rounds cored into the lawn, missing the Phoenix Force warriors.

The gunner turned his fire onto the owner of the villa. The man had still not come to his senses, and now he never would. The rounds tracked him down and crawled up his leg and across his chest, before he dropped at his own front door. The rolled-up magazine fell beside him.

Manning rolled onto his feet and fired a triburst into the vegetation that was the source of the gunfire. The fire abruptly stopped, and a rifle fell off the wall and onto the grass. There was still movement in the vegetation, and Manning unleashed burst after burst, along with Hawkins. Green confetti floated to the lawn, followed by a body.

A Steyr tactical machine pistol fell out of the dead man's hand. Manning continued to maneuver sideways, never lifting the muzzle of his weapon off the wall where the gunners had been. Hawkins was moving the opposite direction, and soon they were both against the wall at the edge of the property, with the bulge of the vent between them. Manning stayed low and approached the brick cylinder. He signaled Hawkins to stay back.

He circled the brick vent, and looked up into the vegetation at the spot where the shooters had been. There was a man staring back at him, eyes fixed wide, flat on the wall.

Manning had switched out the automatic rifle for a Desert Eagle .357 handgun. He stood quickly and found no one else in hiding on the other side of the brick wall. He flattened himself against it, nudging the body off into the grass.

Flat on the top of the brick wall, he found himself looking into the vent. The brick cylinder was at least fifteen feet in diameter, as if someone had started to build a lighthouse and only got the first eight feet completed. Inside the new brick construction were old, perhaps ancient, brick ruins. The entire interior of the cylinder was protected by a grade of half-inch steel bars. Warning signs were wired to the steel bars.

Manning gave a wave at Hawkins, who approached warily and mounted the wall behind Manning. The plan was for Hawkins to search for the hidden device while Manning stood guard. Manning crept forward, following the curved wall top around the vent, and then stopped. He gave an abrupt warning gesture to

Hawkins. They both crouched motionless for a moment while Manning listened to the voices on the other side of the brick wall. He couldn't understand what they were saying. It didn't even sound like Spanish to him. He crept in their direction, rose into a crouch, but found that they were still out of sight. There could be two of them. There could be ten. Two, he was pretty confident, he could handle. If it was ten…

One of them appeared over the top of the wall, spotted Manning just an arm's length away and reacted with a cry of alarm. Manning triggered the Desert Eagle into the man's face. The adversary's gun clattered away, and he collapsed out of sight.

Manning kept the other gunners off guard by charging into their field of view and gunning them down. There weren't ten, but there were three. Two more went down with two more shots from Manning's Desert Eagle. The fourth man cowered against the brick wall, dodging the .357 round that would have cut him down, as well. He triggered his own handgun into the air, almost parallel to the brick wall, but not within line of sight of Manning. He would have to show himself to get a fix on the Phoenix Force warrior.

But Manning wasn't going to wait him out. He raced along the top of the wall, triggering his weapon every second step, knowing he was unlikely to score a hit. But he didn't need a hit. The gunner fled the approaching gunshots, running into the open street and presenting Manning with an easy target. He had two rounds left in the Desert Eagle, and both of them found the gunner's vitals. The gunner dropped in the street.

Manning switched out the magazine in a matter of seconds, scanning the street, the adjoining lawn, and finding no more immediate threats.

"Okay, T.J.," Manning said. "Find that thing."

Hawkins had already grabbed at the steel bars inside the vent and he gave them a heave. They didn't move. The steel grate was bolted in place, and it looked as if the bolts had not been tampered with. Even without the bolts, the thing must weigh hundreds of pounds. So it hadn't been moved when the device was planted, either.

Hawkins felt around the edges of the bars. He scratched his fingers against the bolts in the brick. He reached as far through bars as he could, to touch one of the ancient bricks below, maybe laid by Romans two thousands years ago.

He didn't find it.

Where was the damned device?

THERE WERE TIMES when David McCarter, the leader of Phoenix Force, felt like David McCarter, the hothead who served under Yakov Katzenelenbogen and almost got himself killed through his own impatience, or almost got others killed because of his own temper. He didn't want to be that guy anymore. But sometimes he had to fight hard against the old David McCarter.

Like right now, when he was running out of time and felt he was leading his men into a certain trap. Like when his team was being forced to operate on too little time and too little intelligence, in too much danger.

There were times, too, when channeling the old hotheaded David McCarter wasn't such a bad thing. Sometimes running hot was the most effective way to handle a situation.

The old Subaru spotted the Phoenix Force Land Rover the moment it came to a stop, and even from a distance of a hundred yards McCarter could see the instant alertness of the occupants. He was already con-

vinced that these weren't common pedestrians and they
weren't Europeans on holiday. But before you started
killing people you had to be absolutely certain. They
were parked alongside a circular concrete hole in the
ground. It was twenty feet wide, marked with warning
signs and covered with a steel grate.

If they weren't the guys who planted the devices, and
who were now charged with updating communications
inside of them, then who were they?

Circumstantial evidence, to be sure, McCarter
thought, as he planted the accelerator on the floor of
the Land Rover and steered directly at the Subaru, ruining his tires and filling the air with the stench of burned
rubber. But he didn't care what happened to the Land
Rover after the next twenty seconds. The men inside
the Subaru panicked, jumped out and tried to stop the
rampaging Land Rover by disabling it or killing the
driver. McCarter slammed on the brakes, twisted the
wheel, and sent the Land Rover jittering sideways across
the rocky surface of the cliff top. One of the gunners
fled over the rocks and vanished from sight. The second one triggered his mini Uzi into the looming target
of the SUV. Then the SUV slammed its rear tire into
the concrete ring, slammed its front tire into the hood
of the Subaru and bounced the gunner around the cavity that was left.

The noise became sudden quiet, and Encizo stepped
out of the passenger door. The third man from the
Subaru was unscathed and tried to get Encizo in his
sights. Encizo snapped out one round that took the man
through the brain from a distance of six feet. His corpse
went limp, and Encizo kicked the Uzi off the cliff edge
and into the rocks below.

McCarter had leaped from the SUV and followed the

jumper. He found the man crouched in a tumble of rocks below the ledge. He fired overhead. McCarter, with no finesse whatsoever, blasted into the rocks with two buckshot rounds, and the man in the rocks was dead.

Calvin James had to climb out the driver's side, since the passenger-side doors were crushed against brick and the Subaru. The man who'd been trapped in the crash was crushed and lifeless, but another man had hidden flat inside the concrete ring, taking cover where he could. When he saw the black commando coming at him with the M16, his nerves failed him. He rose off the steel bars, already squeezing on the trigger of his machine pistol.

James put a triburst into his skull. The gunner collapsed on his back on the steel bars, and the Uzi fell from his grip. The weapon threaded itself through a gap in the bars, and the stock hooked on a bar just for a moment. Then it slipped off, and clattered to the cavern floor far beneath.

James found an open gap in the concrete, inside the lip and above the steel grate. It had been sawed out of the concrete long ago and fitted with a locking cover. With the cover already removed, it was easy to see how two hidden latches on the bottom would need to be depressed simultaneously to remove the cover. It looked just like the brick; even if someone was looking for it, it would've been difficult to find.

The device had already been removed from the cavity.

James snapped open the box, and removed the phone. It separated from the nanothermite weapon with a snap of the USB cable.

"We done here?" McCarter said.

"Yeah." James followed Encizo back into the Land

Rover, flipped open the phone and tried to dial in to Tokaido's test number. McCarter stomped on the accelerator and the phone nearly jumped out of James's hand. There were sirens closing in behind them, and cars were running off the road to avoid McCarter.

McCarter was a man with a mission.

James knew just how he felt. He dialed in to the test number, heard it start to ring, and left it on the seat when he exited the Land Rover again. They were already at vent site number three.

The vent was inconveniently placed, so the city planners had simply used it as the centerpiece for a traffic roundabout. It was a concrete ring, three feet high, two feet wide, and this time topped with a fence of linked steel bars. Inside was an eroded mountain of ancient brickwork built by people long dead.

Sure enough, James saw there was a reception committee. How many of these bastards had been blackmailed into taking these fatal risks? How desperate must they be to return to the scene of their crime, to do the dirty work of their unseen employer?

Stony Man Farm reported that, around the world, people were turning themselves in to local authorities rather than jumping through the hoops of their unseen employer. Some of them had truly been appalled by the death and destruction that they had helped to create. Others had simply seen surrendering to the police as their best chance of survival.

But there were others who continued to fight for their own freedom. Even if that meant rearming the devices they had previously armed, even knowing the horror that they could be facilitating.

James wondered if the world would ever run out of people who simply didn't care whether other people lived or died. He for one was getting tired of them. And it was discouraging that there were so many, that they were always there. And here they were again. In place at the third vent site, protecting it, as if waiting for someone to show up and try to stop the damage they were determined to cause.

THE FORD GALAXY VAN was parked broadside to the circular ring of the vent, facing down another roadway, as if they had been expecting trouble to come from the opposite direction. Maybe they had heard about the previous vent attack. Even as the Land Rover came within their line of sight, the van dropped into Reverse and circled backward. Doors opened on either side, and the occupants stepped out behind the cover of the doors and laid their barrels in the crook.

They fired into the Land Rover as James and Encizo ran in a crouch behind their own vehicle and vaulted over the roadside wall. In Santa Ponsa, they were fond of the low, decorative, brick walls. Calvin James didn't know whether he thought they were pretty or not, but he knew they would stop a bullet way better than the doors of the van. When McCarter steered the Land Rover out of the middle of the gunfire, the brick wall received a battering of rounds from the gunmen at the van. James and Encizo sensed a lull and returned fire over the top of the wall.

Their own rounds dented the hood of the van and wormed their way through the gaps between the door and the body of the vehicle. The driver dropped first. Then James scored a headshot on the man on the passenger side. The wounded driver crawled into the vehicle and kept low, yanking his door shut. There was at least one more gunner in the van. He crawled to the front seat, pulled his upper body out of the passenger side and raked the brick wall with machine-gun fire. He pulled back in quickly, before James and Encizo could fire. By then, the driver had put the van into gear. His bloodied face peeked over the dashboard, and he maneuvered around the roundabout, intent on making an escape.

David McCarter had no intention of letting that happen. He had circled around behind the van while the occupants were distracted by James and Encizo. As soon as the van started to move, McCarter hit the gas and circled the roundabout on an intercept course. There was a low-speed head-on collision. The Land Rover had already lost some of its sheen under the hail of rounds, which didn't penetrate the armored body panels but sure scratched up the paint. Its looks deteriorated further when it collided with the Ford van.

But the Land Rover gave worse than it took.

McCarter felt grim satisfaction watching the wounded driver bounce off the steering wheel. The van was still in gear. When McCarter reversed the Land Rover the van moved a few feet before it halted with a screech of rubbing metal. The driver was nowhere to be seen, but the man in the passenger seat, unwounded, was reaching for the steering wheel, jerking it quickly. He got no response from the vehicle. He locked eyes with McCarter, pushed open the passenger door and poked one arm out, firing a 9 mm handgun.

This man had some training. The round bounced off the windshield directly in McCarter's field of vision and left a graze in the glass. The man with a handgun realized what he was not going to get McCarter while McCarter was in the Land Rover.

The rear window of the van imploded and the sole

surviving occupant dropped to the floor. The interior filled with rounds from James and Encizo.

Inside the van, the survivor was in full panic mode. He tried to think clearly. His army training had not prepared him for this. He wasn't going to outgun these guys. His only hope was an escape. When the next volley of automatic gunfire came to a halt, he was going to get up, send a few shots in their direction, just to get them to duck down, then get the hell out of there.

But the incoming automatic gunfire stopped abruptly. The panicked gunman got up on his knees and pointed his 9 mm handgun in the direction of the men behind a brick wall. Before he could fire, he could see that the pair was already on their feet—retreating. The Land Rover was accelerating away from him and his vehicle. The rear hatch of the SUV bounced open, and with a quick squeak of the brakes the Land Rover stopped, which sent the hatch flying open. The two commandos made flying leaps that landed them in the rear of the Land Rover, and the vehicle took off.

The gunner inside the Ford van was reasonably certain that *he* hadn't scared them off.

There was only one thing that could have scared those commandos away.

Which meant that he was himself a dead man.

Seconds later, it was true.

Stony Man Farm

At first the attack attempts had come dependably at three minutes after the hour, every four hours. Whoever was orchestrating the attacks had given up on that schedule. Now the cybernetics team at Stony Man Farm didn't know when to expect the signals to begin to come through the systems that they were monitoring.

Akira Tokaido didn't understand why those systems were still being used at all. Whoever was sending the signals knew by now that every signal they sent was being monitored and even interrupted. And if they knew it, and they kept sending them in this way, they had to have their own reasons for doing so.

Whatever those reasons were, they couldn't be good.

And so, with the sending of every signal, they had been forced into making a decision. Should they turn off the picocell and essentially end this avenue of communication for the terrorists—or should they allow it to continue to be used, under the Farm's control?

It was maddening, but there was really no good reason to shut down the picocell. None of the signals going through it had escaped the control of Stony Man Farm. Every signal sent through that picocell had been interrupted. As far as they could tell, not a single device had been successfully activated since the picocell had fallen under their control.

And there was no good reason that the terrorists could not simply turn to a different picocell. Surely they had backup equipment. Surely they had other systems stationed and ready for use. Maybe dozens of them.

So the only good reason that the terrorists were continuing to use this picocell was as a method of controlling the behavior of their pursuers. Stony Man Farm was allowing itself to be manipulated by the terrorists. Stony Man Farm knew it. The terrorists knew it.

But any access to the terrorists at this point was better than nothing.

Truly, after all this time, after all these attacks, the Farm seemed no closer to tracking the terrorists down.

Stony Man Farm allowed the signals to continue to rebroadcast through the picocell just because they could think of nothing better to do.

An alarm shrilled.

"Incoming!" Kurtzman announced.

Tokaido was already on it. His systems had sensed the transmissions coming through the picocell, and had automatically begun a number of routines designed specifically to alter the signals, as well as trace each signal's destination, and to trace it back to its point of origin.

Tokaido watched the progress of his programs carefully. His eyes were dark. He had slept little since the attacks began. He couldn't even remember having eaten.

And every time these signals began to move through his systems, under his control, Akira Tokaido felt responsible for whatever might happen to them. And every time he expected the worst.

He didn't know it yet, but this time the worst was going to actually happen.

The call came in, the Farm apps altered the commands and the calls were allowed to proceed to their targets in Santa Ponsa. Tokaido's gaze snapped up to the big plasma screen display, which was right now showing an aerial view coming live from the appropriated UAV—Unmanned Aerial Vehicle—hovering over Santa Ponsa. An overlay marked the vent sites. They were computer-generated circles around each of the known, sabotaged vents in the city. The circles had become gray Xs over vents one and two, where the devices were known to have been disabled. In the live screen, vents three, four and five were now receiving the transmitted signals from the picocell controlled by Stony Man Farm. The signals they were receiving were scrambled. In their realm of experience, no scrambled signal had successfully activated a single one of the nanothermite devices.

On the live screen, coming to them from the islands in the Mediterranean, inside the digitally generated red circles the vague images of the vents turned bright orange, one by one.

And Akira Tokaido knew that he had failed again.

Santa Ponsa

THE MQ-CI GREY EAGLE drone hovering over the island of Majorca was equipped with multiple sensors, cameras and synthetic aperture radar. An infrared camera allowed operators to see what the drone saw, even at night.

But the UAV hovering over Majorca had a special infrared camera made specifically for picking up heat signatures. At the MQ-CI's low altitude, with its focus already targeted in five specific preidentified points on the landscape, the sensors were capable of measuring changes in ground temperature in real time and generating significant thermal change alerts in under one second.

The monitoring of the ground temperature was being sent as part of the data feed via satellite from the Mediterranean to Stony Man Farm in Virginia.

As part of Akira Tokaido's alert application, the system would identify these thermal fluctuations, measure their intensity and make a simple judgment call. If the temperature went up too far too fast—such as the rise from 73°F to 612°F within a matter of 1.76 seconds that it had just sensed—the system would sound an alert.

Unlike most of the alerts that Tokaido had programmed, this one fed directly in to the communication system linked with SOG commandos in the field. The result was that, if one of the nanothermite devices activated within the realm of coverage, the commandos would probably know about it even before the cyberteam at the Farm did.

It had been a quick and simple programming job that Tokaido had put in place just hours before, and one that he hoped would remain unused.

And, like everything else he'd been working on lately, there had been a nagging doubt as to how well it would actually function.

McCARTER'S EARPIECE screamed at him. "Fire. Evacuate. Fire. Evacuate."

McCarter never gave the loser in the Ford van another thought. He threw the Land Rover into Drive and accelerated away from the concrete ring of the vent. He stabbed at the quick release of the rear hatch, and he tapped the brakes just right. The hatch was flown open hard enough to fracture the hinge covers.

ENCIZO WAS REACHING over the top of the decorative brick wall to finally take out the son of a bitch in the Ford van when the harsh computer-generated warning nearly split his skull. Instead of going for the guy in the van, Encizo grabbed at Calvin James and practically dragged the man to his feet. It was unneeded. James's eardrums had almost shattered when the warning sounded, and he had been propelled into motion before he even thought about it.

Encizo and James bolted into the street and found the Land Rover inserted directly in front of them. The back end was open to receive them as if by an invisible hand. They threw themselves into the rear of the vehicle.

Encizo could swear he heard a sudden rush of wind chasing after him. He yanked down on the rear hatch, slamming it as McCarter tore away from the concrete ring.

Encizo knew he shouldn't look but he couldn't help himself. In the Ford van he could swear he saw the gunner's face transform from surprise at the sudden departure of his enemies, to understanding, and to terror. Then an arc of white sparks erupted from somewhere inside the vent and oily black smoke belched into the sky, and then the air itself over the vent burst into flame.

A forty-foot-tall tendril of orange flame over the vent grew and expanded and blossomed, overflowing the edges of the concrete ring like a pot of water boiling over. The tide of flame poured over the Ford van, consuming it. The flame flowed into the streets, and toward the nearby homes. McCarter twisted the wheel to take the Land Rover around the corner, and the tide of flame was left behind, a river now, flowing over the rocks toward the nearby shore.

The Phoenix Force leader steered the Land Rover around a screaming police car, headed in the other direction, and shouted into his mike, "Manning! Talk to me! Hawkins!"

"Manning here."

"Hawkins?" McCarter demanded.

"T.J. is here. He's fine. Except his headpiece is kaput. Or maybe it's his hearing that's shot."

"Be there in thirty seconds," Manning said.

McCarter barely slowed the Land Rover to allow Gary Manning and T. J. Hawkins to pile in, then he careened through town, heading back along the coast to the small, private dock where Stony Man's appropriated black-op cruising vessel was tied up. He pulled directly into the automotive bay and shouted at the nearest crewmember to get the boat under way.

Within minutes they were pulling away from Majorca. In the distance they could see a trio of pillars of orange fire burning in Santa Ponsa. Around them were houses engulfed in flame and burning cars and terrified people.

The orange pillars were still burning by the time Santa Ponsa was out of their field of vision.

Stony Man Farm

THEY WATCHED THE NEWS feed from the Mediterranean. There was little said in the War Room. There was little to say. There was little, even, to do.

Brognola appeared on the big plasma screen. The big Fed looked tired. His skin seemed slack. His eyes were dark.

"Okay, Hal is here, Phoenix," Barbara Price said.

"We're here," McCarter said. "What the hell happened?"

"We were set up," Kurtzman said. "The devices in Santa Ponsa were triggered by a call. No specific code or signal. Just the call itself was enough to trigger the devices."

"They're playing with us," Brognola said. "They knew we were onto them, and we knew it, too. They set the trap, we walked right into it. It seems to me we knew this from the beginning. Before Phoenix ever set foot on Majorca."

"True," Price said.

"What about our expert engineer who was supposed to be pulling the gas off?" McCarter asked.

"Our expert engineer was pulling the gas off as best as he could," Price said. "We owe him a debt of gratitude."

"Not good enough," McCarter said, bitterness rising in his voice. "What exactly did we accomplish here today?"

"What we did is save Santa Ponsa," said the well-modulated deep voice of Huntington Wethers, coming in from his feed in Manassas.

"No offense, Hunt," McCarter growled, "but from where I'm sitting, it doesn't look like we saved anything. Those vents still ignited. The fires still happened. People still died."

"Let me tell you boys what would've happened if you had not been there," Wethers said. "We have studied the layout of the known chambers underneath the city. We've got an idea how much room there was and how much hydrogen was pumped into those spaces, and we have even made up a pretty good estimate as to what happened when those devices ignited. We had important insight provided by our translator. One of our temporary staffers let us know which vents to hit first, and why."

From his hotel room in Manassas, Wethers placed an image of Santa Ponsa onto the display. They saw it in the War Room, just as Phoenix was seeing it aboard their vessel on the Mediterranean and Brognola on his display in his D.C. office. It was a recently updated shot from the UAV. It showed black and pits around the still burning vents.

Wethers used a cursor to make a circle in the middle of the town, where there seemed to be nothing.

"Right about here," he said, "is the largest open

chamber belowground. It is also the chamber closest to the surface. Lighter-than-air gas like hydrogen would naturally migrate here. It made an ideal storage chamber. But when it was time to light the vents, that hydrogen had to be forced out. There was a high-explosive charge staged in this chamber. When it went off, it forced the hydrogen out."

Wethers's cursor traveled to the five vents and circled them one at a time. First he circled the two on the bottom of the screen, which had not burned. Then he circled the three at the top, where, at the time the photo was taken, the flames were still alive.

"This is what the terrorists wanted to happen. They wanted their high explosive to force the gases in the catacombs out through the vents at high speed, at the same time the nanothermite devices went off. From what we can tell of the catacombs, the path of least resistance for the hydrogen at the moment the high explosive drove it out of the primary storage chamber would have been to these two vents." Wethers circled the two vents that Phoenix Force had initially disabled. "With the help of my very skilled consultant, we have determined that fifty percent to as much as seventy percent of the hydrogen was forced out of those two vents. Less than half of the hydrogen was channeled to these three vents—the three that actually were ignited.

"In addition, maybe twenty or thirty percent of the gas inside those catacombs was forced by the explosion into deeper tunnels and channels. From there, the hydrogen will naturally rise to the surface. That means most of it will rise to these two vents. They are at the highest ground, and the passageways under the city appeared to give them the easiest exit routes. If those vents had ignited, there would have been two much larger explosions. Maybe twice as large. Maybe three times. But certainly larger, and in more heavily populated areas, and because of their altitude compared to the other vents, they would have been continually fed with fuel for an undetermined length of time. I am not exaggerating, my friends, when I say that we saved Santa Ponsa. If those two vents had gone off, we would be looking at hundreds of burning buildings instead of twenty or thirty. And a lot more dead."

There was silence following Wethers's explanation. It was a different kind of silence. It was a sigh of mutual relief.

Barbara Price felt a swell of affection for her old friend Wethers. She wished he was in the room right now.

"All right," Brognola said with a sort of tired resignation. "So we saved Santa Ponsa. Can we save the world?"

"Not until we know who to save it from," Barbara Price said.

PHOENIX FORCE was no longer on the communication channel. Brognola had disappeared from the screen. Wethers was packing up his gear in Manassas and would return soon to the Farm. But for now, it was unusually quiet in the Computer Room.

Barbara Price felt what many of the others felt. Helpless. Beaten.

But there was one among them now who was beaten down more than the others. She walked across the large room and stood behind Akira Tokaido. He didn't face her. He was looking into his screens. Window after window after window opened and closed around him, as if he were in some eternally shifting digital dimension. The man had been here since the beginning. And for Tokaido, this had begun the moment his software, one of his babies, had failed to let him know that the terrorists were attacking.

Something happened to Tokaido at that moment. Some huge burden had been placed on the shoulders. It was a burden he did not deserve to carry.

"Akira."

"Yeah?"

"You saved them today."

"What?"

She placed one hand on his shoulder. She felt him tense up.

"Your system alerted Phoenix. David, and Encizo and T.J. They are alive now because of your alert system. It gave them the time they needed to get away."

"Oh. Yeah."

"Who knows how many lives you saved when you stopped the second wave of attacks. You own that success. You created it. It is yours."

"I own some failures, too."

"No," she said. "You own what you create. What you created has saved many, many lives. And you've accomplished things nobody else could. But just because you cannot achieve something that's even out of *your* reach, it does not mean it is your failure."

"Somebody owns it."

"The people who are making it happen. Not you. You cannot be expected to program away all the horrible things that happen in this world," Price said. "You can't write an app to stop terror."

Finally, Tokaido turned and looked at her.

"I can try," he said.

CHAPTER FIFTEEN

Ramvik, Norway

Olan Ramm took a tour of his home, starting with the family cemetery, which was tucked in one corner of the gated grounds.

It was small, with maybe forty members of the Ramm family interred here. There were a lot more members of the Ramm family missing—buried else where. Olan Ramm would someday find them all and bring them back home.

But that was for later. All these things that he had planned to recover and restore and reclaim would have to wait. Very soon, he would have the single most important possession of his family returned to him: the land. And everything that was on it.

It would satisfy the demands of justice to have this land restored to him, but more important, it would provide the funding needed to restore what else he had lost, and what all the Ramms had lost, or sold or given away or donated over the years.

The grounds of the estate were filled with his recovered property. Mountains of it. Piles of it. The whole place a cemetery now, with the remains of all the things that had been a part of the Ramm family.

All these possessions could have been saved and preserved. But history had robbed the family of its dignity, as well as its land. Ramm would restore everything.

This whole power play was necessary, but truly beneath his dignity. He had never wanted to embark upon this exercise. Injustice forced it upon him. What was his—what was the family Ramm's—was stolen. It had left the family hollow-eyed and aimless and incomplete. That theft diminished the family as a whole. They suffered through generations of degradation as a result.

But soon that would all be done with. Ramm had found the means and the methods to make things right. His lands would be returned to him. The wealth of those lands would come to him.

He would have the vast resources that would be needed, and he would deploy them to search for and recover on a much broader scale all the pieces that he had yet to find. He would get it all back.

He would find ways to punish those who had profited from the theft of Ramm family property. All of those who had sold him back what was rightfully the property of the family Ramm, he would make an accounting.

He walked inside his home. All those piles of property outside were nothing compared to the stacks and racks inside. They filled the home to overflowing.

He would hire a staff of hundreds to sort through and organize all this paper—which numbered more than ten million pieces, he estimated. They would organize his ten thousand books. They would restore his art and the home itself.

But the Ramm home was just the start of it. There was so much out there that was unfound. There was so much out there that was lost forever.

That would be where the real resources would be needed. If there was a book that the Ramm family had owned three hundred years ago, which was lost now, then it would be found. If it took a staff of a hundred investigators to search through the archives to find the clues needed to establish responsibility for the loss of that one book, then so be it.

Responsibility would be laid. Someone would be accountable and held responsible for the cost of its restoration. It would not be Ramm family money paying for it. The country itself would pay for it. Because the country itself created opportunity for its loss.

Ramm would tax this nation into poverty and enslave its nation and sell its children as slaves to pay for the cost of the restoration of that book. If they resisted the restoration of his rights, then he would execute them until they ceased to resist.

There was no doubt in his mind that the thieves— or their descendants—would be forced to cooperate in the search for and return of every fragment of stolen Ramm property.

The most important box in the old house was the one that contained Olan Ramm's notebooks. In them he had transcribed, by hand, every note, every clue, every lead on every piece of property that had ever belonged to this family. It had become almost a hobby for him to hunt these items down year after year, as he worked to achieve his true goal.

The land was the all-important property that he must recover. When he recovered the Ramm family land claims, and the adjacent maritime properties, then he would have means to recover all the rest of it.

He was deeply disappointed, right now, at the loss of Charles Skyn. The man had run. Ramm was not fooled by the destruction of the factory on his land up north.

Ramm knew that Charles Skyn had taken his car. Just as it was Charles Skyn who had burned his plant to the ground. Skyn had himself stolen from Ramm.

But, like anything else, he would be returned, eventually, and would pay punitive damages.

That would be the real satisfaction in the process of the restoration of his property—enforcing punitive damages.

For every photograph or book or flower that was taken away from his family, at any time, punitive damages would be paid.

Today might be his last day at the Ramm home for some time. He would leave his men here, and take only what he needed, and he would work alone, where he could not be found. Now he would begin to apply his true leverage to the situation. When he asked for the return of what belonged to him, it would be easy for the world to cooperate and agree that he should have it.

So little inconvenience would come to the vast population of the planet by the simple act of agreeing that Ramm's claims were valid. And so great would be their world's distress until they made that agreement.

And Ramm had to admit that he thoroughly enjoyed playing with those who were trying to track him down. As he enjoyed playing with those he hired. That part of it, he would miss.

Skyn had said he was going overboard with the complexity of his employment hierarchy. Ramm disagreed. It was good to have many workers available to do the jobs that needed doing. And to keep them in check it was necessary to have those to supervise them and to watch and record the activities of the hirelings.

And there were those who watched the activities of the watchers.

There were six different levels to the hierarchy. It made for interesting planning. It filled all of a single notebook. He mapped out the system, how it worked and all its checks and balances.

When it was in place, it had given him great joy to witness the system functioning properly. To apply the checks to the balances. To force the hands of the hirelings who thought that their task was done, only to learn that they could not resist. To give the promise of great opportunity to those who had never had opportunity, and then to whisk it away. To manipulate. To make people do what they did not wish to do. That is what he enjoyed.

Soon his new power base would be established, and his ability to manipulate and control people in this fashion would be magnified.

Olan Ramm was feeling such enthusiasm as he made his next round of phone calls.

No more calls to inanimate devices. This time he was ringing up real live human beings.

Stony Man Farm, Virginia

"WE WILL TAKE BACK that which belongs to us."

The voice was stilted English, spoken with an accent and digitally modified.

"There are thousands of public lines to high-level government offices," Barbara Price said. "Doesn't mean you can call the White House and actually talk to the President. They called a few thousand different numbers around the world and it was always the same message."

One came into the public line at the White House and to several public phone lines on Capitol Hill. Public call-in lines operated by U.S. members of Congress received the calls. Public phone numbers for the office of the governor of each one of the United States of America. The prime ministers and members of parliament in the United Kingdom and Canada. The presidents of Mexico and Russia.

Thousands of publicly accessible government office phone numbers around the world received the calls— all exactly the same voice recording, which was on internet news and social sites in seconds, and went viral in minutes.

But even before CNN and the BBC, Stony Man Farm had the recording.

We will take back that which belongs to us. We will take back everything that rightly belongs to us. That is our intention. Interference will result in more destruction. It is as simple as that. Allow us to take back that which rightly belongs to us and we will have no more cause to perpetrate further destruction.

All transportation into, out of and between the Scandinavian nations will cease within twelve hours.

Hermann Schwarz still could not believe what he was hearing.

After all the death and destruction, *that's* the message they give the world?

Blancanales frowned. "It doesn't make any sense. Scandinavia? He wants to close down Scandinavia? Who the hell is this? What the hell is he trying to 'take back'?"

Brognola popped up on the screen and didn't get a chance to speak.

"Working on it," Barbara Price said to the screen.

"Can you track that one back?" Brognola asked.

"No," Tokaido said without looking up. "They didn't go through the Phoenix picocell."

Carl Lyons was leaning over Carmen Delahunt's shoulder.

"Carmen got it cleaned up," Lyons said, and walked to the center of the War Room as the recording played again, minus most of the computer synthetics.

We will take back that which belongs to us.

"Sure enough. It sounds Scandinavian," Blancanales said sardonically.

"Norwegian, according to accent analyzers," Delahunt announced.

"Norway," Kurtzman said, surfing for intel. "Lots of oil comes out of Norway. Yeah, 2.4 million barrels. A day."

Barbara Price touched the headset. "Phoenix?"

Balearic Sea

"UNDERSTOOD!" David McCarter had to shout above the rush of the props. "Keep us up-to-date."

The noise fell off when the hatches closed on the Sikorsky Sea King. The SH-3H was one of the U.S. Navy's workhorse helicopters. It was powered by a pair of General Electric T58-GE-10 turboshafts that would get the bird going at 144 knots—166 miles per hour. The SH-3H variety was specifically designed for anti-submarine activities and had been borrowed from the *USS Carl Vinson,* currently leading a strike group from the central Mediterranean.

"You guys must rate," commented the sailor who locked the doors. "They had us sitting on our thumbs for the last eighteen hours on some little Spanish navy boat, waiting for you to call for a taxi."

"Yeah, thanks," McCarter said.

The sailor was surprised that McCarter spoke with a British accent. He'd heard the others speaking America's own English. They weren't showing stripes but you had to assume they were military—but how do you address them when they don't show stripes? He was dying to know who these guys were and what their business was...

The sailor withered under McCarter's glare.

"What's our ETA to Marseilles?"

"Fifty-five minutes, sir."

"Christ." The Briton growled, then he glanced at the sailor. "Thanks," he said, trying to sound less agitated than he clearly was. "Do you happen to have any Coke?"

"He means the beverage," added the Hispanic-looking guy. "Coffee would be good, too."

The sailor handed them a thermos of hot coffee, then came back a minute later with a single can of soda.

"Will Spanish Coke do?"

"Perfect." McCarter took the can. "They stock Coke on this bird?"

The sailor grinned. "Nah. It's mine. Bought it from the canteen on the Spanish ship. But I don't need it. You look like you do. Sir."

"Thanks."

The sailor disappeared into the cockpit.

"So what's going on?" Encizo asked.

"Stony's filtered the recording. They identified the speaker as Norwegian. Add that together with the fact that Norway's one of the biggest oil exporters—it's not much to go on, but it's all we have to go on."

"So we're going to Norway?"

McCarter nodded. "Navy transport out of southern France. We'll try to get in-country before the deadline for closing the borders. We can assume the Scandinavian countries will follow those instructions."

"So much for not dealing with terrorists," Hawkins said.

"It's not the United States. It's up to each country," Manning said. "You think they're going to risk more attacks just to keep their borders open?"

"So that's all we've got?" Calvin James said. "A country? After a thousand terrorist attacks and a thousand murders and now a thousand robo calls to every government on earth and we've arrowed it down to Norway? And we're not even sure about that?"

McCarter let James rant. He knew how the man felt. He knew that frustration.

"You realize Norway's almost two thousand klicks end to end?" James demanded.

"I've been there, mate."

Stony Man Farm

"WE HAVE PHOENIX en route to Norway," Price said.

"Why'd we miss the Norwegian angle in the first place?" Blancanales asked. "We killed Norwegian intruders in Solon Labs."

"We didn't," Price corrected. "We did a thorough intelligence search after the raid on the labs. We knew one of those men was speaking Norwegian on the phone. At least, that was what we believed from your description of the phonetics. It did not lead us anywhere."

"All of the traces on Solon himself?" Blancanales asked.

"They got us nowhere," Price said. "He was unexceptional, until he came up with some minor innovations in nanothermite technology. Then he got the funding. Then he became a U.S. contractor."

"But it was all linked to this, right?" Blancanales insisted.

"Yes. Solon was almost certainly serving as a spy for someone. Keeping them abreast of the United States military's state of the art in terms of manufacturable nanothermite. We are still trying to track his funding. We've also been trying to identify the surveillance video images we got on the intruders. Those investigations have all come to dead ends."

"It seems all we have is dead ends," Blancanales said.

BARBARA PRICE HAD BEEN in the War Room for thirty of the past thirty-six hours. She gave herself the luxury of a fifteen-minute break. She went to her private room, which was empty and a little cold, and she used it for a quick shower and change of clothes.

She was already running the postmortem in her head. Had they missed something? Could they have followed up on Blancanales's hunch about Norway in some more complete fashion and thus be ahead of the game now?

But that was not a reasonable line of thought. They had run the Norway lead to the ground. They had looked for face recognition on every person who had been inside those offices. They'd checked out all the employees. They had tracked back every lead on Solon himself. The FBI was continuing the investigation of everyone involved with the organization. If they found anything more, it would come into Stony Man Farm.

They had done all that they could.

And then, as she was buttoning her shirt, Barbara

Price thought of one lead, perhaps, that had not been followed.

She headed back to the War Room.

Marseilles, France

THE SEA KING PUT THEM on the tarmac in southern France after a forty-nine-minute flight. Their feet were barely on the ground before they were boarding a U.S. Navy C-40A Clipper, the military's version of the Boeing 737-700C.

The airport was quiet. Every major commercial passenger airline had canceled all flights indefinitely. The United States, Japan and a half dozen other countries had shut down their airspace to all commercial and private aircraft.

The main focus of the terrorist was not on aircraft, looking at the sheer numbers, and no aircraft had been targeted since the first slew of attacks. Small charters, medical transport and private aircraft were flying again in small numbers in Europe and Asia. But not many.

The Navy's C-40A did not have to wait for a runway.

Stony Man Farm

"WHAT'S OUR AVENUE of investigation, here?" Brognola was demanding.

"We're looking into the motive," Price said. "What group would use that term?"

"There's been some anti-Muslim sentiment among some Norwegian fringe groups," Kurtzman suggested. "But none of them have been violent and none of them are well-funded."

"Which is really the key," Price said. "We're looking at any and all groups with Scandinavian interests that have money or have shown signs of newly acquired wealth."

"That should narrow it down right there," Brognola said.

"Not as much as you'd think. There are hundreds of organizations, many of them well-funded. There is a lot of money and a lot of moneyed organizations within and interested in the Scandinavian countries."

"What about individuals?" Brognola asked.

"There are many, many individuals in Scandinavia with money. Putting the focus specifically on Norway, you don't shrink the list much. Norway has the oil. Norway has four or five billionaires. When we crunch the numbers on this operation, depending on how much you estimate for the cost of manufacturing the nanothermite devices themselves, this campaign has cost somebody anywhere from fifty to two hundred million dollars already. But if you assume that there could be an individual out there, running this campaign virtually solo, and you assume that he's obsessive enough to use up most or all of his fortune to do so—well, there are a lot of people out there, believe it or not, walking around with two hundred million dollars."

"There aren't even that many people in Norway," Brognola argued. "How long can the list be?"

"The problem gets back to one of motive," Price said. "Motive, even this excessive, requires desire and rationale. Who out there feels unfairly denied of something, something that they speak of in terms of property, something of such value that they will justify this kind of expense to retrieve?"

"Oil." Brognola shrugged. "We know it's oil. I don't

see the problem here. Are we looking at Scandinavian oil interests or not?"

"Of course we are," Price said. "We have a thousand pages of intelligence on oil interests in Scandinavia, and most of it is focused in Norway. I can give you a list of everyone involved in the Norwegian petro industry. I can give you the names of every CEO that's been fired from any sort of petroleum-related industry anywhere near Scandinavia. You want the staff lists of every anti-oil environmental group that's ever focused its attention on northern Europe? I'll give it to you. We know what we're looking for here, Hal, and if it is here, we will find it."

"I know you will," Brognola grumbled.

"The problem—if anything—is too much information, but nothing is standing out to us in any way," Kurtzman said. "We are sitting on the data, crunching the numbers, we're searching the databases for any evidence of any interests or behaviors or other links. We just can't seem to narrow it down."

Brognola rubbed his head. "Here's my problem. I cannot go to the President of the United States and tell him we have nothing to go on. I have been telling him that almost from the moment this started."

Barbara Price stared at the big Fed on the screen. He stared back, chewing an antacid.

"The Scandinavians are going to capitulate," Brognola said.

"We assumed as much."

"Even the unofficial Scandinavian countries are closing down their borders. Finland, Iceland, the Faroe Islands. No one wants to take the risk of being targeted specifically by this terrorism."

"That is not surprising," Price said.

"But there may be a problem with the Russians."

"What kind of a problem?"

"The Russians already feel as if they have been especially hard hit in these attacks. They are not ready to capitulate," Brognola said. "On the contrary. Russian investigations are getting aggressive, and they are looking for someone to blame."

Kurtzman was poring over information on the screen. "The Russians have been hard hit, because they have a big oil industry and a lot of it flows through pipelines. Compared to the other big oil producers, they haven't suffered a disproportionate share."

"That is exactly what the President said to the prime minister of Russia," Brognola said. "The prime minister was not convinced."

"Is he trying to frame somebody with this?" Price asked.

"No."

"Could it be a staged overreaction?"

"You mean, to disguise his culpability?" Brognola asked.

"I don't think so," Kurtzman said. "I don't see any way that the Russians could turn this situation to their favor. Their petroleum infrastructure has suffered pretty extensively. I would be much more inclined to think that the prime minister wants to do whatever it takes to avoid further losses."

"Well, you've got that right," Brognola said. "The prime minister is ready to send in an air strike if he finds a likely target."

"That's a good strategy if and only if he's correct about the target, and if the air strike is perfect, and if he gets all the principals, and if they don't have an automated system in place to avenge such an attack," Price said.

"I know."

"If he gets it wrong, and infuriates the attackers, who knows what they will do to retaliate," Price continued.

"I know."

"Do the Russians know something we don't know?"

"I don't think so," Brognola admitted.

"We have been monitoring the intelligence agencies around the world. As you can imagine, most of them are focusing their efforts on these attacks," Kurtzman said. "Specifically, most of them are focusing their attentions on the specific attacks inside their own borders. We're sifting through all the data that they are putting on their own systems."

"The President is aware of this. Believe me, I've had to tell him that more than once the last twenty-four hours."

After Brognola vanished from the plasma screen, Kurtzman looked at Price questioningly. "You didn't bring up our new lead."

"When I said it in my head, it sounded too flimsy to offer up to Hal as our best avenue of investigation," Price said.

"It could turn into something."

"If it turns out to be something, then I'll call Hal back and let him know," Price said. She leaned over the table and rang the intercom for the armory.

KISSINGER HURRIED into the War Room.

"I thought you would want to be here when we called your friend again," Price said.

"Yeah. I'm glad you did."

Kissinger, Kurtzman and Price gathered around the phone on the conference table.

"This is Barb," she said when the phone was answered by Harry Envoi. "I assume you've seen the photos?"

The last time she had been on the phone with the CEO, he was outgoing and friendly. Today he was urgent and deadly serious.

"I would have called you myself if I had any way of tracking you down. Those pics you sent—Skyn is there."

A tingle of electricity seemed to move through Price's body. "Which one?"

"Start with photo number 182. Unidentified subject 11."

Price shuffled the stack of photos grabbed from security cameras at Solon Labs. Stony Man Farm had extracted hundreds of photos from thousands of hours of security video stored in off-site servers. There had been dozens of non-staff visitors to the labs over the previous year. Everything from pizza deliverers to paper products salesman. And many visitors whose identity had not been determined.

Face recognition software had been used to group those visitors. Photo number 182 showed a sallow-faced young man in some sort of blue-collar uniform with his first name tagged on the shirt pocket. Unidentified Subject 11 was also in photos 183, 184 and 186, and in sixteen more photos taken at the labs on at least three other occasions. He was always in the same uniform shirt, always with a matching brimmed hat. In several of the shots the name on the tag was legible as Steve.

"That is Charles Skyn. I couldn't see it in the first photo, or even the second, but when I started looking at them together, and I could see past the stupid hat, it started to look very familiar. All at once it hit me. Who it was. I met the guy at some university event in London eight years ago. Other than that I only knew him by reputation. And I was sure he was dead. That was the official finding after his boat was wrecked three years ago. But he's not dead. That's him. If you can find other photos of him, compare them. You'll see it, too."

They did see it. As soon as they put those photos of Deliveryman Steve next to photos of nanotech savant Charles Skyn, it became clear that they were the same person.

Several pieces of the puzzle began to fall into place rapidly.

"These photos were taken on February 4, June 6 and September 1. Each of those dates came within three weeks of the three prototype presentations made by Solon to the DOD," Kurtzman explained.

"We went through hotel and flight records around each of those time periods," Carmen Delahunt added as she entered the War Room and joined them at the conference table. "There's only one high-end hotel in the vicinity. They have records of a Stephen Steeg checking in on February 3, June 5 and August 31. All for one-night stays. Stephen Steeg rented a car at Hartsfield-Jackson Atlanta International Airport on the same days. Stephen Steeg flew in to ATL on matching dates on connecting flights, all of which originated in Oslo."

"Here's Stephen Steeg," Kurtzman said, summoning the image of a Norwegian passport onto the screen.

The picture of Stephen Steeg on the passport was clearly that of Charles Skyn.

Barbara Price nodded and waited for more. She was praying there was more.

Kurtzman said, "Stephen Steeg lists his address as an apartment in downtown Oslo. He lists his occupation as a freelance writer. He has Norwegian records, clearly forged. He has no known criminal record within Norway. He's purchased three cars in the last year, paying with cash each time. His driver's license was issued in Oslo. No living family."

Price nodded. "Please tell me there's more than that, Bear."

"Credit card usage by Stephen Steeg," Kurtzman said, and his face broke into a grim smile. "He frequents an American restaurant in Ramvik, Norway."

"Never heard of it," Price said.

"Not much to it," Kurtzman said. "It's a small town, a good seven hours by car from Oslo." A map of Norway appeared on the screen, and the town of Ramvik was identified with a red dot. It looked like it was right on the North Sea. And, nearby, in the water itself, were several icons for oil rigs.

"That is the Trollway Trio," Kurtzman said. "They're in Norwegian waters. The revenues from that oil field since the 1970s top $80 billion."

"Is there anybody who is trying to claim those revenues?" Price asked.

"Yes," Kurtzman said. "This boy."

He pressed a button on the interface board built into his chair and the video screen filled with the picture of a sullen, dark-eyed, blond teenage boy. It was a mug shot, of the Norwegian variety.

"Olan Ramm," Kurtzman said. "This picture is from his arrest in 1988 when he caused trouble at the Ramvik town hall, demanding the return of title to the lands claimed by his family since 1622. The Ramm family was once Norwegian royalty. They had their lands, as well as their titles, stripped in the early nineteenth century, along with the rest of the Norwegian royalty. By the 1980s, the lands that had once belonged to the Ramm family were producing hundreds of millions of dollars in oil every year."

It was coming together. Price could feel it.

"Good work," she said. "What happened to Olan Ramm?"

"He sat in juvenile prison for three years for beating the town mayor into a coma," Carmen said. "Since then, his name appears only on the records of purchases at various auctions. He appears to be buying back much of the property that once belonged to the Ramm family. Artwork. Antique cars. Books. A suit of armor. Textiles. Ephemera."

"Ephemera?" Price asked.

Delahunt leaned over the table. "Get this. Postcards. Matchbook covers from a family wedding in 1967. He is on record as purchasing the remains of a horse that belonged to his great-grandfather, and had the grave moved to his property in Ramvik. So far we have located more than 2600 records of his purchases, all of which appear to have been efforts to buy back Ramm family property. The most expensive purchase so far was for 2.7 million Norwegian crowns. At least three hundred of the purchases were for items of under five crowns. There appears to be at least two antique buyers who regularly scour the resale market for old Ramm family belongings. They ship these items to the Ramm household on a monthly basis. The items themselves are priced so insignificantly that these buyers appear to be taking finder's fees rather than a cut. Some of this stuff, Barb, is trash. But he buys it all."

"Would you characterize him as obsessed?" Price asked carefully.

"Based on this evidence?" Delahunt said, laughing without joy. "Absolutely."

Aaron Kurtzman pushed a printout across the table and put it in front of Barbara Price. It was the receipt for the purchase of a rusted transaxle to an antique Renault. In the picture it looked like one of those pieces of metal pulled out of a three-hundred-year-old shipwreck. It was warped and unrecognizable as anything usable. The translation said that it had come off of a Renault belonging to a T. Ramm in 1971. The seller insisted that the buyer understand that this part was absolutely beyond salvage or use. He was selling it to Olan Ramm in 2009 for the equivalent of two dollars. Shipping was over eight hundred dollars.

"I would say that qualifies as obsessed. And this qualifies him as rich," Kurtzman said. On top of the receipt he placed an accounting sheet that showed Olan Ramm's net worth to be on the order of 312 million dollars.

"He could've done it," Price said. "He has the means and motive."

"He's liquidated almost half of his paper holdings in foreign companies in the last six years. He used to be worth more than a half billion dollars," Kurtzman said. "The liquidated funds are unaccounted for."

Price nodded tightly. "He used them to fund the attacks."

"Yes. Almost certainly," Kurtzman agreed.

There was just one more piece needed. She looked at Delahunt, turned her eyes to Kurtzman.

"Tell me," she said, "that you can link them together. Charles Skyn and Olan Ramm. Definitively link them."

"Barb," Kurtzman said, "we can link them together."

He showed her a listing of—what *was* it a listing of?

In the second she'd seen the list her eyes and brain absorbed several incongruous words. Had she really just seen *gift box* and *Hot MILFs?*

"May I?" Price took the list from Kurtzman.

It was a list of internet purchases made under Charles Skyn's fake name, Stephen Steeg. In the past twelve months Steeg had ordered thirty-seven items online. A gaming system and several games of the fast-cars variety, a gourmet gift box of the best British sausages and cheeses, a set of expensive luggage, a single-serve coffeemaker and some boxes of coffee pods to go in it and quite a number of DVDs with the words *MILF* or *Cougar* in the title.

The items themselves didn't seem helpful. What was important was that Steven Steeg had ordered them all to the home address of Olan Ramm.

"He's living at that house."

"For at least a year," Kurtzman agreed.

CHAPTER SIXTEEN

Ramvik, Norway

The Navy's C-40A opened up at ten thousand feet and five figures jumped out. The C-40A turned around and headed back the way it had come, scheduled to get on the ground as quickly as possible at the first airfield it could find in the UK. Safely outside the danger zone of Scandinavia.

The five falling figures blossomed in the night sky and fell gradually into the unlit, uneven fjord lands outside the small town of Ramvik.

DAVID MCCARTER COULD FEEL the darkness around him, but something in him still felt exposed. It would be disaster if the insertion of Phoenix Force into Norway had been witnessed.

But there were no witnesses. There was no one to see, and their landing had been dark. They were five miles outside of the town of Ramvik, and the area was entirely depopulated—except for the Ramm house. This region of the rocky fjord lands was too far away from the tourist hub of Bergen to see holiday travelers. A fertile belt surrounded the town of Ramvik and there were farms and grazing lands to the south of it. Here, though, north of the town, it seemed as if nothing lived.

McCarter could see only one of his teammates.

Encizo had landed within 150 feet of McCarter and remained within his line of sight if he kept his night-vision glasses on. The three other members of Phoenix Force checked in within seconds of each other. They had all made successful jumps. They had all found their landing targets. They were all in readiness to hit Olan Ramm.

"Stony, we are on the ground. Heading to the Ramm estate."

"Technically, you are already on it," Barbara Price said. "Ramm owns every square foot of property within two miles of where you are at this moment. His walled-in property should be visible to you within a klick."

"Move out," McCarter said.

Rafael Encizo proceeded at a steady pace over the rocky landscape of the Norwegian coast. A veteran of more missions than he could count as a part of Phoenix Force, Encizo knew this team. He knew these men. There was not one among them that he would not trust with his life—as indeed he did every time they entered combat together.

Encizo knew that there had been few times in their years together when they had experienced such pressure to succeed.

There had been days of frustration because the mission seemed directionless, lacking in a goal. The terrorist attacks had been devastating, and widespread, and until just a very short time ago, there had been no one to blame. Nowhere to channel the anger or the effort.

Then, as they were watching the countdown to the border closure approach, and as their Navy aircraft flew them finally over the Scandinavian peninsula, the word had come from Stony Man Farm. They had done what hundreds of intelligence agencies had failed to do. Stony Man Farm had found the terrorists.

Found *him*. One man. Olan Ramm. And his sidekick, some sort of scientist genius named Charles Skyn.

All it took was having those identities, and everything changed. The group anxiety transformed into urgency. The pressure changed to eagerness.

After the endless hours of uncertainty, Stony Man Farm, and especially Phoenix Force, had a goal, a geographical destination and a human target.

Encizo had hiked the fjord lands of Norway, years ago, for pleasure. But it was a different place tonight. It was dark, but high contrast. Every detail got his attention. Every stone underfoot was stark in his vision. He felt as highly tuned as he had ever felt going into battle.

When Encizo heard David McCarter speak through his headset, the voice was as crisp and clear as if the man was standing a foot away from him.

"I see it."

Encizo now saw it, too. An old stone wall traveled over the contours of the land, and the dark hulk of the Ramm family home was visible on the other side of the wall.

After another twenty paces the burning vividness through his night-vision goggles was too much and Encizo pulled them off his eyes. There were lights on the grounds of the home, beyond the old stone wall.

The wall formed a rectangle, more or less, with an entranceway on each of the four sides. On the front, a large gated entrance faced the road into the town of Ramvik proper. Encizo was approaching from the back side of the building, closing in on the southwest corner, slowing his pace and staying sharp.

The original wall at this point was waist-high, constructed over many painstaking years out of local stone. The stone had been fitted together so perfectly, there was no need for mortar to give the wall durability.

That was all the security the Ramm mansion grounds had needed for a few hundred years—a border to give the grounds definition and maybe keep in sheep. Not to keep out intruders.

Then, in very recent decades, the nature of the wall had changed radically. Mortar had been poured over the existing stonework, cementing it in place and ruining its hardscape beauty. Atop the old wall, a new section extended upward, consisting of concrete brick that took the wall to a height of ten feet.

Protruding from the top of the brick section of the wall were steel rods and a sloppy tangle of barbed wire. It looked as if someone had taken a POW camp out of Somalia or Afghanistan and transported it to the beautiful, peaceful, empty fjord lands of Norway.

It didn't belong.

The thought became heavy in Encizo's mind. This place and this man did not belong here. Did not belong in Norway, did not belong in this world.

And Encizo would be more than happy to make it all right again.

There was no evidence of a security system outside of the wall. He got close, made his inspection, then headed along the long, rear west wall to the back entrance.

Waiting for him was David McCarter. He was examining the wide gap in the brick. It was gated, and the gate was reinforced steel, with a coded electronic lock. An ancient wrought-iron gate, which had served this estate well enough for a few hundred years, was open, and broken off at the hinge.

Calvin James materialized from the darkness, coming from the north, and paused on the other side of the rear entrance.

McCarter spoke so softly, that even standing a few feet away, Encizo heard him best through his earpiece. "Find anything?"

Encizo reported finding nothing.

"No sign of electronic surveillance," James agreed. "No sign of a security force."

ON THE FRONT SIDE of the building, Gary Manning, accompanied by T. J. Hawkins, was discouraged to find the front gate ajar. The electronic lock display showed dashes. On the one hand, it made their entrance that much easier. On the other hand, what did it mean about the security needs of the house? Was Ramm even still in residence?

Manning reported his findings to McCarter. Then he and Hawkins slipped through the open gate and into the grounds of the Ramm estate. There were just a few cold floodlights glaring on some isolated points of the grounds, casting long, broken shadows of the contents.

"What the fuck?" Hawkins said.

ENCIZO STEPPED UP onto the ancient rock section of the wall, which gave him room to stand. A quick touch of the wire cutters revealed no electrical current. He snipped at the barbed wire and separated entire tangled sections of it, yanking it off the wall, clearing a three-foot-wide passageway. He hoisted himself up onto the top of the brick and scanned the grounds below. He pulled on his lowlight classes, and looked again.

"Encizo?" McCarter asked. "Is it clear to go in?"

"I think so," Encizo said.

There was a moment of consternation, then McCarter said, "Encizo, can we go in or not?"

"I'm going in," Encizo said. And with that, he slithered over the wall and dropped to the grounds inside. A moment later, almost soundlessly, Calvin James landed beside him, and then David McCarter.

"Holy shit," Calvin James said under his breath.

HAWKINS AND MANNING found the front grounds of the Ramm estate covered in junk and trash. There were piles of rusting metal, there were cars that had been sitting unmoved for years and there were pieces of wooden furniture that had rotted nearly out of recognition.

"Back home we call them Texas trash, the people who live in places like this," Hawkins said in a whisper. "I wonder what you call them in Norway?"

There was a stack of two-by-fours—hundreds of them piled so long ago that they had sunk into the ground and rotted into mush. Just to the right of the entrance gate was a tangle of corroded metal, and only after examining it closely did Hawkins realize that it was the remnants of fifteen or more bicycles. A tricycle, an old tandem bike, a classic Roadmaster, and even one of those ridiculous high-wheel bicycles from 120 years ago. It was as if there had been a Bicycles through the Ages parade that ended in a horrific pileup, which was then left untouched for years.

And that was just one of the piles. As Hawkins moved slowly along the wall, his eyes peeled for signs of digital or human security, he was taking in dozens, maybe hundreds of sets of cast-off and discarded items.

"I changed my mind. This is not like Texas trash. Texas trash doesn't junk up their yards in precision grids like Norwegian trash do," he whispered to Manning.

"T.J.," Manning said, "I don't think anybody, anywhere, does it like this weird fuck does."

"We're inside," Hawkins advised. "You seeing what we're seeing?"

"I DOUBT IT, T.J.," McCarter said. What McCarter was looking at was a three-yard-square section of the grounds that was piled with sound equipment. Old tube radios, a Victrola, the remains of what might have been an old wax cylinder player, dozens of audio components systems dating from the 1950s through the 1980s, and even a few obsolete MP3 players. Most of it was so old, and had been lying there exposed to the harsh Norse winners for so long, that it had almost melted into the soil. Incongruously the brushed aluminum of some old control panel here and there continued to catch the dim light of the distant security lights and almost sparkle.

McCarter bent low and examined the ground from inches away. There was a faded orange stripe sprayed on the earth to demarcate this square. Now that he was down there, at their level, McCarter could see that some of the trash pieces retained old dangling tags or masking tape labels. He could still read some identification numbers hand-lettered in black.

McCarter straightened and gazed down the row. He was coming to understand what he was seeing. A carefully ascribed grid had broken the hundred or so acres of the enclosed grounds into uniform squares for the organization and storage of all the old Ramm family possessions.

Olan Ramm was known to be buying or stealing back everything that he could find that had once belonged to his family.

Now they knew what he did with all that stuff. He

was giving it an identification code, and then "storing" it in these carefully marked spaces. Somewhere inside, McCarter had no doubt there would be records of the identification codes of each and every one of these items.

Upon landing, Calvin James had erected a satellite transponder to give them easy access to communications with Stony Man Farm, and McCarter's video pickup was feeding images back to them even now.

"Stony, do you believe what you are seeing?"

"It fits the profile that we were developing for Olan Ramm," Price said.

"Is it the same thing up front?" Encizo radioed.

"Same piles," Price said. "Different junk."

"Our man isn't interested in the stuff itself," James said. "The only thing he cares about is having possession of the stuff, and keeping track of the fact that he has possession of the stuff. Not to use. Just to have. What does that say about him?"

"What we already knew," Price said. "He is obsessed."

"Psycho-fucking-pathically obsessed," James said.

"Enough gawking," McCarter said. "Let's go put this obsession to rest."

FILLING THE GROUNDS with piles of junk was not a smart move from a security point of view. From the front and from the rear, the Phoenix Force commandos found ample cover for their approach to the old Ramm family house.

There were shadows behind mountains of discarded bookcases. There was an easy, unseen channel of approach behind a row of old, dead appliances. McCarter, James and Encizo found themselves at the back main entrance to the building without ever feeling as if they had been exposed. And there was no sign of a security system that would have been watching them. Not yet.

Silently, Encizo signaled McCarter and James before they could start work on the main rear door. He had spotted a small courtyard, long overgrown, and he led them into it. The tiny space was dominated by the dry, years-dead figure of a denuded pine. The little courtyard had become the place to deposit old desks. Wood, composite, steel, centuries-old or from the 90s. All tossed together, as if for a bonfire, around the base of the dead pine.

There was an old wooden door to this wing of the house. Undersized, on a high stoop, with a latch. A simple padlock would've secured the latch, but there was no padlock in place.

Encizo scanned the roofline, and scanned the windows, which were dulled with years of grime. No sign of any visible security system on the house itself. He stepped high, and carefully, among the ruins of old desks, and found his way to the old wooden door. He touched it. He listened. He pushed it open.

David McCarter had hit the ground in Norway in high spirits. They had a target. The target was almost in their sights.

Now his optimism waned. The information from Manning, that the front gate alarm was inactivated, was a bad sign. It could mean the occupants of the building had left it, and felt no good reason to secure it.

And the familiar worry had come back—of walking into an incendiary ambush. He knew what a single block of that nanothermite was capable of. He knew how easy it would be to place a trap for intruders here.

And what made him uneasy was the disregard Olan Ramm had for his possessions. McCarter would have thought the man would do anything to protect all the trash that he had gone to so much trouble to retrieve. But the junkyard around him said differently. It said the man cared only about taking back those possessions. Ensuring that no one else had what, in his warped brain, was his property. He cared nothing about the items themselves. Once he was satisfied that he had again taken control of that piece of property, he could throw it in a pile and let it rot. Be it a hundred-dollar iPod or a twenty-thousand-dollar seventeenth-century French secretary desk.

The thought kept occurring to David McCarter: if you would let it rot, then you would probably let it burn.

He almost gave in to the impulse to order Encizo away from the door. But then, Encizo moved the door open gently and slowly, and stepped inside the Ramm mansion.

"I'm in," Encizo confirmed. "Man, you thought the outside was bad."

McCarter and James quickly entered with Encizo. The interior of the house was dark and silent, but they did not feel alone. The place felt crowded.

Encizo was riffling through some papers from a stack of boxes nine high against one of the walls.

"What do you have there, Rafe?" Price asked. "We can't read it."

"Aina Ramm," Encizo said. "These boxes are all labeled, Stony. This entire stack of boxes is the papers of Aina Ramm. She must've been somebody important."

Encizo was being sarcastic, and Barbara Price knew it. But she explained anyway. "Second cousin, once removed, spent most of her life knitting. Died in 1968 at age 74."

Encizo moved close enough to the next stack of boxes to read the labels. And then the one on the other side of the hall. Hannah Ramm, died 1980. Nicholas Ramm, died 1939.

The stacks went on as far as he could see.

"Forget this shit," McCarter said. "Let's find this freak."

GARY MANNING WAS LESS impressed with the sheer volume of trash that had been accumulated in this household. He barely glanced at the stacks of boxes of papers and shelves of books and racks of small household items and junk. He was sure some of it was valuable, and he was just as sure that most of it was worthless.

Manning had once watched ten minutes of an episode of a reality series that focused solely on people who hoarded stuff and filled their homes to the gills with junk. Ten minutes had been enough of that program for Manning. In real life, it was no more intriguing to him. He wanted to get at the human trash behind the physical trash.

Hawkins nodded to the right. Down the tight corridor made between two piles of wooden crates was a closed door, and a dim glow came from underneath.

With Hawkins at his back, Manning moved to the door, finding he had to turn sideways to accommodate his bulk. He twisted the knob, nudged at the door and leveled his M16 at the occupant of the room.

A man choked on his beer, spitting a mouthful of it on a laptop computer playing a British sitcom. He tried to speak, even as he was hacking on the inhaled beer, and by the time he could breathe properly he was face-down on his filthy cot, his hands trussed behind him.

The barrel of the M16 was so far down his throat it was making him gag. Which didn't help him breathe any easier.

"Where is Olan Ramm?"

The man shook his head.

Manning withdrew the barrel of the M16 from the man's throat and pressed it deep into his eyeball. He wanted this guy to know just how serious he was.

"Well?"

The man began to protest in Norwegian. Too loudly. Manning bore down on the weapon, compressing the eyeball through the lid, and the figure shuddered and moaned in agony.

"You will speak quietly," Manning said. "You will speak in English. You will tell me where to find Ramm. If you fail to do exactly what I have said you will do, I will burst your fucking eyeball, then I'll shove this thing down your throat and shoot your guts out from the inside. Do you understand?"

"Yes," the Norwegian choked.

"Well?"

"Back bedroom. Top of the house. That is where you will find him."

"How many others in the house?"

"Me, Ramm, three more."

"You're staying here," Manning said. "When I come back, I'm going to keep all my promises. First your eyeballs. Then the gut shot. Unless everything you have said is true. Care to make any corrections?"

"Five more. Otherwise it's true what I've said."

Manning thought the man looked panicked. He was trapped, cuffed to his bed, unable to free his hands or legs. He didn't seem like he was bluffing. He seemed afraid.

It was the best Manning was going to get.

MCCARTER AND THE OTHERS listened to Manning's quick report. McCarter could hear the doubt in Manning's voice. But, even more so than Manning, McCarter was determined to follow through, regardless of the risk. If Ramm was indeed in this house, McCarter would be sure that he was found and exterminated.

He led the way through the narrow alleyways between the stacks and piles that filled the great house. It had once been an open, spacious home by the standards of the seventeenth-century aristocracy of Norway. Now it was an overstuffed warehouse.

They ascended to the third floor at the rear—a third story added in the twentieth century. The wide window at the end of the hall looked out into the night. All he could see from this view now were a few huddled piles of trash directly below them.

The hall was narrow and made more narrow by stacks of furniture against either wall, held in place by a few wooden studs nailed into the floor and ceiling.

McCarter took the lead at the door at the rear of the house. This must be Ramm's room. Either he would be in there, and he would be dead in seconds, or they could be walking into a trap. McCarter turned the knob.

The house started screaming.

ENCIZO SNAPPED HIS EYES shut at the moment the sound started, and pushed his low-light glasses off his eyes. The lights came on, turning the oppressive darkness into blinding brilliance. He and James were standing between the framed-in junk furniture, and when a pair of gunners stepped into the open at the front of the house, they could not have had a more direct shot at the Phoenix Force warriors. Encizo jumped back, snatching James by the collar.

James had reacted to the same danger. He had leaped in the direction of Encizo, and the two of them were practically ejected by their own efforts into the cover behind the racks, but they missed being in the way of the blast of a hunting rifle that ripped into the wall where they had been standing. Encizo found himself being dragged back to his feet by Calvin James.

"Hurt?" James demanded.

"No," Encizo said. It was a lie. He had hit a stair edge with most of his body weight compressing against his upper rib cage. In all the tumult, he may have heard something crunch inside. Or maybe not. It hurt like hell but he'd worry about it later.

James dived to the floor, and reached out at floor level, sweeping a figure eight as he bore down on the trigger of the Heckler & Koch MP5. The submachine-gun fire chopped through the torso of a rifleman who was cocking his weapon for the next round. A second gunner stepped over the body, and filled the long corridor with machine-gun fire of his own. He was still trying to find the target when James took him with the triburst to the chest. He pulled back into the cover and triggered the weapon at the small grille in the ceiling that was issuing the alarm blare. It turned off, but at least three more alarms were whooping in other parts of the home.

James changed out the magazine on the MP5 and signaled his intention to Encizo. The Phoenix warrior nodded.

James hurried up the corridor while the coast was

clear and stepped into an open space at another door. It was a tenuous position. If there was anyone in the room behind him, and they emerged while he was watching the hallway...

A new figure appeared at the end of the hall, almost invisible behind the stack of old sofas caged in two-by-fours. He pumped a shotgun, twisted into the corridor and emptied both shells before he realized the corridor was empty. Then James appeared and triggered the MP5 in a downward slash that opened the shotgunner from shoulder to hip.

The door that was the back wall of James's hiding place opened cautiously. James hurried it up with a swift kick. The man who had been opening the door was thrust aside. His companion was startled to find himself face-to-face with Calvin James and pulled up his 9 mm handgun but never made target acquisition. James cut him down and turned the submachine gun on the doorman, triggering a second burst with almost no lag time. The doorman's chest blossomed blood and he fell.

James stepped over the bodies, thrusting his subgun into a cavity behind one of the ubiquitous piles of trash. It was the only place left in the room that could hide another attacker. The space was empty.

"Hold, Cal," he heard from his headpiece.

It was Encizo, who was supposed to be going in with McCarter. Why wasn't he? Calvin James would have to worry about that later. He heard the creak of a step in the hall, somehow reaching him over the wail of the warning sirens from the floors below and the ringing in his ears from the recent gunfire. James placed himself in the hiding space.

Only then did he see an imperfect reflection of the room in a darkened, old tube TV set. Calvin James momentarily chastised himself for having missed that detail. That was a mistake that could get you killed. If there had been someone hiding in this spot, they would've been able to watch Calvin James enter the room, and been able to perfectly anticipate the moment to take him out.

To be honest, it wasn't that clear a reflection. It didn't give him anything close to a clear view of the room or the hall beyond, but the image was good enough to show him when the dead stillness turned to movement. He could see a figure in the poor reflection. He saw it turn into the room, assess the bodies and then return its attention to the corridor. The figure's two-handled handgun now pointed away from Calvin James.

James stepped out of his hiding place. The figure in the hall spotted the movement in his peripheral vision and spun to engage him. Parabellum 9 mm shockers from James's MP5 cut through soft tissue below the gunner's rib cage and cracked his vertebrae, and the gunner with the CZ 75 was dead on his feet. He fell hard.

James jumped aggressively into the corridor and returned to the place where he had left Encizo.

"We're coming up," Manning said into his headset. The sirens had ceased.

"Encizo?"

"In here." Encizo appeared in the door, looking at ease.

Hawkins, and then Gary Manning, stepped over the bodies at the end of the hall and joined them in the room that had been designated as Olan Ramm's.

There was a bank of flat-screen monitors on a folding table, each showing a different section of the interior of the house. It was far from being complete security coverage. In this house, with this mess, it would have taken a hundred cameras to see into every nook and cranny that could possibly hold an intruder.

And there was a dead man on the floor, next to the chair, where he had been viewing the screens when McCarter entered the room. A single headshot had efficiently ended him.

David McCarter, Calvin James could see at a glance, was not a happy man.

"That guy is not Olan Ramm," James said.

"No," McCarter said bitterly, "it's not."

Stony Man Farm, Virginia

BARBARA PRICE FELT NUMB. She stared at the frozen image of the dead man on the floor of the house out in the middle of nowhere, Norway. A dead man who was not Ramm.

It was a split screen. On the other side scrolled the transcription of the second message from the perpetrators of the attacks.

We will take back that which belongs to us.
We call upon Norway's Parliament to pass the following laws.
The Nobility Law, illegally instituted in 1821, will be abolished. Property, land and holdings stripped illegally from the noble families will be restored. Ownership and profits from all enterprises located on restored land and maritime properties will be restored. A Norwegian king will be identified using the Norwegian Yearbook of Pure Nobility, and will have veto power over all Norwegian laws and judicial decisions. Noble families that supported the illegal system initi-

ated in 1821—including the family of the current King Pretender—will be deemed Traitors to the true King of Norway. They are to be exiled or executed.

We call upon the nations of the world to encourage the Norwegian Parliament to pass such laws within the next 60 minutes.

"It's ridiculous," Kurtzman said. "It's outlandish. Crazy."

It was all those things.

Hal Brognola's face appeared on the screen from his office in Washington, D.C.

"Barb?"

"We're seeing the new message. It's like a bad joke."

"But no one is laughing. What has Phoenix found?"

"They are ripping the place apart, Hal. So far they have come up with nothing. The place is a junkyard. If there's anything there, anything of value that would help us now, it could take months to find."

"That is not good enough, Barb. We are going to run out of minutes very, very fast."

Price maintained her composure though her eyes blazed. "Don't you think I know that? There is nothing for us in Ramvik, Hal. No computer systems to tap into. No documentation of intended targets. No list of hired saboteurs. No leads. No clues. Nothing to give us direction."

"Barb, I also don't have to tell you what's going to happen at the end of the sixty minutes."

"You're right. You don't."

THE MEMBERS of the Norwegian parliament had made it very clear that they could not follow the demands made by the terrorists.

The news channels were full of speculation, most of which focused on the possibility that the demands were some sort of bizarre hoax. It seemed outrageous, even comical, that this could be the motivating factor behind the terrorist attacks.

Then the hour was up.

At Stony Man Farm, the alarms began screaming.

Washington, D.C.

BROGNOLA WATCHED the destruction, feeling as hopeless as he had ever felt. This time the attacks focused on bridges.

A bridge was an ideal target for Ramm's nanothermite devices. The very nature of bridge construction meant that compromising a few points of support could undermine the entire structure, and bring it all crashing down.

The Su Yang suspension bridge in China went down when nanothermite devices burned through suspension cables and the central support tower simultaneously. It may have taken as few as eight of the devices to do the job. The tension on those cables and the load on the tower was so great that partially liquefying the metal was enough to compromise the integrity of the structure. Six hundred feet of its eight-hundred-foot length collapsed into the Su Yang River.

The Roebuck bridge in the Tennessee mountains disintegrated when a single reinforced concrete central support was burned in two. Four to six devices cut the column at an angle steep enough to cause the column to topple like an enormous tree. At least fourteen cars followed the column into the Roebuck Gorge.

Those were the high-profile disasters. The worst

losses came from the bridges and simple spans that went unnoticed, even by the thousands of drivers who used them every day.

Twenty-eight bridges collapsed in the United States. Fourteen in South America. Two in Canada.

Three bridges fell in Japan. Ten in China.

Eight automobile traffic bridges went down in Russia and the human toll was more than thirty.

But there was also a new type of target in Russia: at least twenty pipeline suspension bridges had been taken down, cutting oil and natural gas lines that had so far survived the attacks and had continued to operate. These bridges carried no traffic or people—only oil or natural gas.

Included among them was the giant Kitski 2 Pipeline Suspension Bridge. Kitski was a new, eighty-million-dollar suspension bridge highly touted as Russia's environmentally responsible future of oil transport. Photos had circulated worldwide showing the gleaming, high-altitude pipeline soaring majestically among beautiful, centuries-old pines. Nature and technology not just in harmony, but beautiful together.

The support towers, suspension cables, shutoff valve stations and the pipes themselves—all ignited. Burning rain fell into the forest and the world had a new image from Kitski: dangling mechanicals and the oldest living stand of Siberian pines consumed in bright flame.

Two bridges fell in Stockholm, taking down twenty-two vehicles.

Two bridges fell in Denmark, taking eight vehicles.

In the rest of Europe, another dozen or so bridges had their supports burned out from under them and collapsed. The death toll in the EU alone topped one hundred.

But not a single bridge fell in Norway.

Ramm knew what he was doing. Leaving Norway unscathed meant that global sentiment would increasingly turn against Norway. It was the nature of human beings. The pressure on Norway's parliament to give in to the demands of the terrorists would be immense.

Stony Man Farm

Demands were issued again. The deadline, this time, was four hours away.

That son of a bitch, Price thought. He knew he couldn't get his demands met in the first one-hour time limit. It was a setup. He wanted to tighten the screws. He wanted to make absolutely certain that he was going to get what he wanted.

"We might have something," Kurtzman said hesitantly.

She looked at him. Kurtzman looked at Tokaido.

"Desperate times…" Tokaido said.

"These absolutely are desperate times," Price said. "And at this point the world is ready to take any measures, however desperate they might be."

Tokaido looked uneasy. "Maybe."

"Spill it, Akira," Price said.

"We know how to track down Ramm. But it would take some drastic measures to do it."

CHAPTER SEVENTEEN

The White House, Washington, D.C.

Hal Brognola sat in the chair across from the President of the United States of America and told him what drastic measures would be needed. It didn't take him nearly as long to lay it all out as he had thought it would.

The Man looked at him.

"Why? Again, tell me why we would need to do this?"

"Mr. President, we don't know where he is sending from. We don't know how to track him down. He can use a different phone with every call he makes, and he is doing so now."

Brognola explained that the attacks were now cycling through different cell networks around the world. No more dedicated sending channels.

"He doesn't need any special cellular hardware, just a phone that he can buy off the shelf at any drugstore or department store in the world. We can't track him down that way. We have to find a way to isolate him and identify him at the moment that he is sending his signals."

The problem was that, at any given moment, there were millions of calls going out around the world.

"We can't search it all, not quickly enough. We have to silence the chatter. We have to cut the number of calls to a number small enough for us to deal with in real time. *That* will give us a chance to actually track him down."

"And you cannot do this? This shutting down of the phone systems?"

Brognola shifted in his seat, suddenly very uneasy. "We can't break into the hundreds of cellular systems operational around the world and switch them off at the instant that we need to. Not without permitted access. That's where we need you to intervene."

The President nodded. He was an intelligent man. "What you want me to do is get on the phone with heads of state, presidents and prime ministers, anyone who can make this happen, and ask them to give your people access to their systems for five minutes, starting three hours from now?"

Brognola nodded.

The President continued, "I'm supposed to ask them to allow us to penetrate their systems and shut down the communications networks in their nations. Do you know what will result from that? The cost in revenue alone will be in the billions."

"But we could be saving lives. We could be able to stop this from happening. We could take him down."

The President rubbed his brow and glared at the single piece of paper in front of him. It was an internet protocol address, a single string of numbers. He was to provide this string of numbers to the heads of state, who were to provide it to cellular network operators in their own countries with orders to allow top-level access to their master system control for five minutes. To anyone from this IP address.

"Tell them this," Brognola said. "Tell them to consider what damage could be done to their cellular phone systems in five minutes. Ask them to weigh that against the damage that could be done in their country if these attacks continue every four hours for the next day. Or two days. Tell them to consider that."

The President nodded. "Hal, what if they go along with it? What if they give you this access? What if you succeed in shutting down all these cellular systems, all at once? Will your people be able to find him? Really, find him, track him down, take him out?"

"They think they can." Brognola paused. "I *know* they can."

"It seems to me that about this time yesterday, you were feeling less confident in your people."

Brognola nodded at the floor. Resting his elbows on his knees, he said, "Mr. President, if I was doubting the capabilities of those people, that was a sign of my weakness, not of theirs. I tell you this — if anyone on this planet can stop Olan Ramm, it is my people. If not them, then no one."

The President looked at Brognola. "You are going to have to hope that your confidence in them is warranted. And I have to hope that the confidence I have in you, Hal, is warranted. I'm putting my ass on the line in a very big way. I'm to ask some of the most powerful people in the world to trust my judgment. A lot of those people do not like me very much, and they have to trust me without a second thought. The fallout from this is going to be huge, and that's if it works the way it's supposed to. If it fails, if it explodes in our face…"

Brognola nodded. "Desperate times, Mr. President."

Stony Man Farm

"THERE'S A PROBLEM," Brognola reported. "With the Russians."

"What's the problem with the Russians?" Price asked.

"The Russians are in the hole for tens of billions of

dollars from these attacks already. Maybe hundreds of billions. They are not willing to cooperate with our plan on our terms."

"Under what terms, then?" Price asked.

"They want a live feed, directly from the United States, from whatever intelligence agency it is that is managing the blackout. They want to know—at the same instant that we know—the location of Ramm."

"Oh, God."

"It gets worse. They have made their intentions clear to strike that target. They intend to be in the air, armed and ready to make a strike against whatever that target is, as soon as they can reach it. They have agreed to be a part of blackout plan only on this condition."

"Our intention is to find Ramm and take him out. That is our goal," Price said.

"But the Russians are not going to trust us to follow through. They have said as much. They will give us just whatever time it takes to get their planes from the Baltic Sea to Norway to find Ramm and take him out. If we can't do so, they will strike that target."

"Do you know what you're saying? We're sending Phoenix Force to those coordinates. That's our plan. Are you really telling me that the Russians fully intend to strike the coordinates where Phoenix will be?"

"That is what I am telling you, Barb."

"That is unacceptable. I am not sending Phoenix to certain death. We will not abide by those terms."

"Then the operation will be canceled," Brognola said. "The Russians have made it very clear that these are the only terms upon which they will cooperate."

"Wait," said Kurtzman. "I think we can do it."

He rolled his wheelchair up behind Price. "Barb, we're almost certain that Ramm is in Oslo. It's the only location inside of Norway that makes sense. It's the only place where he could find enough cellular traffic to remain hidden. Whoever has been helping him put together this transmission system would know this. They would know that there are few places in Norway with enough cell chatter to hide these specific sorts of calls. If Ramm is in Oslo, if we track him, we can get Phoenix there before the Russians."

"How can you be sure?" Price asked. "Russian fighters could get from the Baltic to Oslo in less than half an hour. That is not much time to find one man in the city of almost 600,000 people. Even with his exact coordinates. How much time will it take for us to get the word out to the Russians if we do take Ramm down? And what evidence will they want? Once they order that strike, what will it take to convince them to stop it?"

"They'll have to just take our word for it," Kurtzman said.

"Why would they do that?"

"Because," Brognola said, "we'll be speaking for the President of the United States. They'll be trusting us because the Man's credibility as a world leader is on the line. If we lie, and if we tell them we have stopped the attacks when we really haven't, and the Russians find out that they missed an opportunity to stop the attacks themselves—the repercussions would be monstrous. I tell you this—we will not lie to the Russians. If we don't get Ramm, we will let the Russians get him. I know what I'm saying, Barb, but I also know what it will mean to the world if Ramm is not stopped."

Price stared at Brognola's image on the screen. Stared through him and far past him. Then she nodded her head and said she understood.

Brognola seemed to have something more he wanted

to say, but then he signed off. His image faded from the screen.

The Stony Man mission controller put on her headset and called up Phoenix Force.

Over Tyrifjorden

"STONY?" McCarter said.

"David," Price said, "I need a private line to T.J."

McCarter was not quite sure what to make of that. "You got it."

McCarter pulled off his headset. "Cal, Gary, Encizo, headsets off."

Phoenix Force had hired a helicopter out of Bergen. It was a big sightseeing chopper, with large windows for breathtaking views of the fjords. It was the only transport they could get. The pilot was willing to fly, despite the danger, despite the strange nature of his passengers.

Even in Norway, money talked.

"Barb?" Hawkins said.

"T.J., I'm going to explain the mission parameters to you. When I have done, you will tell me—yes or no—if you accept your role in this mission."

"What? Since when—"

"T.J.! Not another word until I'm done explaining the mission parameters."

"Okay," Hawkins acknowledged.

When Price was done, after she'd explained all the risks, she said, "T.J., it's too dangerous not to give you a choice. Do you want to be a part of this? Yes or no."

DAVID MCCARTER WATCHED T. J. Hawkins listening to Barbara Price. Hawkins was silent for more than a minute before he said, "Yeah. Yes, of course."

Hawkins removed his headset.

"Encizo, Barb wants to talk to you."

Encizo donned his headset. He listened. His face grew hard. "Yes," he said finally. "And never ask me that again!"

He ripped off his headset. He put it back on.

"Sorry, Barb."

He took it off and nodded at Gary Manning.

Manning listened. Manning answered. "Yes."

When it was James's turn he looked at the headset with distaste.

"Yes," he snapped before Price even start talking.

"I'm not giving you the option of answering until you've heard the risks," Price said.

"Fine."

McCarter watched James. Now he had an idea what was going on. He wondered what could have made this mission so different, so excessively dangerous that Barbara Price would affront these seasoned and loyal warriors with a back-out option.

"Yes," Calvin James said.

Finally it was McCarter's turn. He dreaded putting on the headset. But he did and he listened to what Price felt she had to tell him.

"David," she said after she mapped out the mission parameters, "I'm not asking you to decide for yourself. I'm asking you to decide for your entire team. Under the best possible circumstances, if this works flawlessly, Phoenix Force is going to be in the line of sight of a Russian air strike. If you go in, and you do not succeed in killing him, the Farm will not be in a position to save you."

It wasn't just the danger. It was the risk of death at the hands of Stony Man Farm itself.

"Yes, Barb," McCarter said. "You do what has to be done. I understand. We all understand."

Stony Man Farm

THERE WERE THIRTY-TWO minutes left in the countdown when another wrinkle materialized.

Carmen Delahunt was the one who responded to the curious alarm. It did not have the distinctive shrillness of an attack alarm. It was a less urgent alert activated by one of the Stony Man Farm internet trolling apps. It could be any of a hundred things.

It was not what she had expected.

"Interesting," she said, eyes sparkling.

Tokaido seemed to be operating three computers simultaneously, as he prepared for the moment the countdown ended.

"Carmen, what in the world are you so happy about?"

"I'm happy to see our old friend Steve Steeg is in town," she said.

Tokaido felt a smile grow on his face. "My man Steve! We should get him together with our guys."

ABLE TEAM WAS HANGING OUT in the barracks with nothing to do but wait. Reading magazines. Pestering Cowboy. Schwarz had clicked through all the cable TV channels without finding anything to hold his attention, so he started over again, and Carl Lyons, swear to God, was about to grab that damned remote and shove it up Gadgets's—

The phone rang. It was Price, calling from the Farm.

"We came up with a little busywork for Able Team."

"Busywork," Lyons growled, "is better than no work."

AMONG THE MANY DISPLAYS in the War Room at Stony Man Farm was a bank of television screens dedicated to the news networks. They were all reporting the failure of the Norwegian parliament to vote into law the demands of the terrorists. Members of the parliament were being interviewed by the dozens. The vote itself was illegal, since it would violate the Norwegian constitution in more ways than they could count. No such law would be legal if they did cast the vote. It was not acceptable. It couldn't be done.

Besides, what did it matter? the members of parliament demanded. If this organization intended to extort billions of dollars from the country of Norway, then they would do it, with or without the symbolic passage of laws with no legal standing.

Pundits decried the Norwegian parliament as mass murderers on the one hand and lauded their courage on the other, and the countdown grew shorter.

The networks scrambled to assign culpability. They reasoned that whoever had the most to gain from the machinations of the terrorists might be the leader of the group. That would be whoever turned out to be in line for the Norwegian crown according to the preposterous demands of the terrorists. Nobody, however, could seem to get their hands on the Norwegian Yearbook of Royalty that the terrorist demands had named.

The royal families of Norway were getting more attention than they had in centuries. Many of them retained titles in name only. Others had titles that stemmed from intermarriage with Danish royalty. Some still had money. Others were destitute. Many of the descendants of Norwegian royalty were now middle-class, unexceptional citizens of the country. The nobility of their forebears was little more than a genealogical anecdote.

The countdown continued. With only ten minutes left, Norway's parliament gathered yet again—the third time in four hours, and in a flurry of activity decided yet again that they could not pass such laws, and that any such laws would hold no legal authority under the Norwegian constitution.

Stony Man Farm

PRICE LOOKED at the clock. The time display had been her enemy for days. Now she just wished that the time was up.

Everything was ready. The systems were in place.

With one minute to go, Tokaido and Kurtzman began the automated process of opening up connections through their dedicated IP address to the top-level controls at all the cellular systems in northern Europe.

There were some log-ins that failed to connect. This was expected. Huntington Wethers and Carmen Delahunt jumped on those, using a predetermined system of priority to troubleshoot the problems and prestaged hack apps to get past the systems that were uncooperative.

They were nearly all accessed in seconds.

The countdown reached zero.

With the push of a key, Aaron Kurtzman turned off nearly all the cellular systems in Western and Eastern Europe and the CIS.

With the push of a second key, eighty percent of the cellular communications in Asia and the South Pacific went silent.

And with the press of a third key, the cellular systems across North and South America went from on to off.

The world became eerily quiet.

Barbara Price could feel herself holding her breath,

but Kurtzman and Tokaido were in a frenzy of activity. Kurtzman was methodically turning off cellular systems across Scandinavia. The President of the United States had not contacted the leaders in Sweden or Denmark or Norway. Brognola had not asked him to.

Those three countries had deliberately been left off the list. It was a gamble, one of many being taken by Price and Kurtzman.

It was imperative that they control the systems in Scandinavia, but they were certainly not going to go through official channels to do so. Tokaido had quietly hacked into the biggest providers and opened his own channels, which Kurtzman was now exploiting.

Within fifteen seconds, Oslo was the only city in the world with a fully functional cellular system. In a city of almost 600,000 people—in a nation holding its breath for an inevitable terrorist attack, where the eyes of the world were focused at this precise moment—there simply weren't that many people on the phone.

For the first time since this all began the search systems at Stony Man Farm had a volume of calls to examine both dynamically and comprehensively. In 5.1 seconds the systems processed the Oslo phone traffic, analyzed it, searched for patterns, identified those patterns and pinpointed their source.

Oslo

CALVIN JAMES WAS BEHIND the wheel. He'd been studying the maps of Oslo every minute since arriving. Phoenix Force had a rental Highlander, big and black, and a full tank of gas, and they were armed to the teeth.

They were ready to find Ramm. They were ready to hunt him down, and hunt him down fast. And if Phoenix Force went down with him, well, it wasn't too big a price to pay.

Oslo was quiet now. The city was waiting. There was almost no one in the streets. That was good news. No traffic to worry about. Few pedestrians to get in the way. Calvin James was ready to drive up the side of a skyscraper if that was what it took to get to Ramm.

All he needed was—

"Coordinates," Barbara Price said. She read them off.

James put his foot down on the accelerator so hard he thought he might've wedged it into the floorboard.

McCarter was giving him the street directions that would take them to the numerical coordinates.

"Left here."

James felt like a driver on an IndyCar oval, the kind that was so smooth and so perfectly banked that the drivers only decelerated when they hit the wall. He took the corner without slowing. Some sort of street sign was flattened by his rear end. Nobody inside the Highlander even noticed.

"Right in one hundred feet, then take a fast bloody left."

James almost laughed. McCarter sounded like a dashboard GPS off the mean streets of Brighton. He took a hard right, and put his foot on the brake just enough to keep the big SUV from fishtailing as he cranked hard left.

"Slow to fifty," McCarter said.

He was looking out the window. It was a bank of apartments. New walk-ups. They looked expensive.

"Park it."

James hit the brakes. The SUV shuddered to a halt in front of a dark brownstone. Phoenix Force debarked from the Highlander and faded into the darkness between the buildings.

Calvin James couldn't believe a city—even a city as small as Oslo—could feel so still.

In the darkness between the buildings, McCarter displayed the closeup of the map on a smartphone. The coordinates were forty feet away from where they stood. They were two doors down from the man who was guilty of a thousand murders.

McCarter issued his orders in seconds. "Cal and me, front. Rafe, Gary, T.J., back. Don't let him get away from us."

And then they separated.

Stony Man Farm

ON ONE SCREEN was Brognola. Except for the chewing of an antacid tablet, the image did not move.

On another screen was a conglomerate of radar images, showing air traffic over Scandinavia. The screen was blank. There was no air traffic whatsoever.

Five screens relayed the video pickups from Phoenix Force—but at the moment they displayed only chaos and darkness.

Oslo

THE FRONT DOOR was locked. McCarter sacrificed twenty long seconds to the process of picking the lock. He got it and pushed open the door, all his concentration focused on silence.

"Manning, move to cover the front exit," he said into his headset.

He couldn't let this guy get away.

He entered, scanned the main room, found it empty of furniture.

He and James found the first floor empty. McCarter was already on his way up. The house was dark and felt empty.

McCarter felt as if he had a steel spring in his guts, wound so tightly it was about to snap.

McCarter felt as if he was about to snap.

The steel spring was ratcheted even tighter when he reached the second floor, and found it dark, cold and silent. No one here. James was at his shoulder, his eyes livid, as it he was challenging the darkness to not give up Olan Ramm.

But it was plain that there was no one here. There was no furniture. There were no piles of junk and trash, the signature of Ramm. This place didn't feel like a place that Ramm would even want to be in.

A thump drew McCarter's and James's attention to the ceiling.

In the far corner of the empty loft there was a ladder into the blackness above. McCarter hurried to it and climbed as quickly as he could in silence. He reached a blackened hatchway. It gave way to his touch.

McCarter glanced down at James. He was going in. James nodded.

What McCarter meant was he was going in there and he was going to do whatever it took to make sure that he killed Ramm. Maybe he wouldn't come out of there himself, but maybe he'd kill the man fast enough to keep the bloody Russians from wiping out the whole bloody lot of Phoenix Force.

James understood that, too. James was going to be right behind him.

Stony Man Farm

PRICE WATCHED THE CLOCK. She watched the air traffic display. She watched the Phoenix video displays.

They all gave her nothing.

James and McCarter were inside the building. Was it the right building? It had to be. Their displays gave her only shifting shadows. There was a glimpse of the ladder from McCarter. Then, for a moment, she saw McCarter on the ladder, from James's video feed. McCarter was above James. He had his head against some sort of trapdoor in the ceiling. As McCarter pushed up, using his head, the trapdoor opened, and bright light illuminated McCarter's face.

The audio feed was filled with the rattle of machine-gun fire.

Oslo

MCCARTER DROPPED HIS head, and the trapdoor cracked shut, then light streamed through a pair of ragged holes that appeared in the wood. McCarter didn't wait for the sound of the burst to end. He simply estimated when it would end, hoped he was right, and thrust his body up through the hatchway.

He fell forward on the floor of the attic room, and twisted to the side to avoid the next burst of machine-gun fire, which ate up the boards where he had been lying. Then he twisted his body back into position and fired the MP5 at the source. There was a caw of sound. Human, but he couldn't tell if it was a laugh or a bark of terror. McCarter yanked his legs out of the hatchway and got to his feet. Then the machine-gun fire came at him again, and he felt the rounds hammer into his body.

It was as if three bricks had been lobbed into his left side. Something broke. Something bled.

McCarter refused to hear the screams of pain from his left shoulder and allowed the force of the impact to push him around in a circle. When he faced the source of the machine-gun fire he triggered his sub-gun again. The torrent of rounds cut through sort of a room-dividing drapery, until the magazine was empty. He slipped out the mag and inserted a fresh one, but before he could make use of his weapon again, a shotgun blast flapped the drapery at him. Buckshot tore at his legs. McCarter dropped as Calvin James rose through the trapdoor and unloaded half a magazine at the flapping drapery. James raced across empty space to face whatever was behind the drapery, and triggered again.

James's rounds cracked against a closing shutter. Beyond it was the night sky of Oslo.

James ran for the shutters and punched them open. Machine-gun fire tore into the opening, and James retreated inside, biding his time for a heartbeat before thrusting his upper body through the opening and achieving target acquisition.

There was a man there, desperately slapping at the magazine of a machine pistol. The magazine dropped. Calvin James fired. The skinny blond man uttered a surprised sound and fell from sight.

James clambered onto the roof. The blond man was flat on his back, and had somehow managed to insert a new magazine in the machine pistol. He fired at James and James fired at him.

James heard the thump of a round against his hip and, just an inch lower, the sudden cold of a penetrating round. His right leg stopped working. Calvin James toppled onto a steep incline of the roof. He grabbed at a shingle, but it ripped free. He grabbed at a second one. Its two nails held it in place long enough for James to drag himself onto his stomach, push against the surface of the roof and crawl away from the precipitous drop a foot from where he had fallen.

He pushed up onto his knees and the machine pistol spit. James fell flat.

His right leg was dead weight, but the rest of him still worked. He gritted his teeth against the effort, forcing himself onto his knees, and fired at the blond-haired man who was crawling toward him and firing back. The blond-haired man dropped. Calvin James felt a rush of sound that filled his head. He felt as if he had been hit again, but he couldn't feel the wound. And it didn't matter. It didn't matter...

He pulled his body over the coarse shingles with one hand. There was a moaning from beyond this rise in the roof, and it was the blond man, and the blond man was Ramm, and Ramm was still alive. But Calvin James was still alive, too. His left leg appeared to be helping him move. Some sort of wind storm was happening in his skull, disorienting him. But he would keep going. He pulled his body up and faced Ramm from a distance of less than a foot. Ramm already had James covered with his machine pistol, and James had his gun pointed right at Ramm.

They would see who would die first.

McCARTER FELT AS IF he were digging his fingernails into the very wood surface. After several feet, he found the strength to get to his knees. And then to his feet. He staggered to the opening, it showed him the cool night sky. He reached out, grabbed for the roof ledge above and yanked his body through the opening. He glimpsed the ground thirty-five feet below. It wasn't that far a drop, but far enough to kill a man.

His fingers were bleeding against the rough-surfaced shingles, but the burst of gunfire beckoned him. If guns were firing, it meant Ramm was not dead yet.

He saw blood. It glistened against the shingles. He raised his head above a rise in the rooftop, and he saw the blond head of Ramm. And he saw the glistening, dark, bloodied face of Calvin James. They were close enough to touch each other. Their weapons rose quickly.

McCarter felt time slow. It seemed he had all the time he needed to think this through. Not that there was anything he could do about it. It was simply a matter of who fired first. There would be no missing. Not from so close. In another heartbeat, one of them would be dead.

And it would not be Calvin James, if McCarter could do anything about it.

Encizo pulled off his wire-framed glasses for a full, unrestricted view.

There were people on the roof.

"Christ," Hawkins said. "That's him."

Manning had reappeared and shouldered his assault rifle.

"Wait," Encizo said, waving off Manning. "Shit. It's Cal and Ramm."

And then they saw McCarter.

And then they heard the shots.

Calvin James felt a thunderstorm break between his ears, and clouds of darkness close in on his vision but he didn't care. Because he knew he still had enough strength to trigger his weapon. And he knew that he wouldn't die before he had triggered his weapon. And even if Ramm gunned him down, it would be too late for Ramm.

Calvin James thought all these things in the time it took him to squeeze the trigger on his MP5. The weapon fired deep into the chest of Ramm.

McCARTER IGNORED the screaming inside his ribs and ignored the realization that he couldn't beat Ramm to the trigger; he just acted with all the speed he could muster. He raised his gun and pulled the trigger.

Ramm was hit in the chest with a torrent of rounds that cut through his rib cage and his sternum, forced his body back and forced his aim up, and the burst from the machine pistol sailed high into the night sky of Oslo. But the rounds from James's submachine gun just kept coming. They chewed through Ramm's heart, they shattered his spine, they exploded from his back.

David McCarter pumped a burst into Ramm's throat that sent his head flopping back, and a flood of blood poured down his chest. His feet flopped away from under him, and Ramm landed on the edge of the roof on his back, upper body dangling over the side, and for a second he hung there.

Then, he slipped over, somehow still conscious. But not for long. As he fell the rounds slammed into his head and his chest and his legs, and they seemed to rain into his body—until he hit the ground and was still.

David McCarter staggered toward James, who had also slipped off the roof. There was blood. James must've been hit by Ramm in that last burst. He must've been hit.

"Stony." He didn't hear an answer. He didn't know if he was being heard.

"Stony. Help James."

McCarter sat weakly, aware he was fading himself. He heard the shouts from below. It was Encizo yelling up at him. McCarter knew his radio must be busted. He felt busted. And James…

James, he was sad to say, looked really, really busted.

McCarter was too weak to do anything except lie down beside his busted friend and stare into the clear night sky of Norway, and wait for the air strike that may or may not be coming.

Stony Man Farm

HAWKINS WAS SHOUTING at them through his headset. "Ramm is dead! Tell the Russians we nailed him. If they don't believe us then send them this."

The huge plasma screen that dominated the War Room suddenly filled with the image of a blond skinny man, with surprised-looking eyes. The body below the neck couldn't even be identified as human. It looked like he had exploded.

"Bear?"

"We're sending it."

"Have they responded?"

"Not yet."

"Phoenix, get out of there," Price said. "Russians have not acknowledged."

"—going anywhere, Stony," Manning said. "McCarter is down. James is—James is down. We need a medical chopper."

"Rafe, the Russian's may still be en route!"

"Acknowledgment!" Kurtzman said. "They called off the strike."

Price didn't feel relieved.

"We're on the roof with Cal and David," Manning

said. "We need a chopper. Trauma team. McCarter's got impact trauma, maybe deep tissue. Broken ribs."

"What about Cal?"

"Stony," said Manning, "I don't know about Cal."

CHAPTER EIGHTEEN

Brooklyn, New York

Hermann Schwarz could not believe how he felt. He should be ecstatic.

Able Team had just got the news from Stony Man Farm. Ramm was dead. Their plan had worked. They had stopped him, they had found him and Phoenix Force had killed him dead.

They'd seen the picture of Ramm.

Phoenix Force had made very sure Ramm was very dead.

Schwarz should be feeling huge relief, but the Farm had passed on more news.

Ramm had gone down fighting. And Phoenix had gone in hard and determined. McCarter and James had put themselves in harm's way, just to be sure that Ramm couldn't escape. And Ramm had cut them down. McCarter was in bad shape but he would live.

"And Cal?" Lyons had asked.

"He's alive for now," Price had said, but offered no further details.

THEY DROVE PAST the corner building on Hamilton Parkway before parking half a block down from Skyn's brownstone.

The four-story building in Brooklyn had been reno-

vated once into three two-bedroom apartments, as well
as a full main-floor medical center. Post-renovation,
changes had been made to knock out the walls between
the different apartments, to create a single six-bedroom
living space on the top floor.

From the information supplied by the Farm they
knew that the urgent-care center on the main floor remained in operation.

The renovation had created extra exits. No less than
four doors on the front of the building, three at the rear,
not including two fire escapes and a cellar access door.

There were a lot of ways to get in, and it would be a
lot of ways in which Charles Skyn might escape.

But Charles Skyn wasn't going anywhere.

There was some sort of an unspoken purpose that
had settled over Carl Lyons, Rosario Blancanales and
Hermann Schwarz. It was kind of reckless determi-
nation. They were going to go in there, and they were
going to find Charles Skyn and take him out, regardless of the consequences. They would put themselves
in harm's way to exterminate him.

Carl Lyons tried not to think about it. He knew that
Able Team was going into this battle with a chip on its
collective shoulder. With a score to settle. It was personal, and that could make people careless. He was the
leader of Able Team, and he should say something. He
should warn himself and the others to be professional.
To fight with purpose and not passion.

But he didn't say anything. The words would've been
wasted, on himself and on the others, and he didn't want
to say them anyway. It seemed somehow wrong, disre-
spectful, to take away that anger.

He would not disrespect Calvin James by urging that
the men of Able Team disregard their concern for him.

Funny thing. They were going into battle against a man who was guilty in a thousand murders, but what drove them this night was the fate of one man, who, last they heard, was "alive for now."

Schwarz exited the vehicle first, in jeans and a jacket and a baseball cap that hid his headset. He carried a knapsack over one shoulder and seemed absorbed in a cell phone as he stood in front of the corner lot belonging to Charles Skyn. He glanced up and down the street, found it empty and vaulted neatly over the gate. He crept like a shadow to each of the darkened windows and the doors, placing a device on each windowsill and at the bottom of each doorway. They looked like thumb drives. Small, smooth, plastic two-piece electronics.

At the side of the building he performed the operation again, placing an item at the bottom of each window. When he reached the rear of the building, he armed every window and fire escape, and all but one door.

Blancanales and Lyons were waiting for him in the shadows.

Schwarz would arm the devices via his smartphone.

The devices were passive infrared motion detectors. Powerful for their size, their signals were monitored by the Farm as well as by an app on Schwarz's smartphone.

As he activated the detectors, he assigned each a number, one through twenty-one. Anyone coming to or departing from any of those access points would be sensed by the detector, and a signal would be sent to Schwarz's phone.

They took the cellar entrance in. The lock was old, and mechanical, and easily picked. The noise was the farthest removed from the residential area of the building. Lyons had it open in half a minute. They stepped inside and closed the door behind them.

The cellar had two purposes. Mop and bucket storage. Utility company meters. That was it.

They went up the concrete stairs that seemed to date back to an original building on the site maybe a hundred years ago. They were that old and smoothed by time. The door at the top of the cellar stairs led them inside the ground floor of the medical center, where diagnostic equipment worth a million dollars was protected by a commercially monitored, insurance-certified alarm system. As far as the monitoring company was concerned, there was no activity at the urgent-care center at this address on Hamilton Parkway in Brooklyn, New York. The Able Team intrusion, thanks to help from the Farm, did not register.

The urgent-care center was dark and cool. The specimens refrigerator hummed in one of the offices. A clown fish gaped at Hermann Schwarz from a big aquarium.

Schwarz wanted to shoot it. It would have to wait.

There was an exit from the medical center into the residential foyer area. The door handle was decorated with red-and-white stripes. The decal informed them that opening the door would activate the emergency alarm.

Lyons pushed through the door.

The building remained quiet.

He closed it behind them. It could not be opened from the outside.

They were inside the main floor's exit hallway. They were inside Charles Skyn's home. The back door was locked, chained and dead-bolted.

They had not said a word. Not since getting into the car. They didn't need to speak. They all knew everything they needed to know about this building and about this mission and about what they intended to accomplish.

A set of short stairs took them up to the door to Charles Skyn's section of the building. The door was open, and they could hear the sound of a television playing the news. CNN was reporting on the events in Norway as Able Team stepped silently into the apartment.

Lyons stood in the center hall as Schwarz and Blancanales checked the two rooms on either side. Lyons knew they would find nothing. He knew Skyn was alone.

The two Able Team warriors made a quick sweep of the bedroom on the right. It was empty. The television noise was coming from the room on the left, the one with access to the recently added all-weather terrace on the roof—an octagon of glass for enjoying a 360-degree view of the Brooklyn neighborhood.

From the street they had seen the flicker of light coming from the terrace room. That's where Skyn had his television. That's where he'd be.

The apartment was dark.

LYONS HELD UP ONE HAND. His teammates stopped to listen to footsteps. Bare feet on a hardwood floor. The sound of a refrigerator opening was accompanied by an increase in the illumination from the kitchen. There was a rustling of bottles, the flip of a beer cap being removed, then the light went away with the sound of the refrigerator closing. Bare feet walked from the kitchen, across the hardwood floor of the living-room space and up the open stairs to the loftlike terrace.

Lyons gave Charles Skyn time to settle into his recliner, flip to MSNBC and take a big swallow of beer.

Able Team strolled into his living room.

Schwarz planted himself firmly in the middle of the sparsely furnished room. He could see the top of Charles Skyn's head, where he sat in his recliner in the loft, the windows reflecting the TV display around him. Schwarz wanted to be one of the guys to go up there. To get him. But staying here was fine, too. He'd be here, with his MP5, with 30 rounds, with which to chop down Charles Skyn if Charles Skyn tried to run.

Charles Skyn would not get past Hermann Schwarz.

Blancanales and Lyons headed up the stairs. They were trying to keep quiet. But they didn't need to try hard. The TV was blasting.

Carl Lyons stood at the top of the stairs, where Charles Skyn could've seen him with a slight turn of his head. There was one flat-screen TV, and one recliner, and a side table holding one beer and remote control.

Blancanales picked up the remote and muted the news from Norway.

Charles Skyn became aware of Carl Lyons for the first time. His mouth dropped open.

Carl Lyons stepped across the room and stood next to the television. From where he stood, eight windows reflected the silent television screen, and at that moment the news network decided to run a video retrospective of the attacks of the past few days.

It was all there, five seconds at a time: the burning bay in China, the burning reporters in the van in Wyoming, the collapse of a bridge and several cars in Arizona. The pipeline in Alaska splitting itself open, one gash at a time, and spilling burning blood onto the tundra. A commuter train crumpled on its side in Chicago. The black, burning stain on a field somewhere in Russia where an aircraft had gone down.

"All yours," Lyons said. "You own it all, Skyn."

"Who the hell are you? What are you doing here? I haven't done anything."

"You're Charles Skyn."

"I'm not. I'm Cecil Ford. You've got the wrong guy."

"You were Charles Skyn," Lyons said. "Then you were Stephen Steeg. In the past 48 hours you've become Michael Althouse, Lance Morelski and Lewis Corrington."

"You don't know what you're talking about!"

"And now, again, and forever, you are going to be Charles Skyn."

"You're not cops. Are you from Ramm?"

"Olan Ramm is dead. We killed him. We shot him. We shot him again. We threw him off the roof, and we shot him all the way to the ground. Not me personally, you understand, but friends of mine. But some of my friends got hurt. By Ramm. And part of the blame lies with you."

"No. I left. I didn't have anything to do with this. I thought it was deplorable. I had to run away. I only got away a few days ago. I had to hide, because I thought Ramm was going to track me down."

"Save it," Lyons said. "Those were your devices. Your devices have killed a thousand people. Give or take. You own those murders."

Skyn snorted. "Whatever. You want to arrest me? Arrest me. I've got contingencies in place. I guarantee it. I'll come out clean."

"You know what?" Lyons said. "I believe you. I believe you could come out clean. I believe you are way smarter than me. I bet you've got all kinds of excuses and alibis and ways to create reasonable doubt. But you and I both know that those murders are yours. They belong to you."

"So the fuck what? You're right. I am smarter than you. And I don't care what you think about me."

Charles Skyn got to his feet, turned around and put his hands behind his back.

He didn't hear Lyons coming to cuff him. But, for the first time, he noticed the other man in the room. Rosario Blancanales was standing there watching him with a grim sneer.

And there was a third man in his apartment, Skyn realized, down below. In his living room, in wire-rimmed glasses. The second guy and the third guy had submachine guns.

Charles Skyn knew ordinary cops didn't carry submachine guns.

"You can't do anything to me!"

"What?" Blancanales said. "No contingency plan for a bullet in the brain?"

Skyn turned back to Lyons. He didn't know who this man was, but the more he looked at him, the scarier he was. He looked like a guy who *would* shoot him in the head, even with him just standing there unarmed and helpless, even with all his knowledge and craftiness and perfect strategies, no matter how carefully he had prepared for just such a thing to not happen.

"Yeah, I can do that," Lyons said.

And now Charles Skyn saw the gun the man was holding. A big, heavy handgun. And he brought it up and pointed it at Skyn's head. He was five feet away.

He wasn't going to miss.

"No!"

"Yes."

The big handgun made a very big noise.

Part of Charles Skyn flopped into the recliner. The rest of him dripped down the wall.

"He's not coming out clean this time," Blancanales muttered.

EPILOGUE

The planes were flying again, although after a week the air travel backlogs were only just clearing.

The oil was being cleaned up on land and on sea. The process would take years.

There were bridges to rebuild.

There were hundreds of funeral ceremonies to perform all over the world.

There was a molten pool of metal in the woods some three hundred miles north of Oslo that would be excavated, once it cooled. The core, testing had shown, was still five hundred degrees Farenheit.

A chartered jet waited at Oslo. Nobody paid much attention to the men who crossed the tarmac to board the aircraft. They were in civilian clothing and looked unexceptional, except for the one in a wheelchair. He looked hurt and tired.

They all looked tired. Overwrought. Ready to get back home.

There were stairs into the chartered plane and the black man in the wheelchair tried to get up and walk them. The others carried him up the stairs, to his embarrassment. He struggled the entire way. But by the time he was inside, the fight had sapped all his reserves.

They said it would be a few weeks before he got his

strength back. Then it would take another six weeks in the gym to loosen up the stiff, deeply bruised muscles.

The men collapsed into the cramped interior of the small jet and soon felt it rolling on the runway, and then they were lifted into the frigid sky.

The attendant was a cute Scandinavian blonde named Gunilla. She couldn't seem to get a smile out of any of the men. They looked like they been through hell lately.

Hadn't everybody?

She watched as the one who seemed to favor his left arm pulled out his own personal liter bottle of Norwegian Coca-Cola. He shot-gunned it, sucking the bottle until it was empty and collapsed upon itself with an ugly noise. Then he pulled another liter out of his knapsack.

The blonde felt bad for this bunch. Gunilla knew people. She was intuitive. This group of big, powerful-looking guys didn't seem like the dreary businessmen she usually flew with. These men, she imagined, were normally a pretty upbeat bunch. But lately they'd been through some bad times and they were having trouble snapping out of their funk.

Gunilla pulled out the big guns.

"Norway aquavit," she announced. "This is very special stuff. Surely I can interest you?"

The two men in the seats closest to her didn't say no. They just shook their heads.

The other man, the one with the wire-framed glasses, was already snoring against the window.

But she did get one positive response.

She poured a glass of aquavit and took it to the rear of the cabin.

"Are you allowed to be drinking?" she asked, smiling.

"Not only allowed—I'm supposed to have four aquavits every day," croaked Calvin James from his seat. "Doctor said so."

"Don't listen to him," David McCarter growled. "He's addled by drugs. He's supposed to stay flat on his back and he only gets Norway goat porridge to eat."

"You mean, Norway Grøt porridge?" Gunilla asked.

"That's it."

"He's lying," Calvin James whispered. "I'm on nothing but Tylenol."

Gunilla gave the snifter to Calvin James. He sipped it and smiled.

"That'll cure what ails me."

"This special aquavit has been to Australia and back, in a barrel of oak, to give it the perfect complexity and flavor."

"It's good anyway."

Gunilla knew he was joking. She didn't quite get it but that was okay. She liked this American black man with his wounded smile. The only part of him that really showed was his left shoulder, but it was a muscular, meaty shoulder. It made her want to see more. And she was terribly interested in knowing how he'd come to be so injured.

"You guys got into some trouble, yes?" Gunilla asked, taking the seat next to Calvin James.

"Yeah. But the trouble's over for now."

James thought he must look like hell, but that wasn't putting off Gunilla. In fact, she looked like she was settling in to keep him company for the entire flight.

That was just fine with Calvin James. He liked Gunilla. He liked her aquavit.

"These grumpy boys," Gunilla asked, loud enough

for the grumpy boys to hear, "where are they taking you?"

Calvin James smiled.

"We're going home," he said.

* * * * *

TAKE 'EM FREE
2 action-packed novels plus a mystery bonus

NO RISK
NO OBLIGATION TO BUY

GE11B

James Axler
Outlanders®

GENESIS SINISTER

A vengeful enemy plots a horrifying new assault on humanity.

Tiny stones wielding a powerful force lie scattered throughout the Gulf of Mexico, remnants of a past war between godlike aliens. In the wrong hands, they could be used as biological weapons—which is why Kane and Grant are tracking a notorious pirate said to possess an entire collection. But they quickly realize something bigger is happening: the genesis of a new age. And that means annihilation for mankind.

Available November wherever books are sold.